Praise for *The Ninth Day*

The story is riveting; the two periods intertwine seamlessly and, speaking as someone who was arrested in the Free Speech Movement, the Berkeley sections feel true and authentic. In this gripping tale, Hope must conquer her fears and make difficult decisions in both worlds. —Margot Adler, journalist and author of *Drawing Down the Moon* and *Heretic's Heart*

Thank you, Ruth Tenzer Feldman, for gracefully transporting me to both 1964 and 1099, for an equal parts brave and tender heroine who rises up to meet unthinkable challenges and finds out she's made of strong and beautiful stuff. Reading this book felt like looking at a night sky full of stars and having a wise someone connect the bright spots for me, revealing constellations rich with story, myth, and magic. Once I entered this world, I found it hard to leave. I had to find out what happened next. *The Ninth Day* took me a mere three days to devour. —Jen Violi, author of *Putting Makeup on Dead People*

As Miriam Hope discovers that the past and the present are intertwined, she also discovers her own voice and realizes she can choose her future. *The Ninth Day* is a historical coming-of-age story that reminds us all of the power of family, love and mystery." —Maureen McQuerry, author of *The Peculiars*

In *The Ninth Day*, Oregon Book Award-winner Ruth Tenzer Feldman offers fans of time-slip fantasies an intriguing journey through the *olam*, a Hebrew word meaning both "universe" and "forever." Led by a spiritual being actually named in the Bible, sixteen-year-old Miriam Hope navigates a challenging nine days as Feldman cleverly links the student free speech uprisings of 1964 Berkeley and a horrifying incident during the 11th Century Crusades, managing this by connecting the chemistry of LSD and the rye-rotting fungus of ergot, prevalent in medieval times. —Linda Crew, author of *A Heart for Any Fate*

THE NINTH DAY

Also by Ruth Tenzer Feldman

FICTION

BLUE THREAD

winner of the 2013 Leslie Bradshaw Award
for Young Adult Literature

NON-FICTION

THE FALL OF CONSTANTINOPLE
CHESTER A. ARTHUR
CALVIN COOLIDGE
JAMES A. GARFIELD
WORLD WAR I
THE MEXICAN-AMERICAN WAR
THE KOREAN WAR
HOW CONGRESS WORKS
DON'T WHISTLE IN SCHOOL
THURGOOD MARSHALL

The NINTH DAY

Ruth Tenzer Feldman

OOLIGAN
PRESS

The Ninth Day
© 2013 Ruth Tenzer Feldman

ISBN13: 978-1-932010-65-7

Ooligan Press
Portland State University
Post Office Box 751, Portland, Oregon 97207
503.725.9748
ooligan@ooliganpress.pdx.edu
www.ooliganpress.pdx.edu

Library of Congress Cataloging-in-Publication Data
available from publisher

Cover design & photo by Riley Kennysmith
Interior design by Robyn Best

Printed in the United States of America

Publisher certification awarded
by Green Press Initiative.
www.greenpressinitiative.org.

 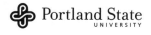

For Michael

And the evening and the morning were the first day. –Genesis 1:5

The

clock

starts

now.

The **First** Day

PARIS
25 Kislev 4860
ANNO DOMINI 1099, FESTIVAL EVE AND
FEAST DAY FOR SAINT DANIEL THE STYLITE
Sunset, Saturday, December 10–
Sunset, Sunday, December 11

BERKELEY
25 Kislev 5725
Sunset, Sunday, November 29, 1964–
Sunset, Monday, November 30, 1964

PROLOGUE

After the sighting of the third star,
on samedi, 10 décembre 1099
PARIS, ROYAL DOMINION OF KING PHILIP I

SERAKH, DAUGHTER OF ASHER, appears in a burst of blue. Breathing the damp night air, fetid with waste and rotting fish, she crouches in a deserted alley on an island in the river Seine. Hidden in the darkness, she searches for signs of alarm at the flash of light heralding her arrival.

Nothing.

Satisfied, Serakh rubs the back of her neck to ease the stiffness that comes with her travels through the *olam*. As she struggles to unravel the knot of worry that comes with each new task, she murmurs a petition to The One. "Let me be worthy. Let me do Your will. Let it be so."

The alley echoes with the moans of a woman in childbirth. Nothing else comes to Serakh's attention. This woman must be why she is here. So be it.

Serakh hides her thick white braid and most of her face in a rough linen scarf. She picks her way through the muddy snow to the heavy wooden door of a low stone building. She touches a small rectangular box on the doorframe and kisses her fingertips.

The door creaks as Serakh opens it, but no one comes to greet her. A faint smell of burning oil rises from a triangular wedge of beaten metal hanging on the wall opposite the kitchen hearth, a menorah from a place and time that is not hers. A tiny flame flickers in one of the eight shallow cups that form the menorah's base and in another cup that sits near the top.

The start of Hanukkah, she thinks, using the holiday to orient her to the Hebrew calendar. *The twenty-fifth day of the month of Kislev, but what year?* Serakh flexes her toes to drive the cold from her sandaled feet as she studies the menorah and the simply furnished, low-ceilinged room. Potato barley soup simmers in an iron caldron over a log fire in the stone hearth. A small leather pouch slouches against a pewter pitcher on a rough-hewn oak table. A broom of bound twigs rests against a shelf that holds a two-tined fork, a loaf of light brown bread, and a wedge of sharp cheese.

This is the time of moated castles, plagues, and superstition, she decides. Her long robes and headscarf, the kind she has worn for generations, will still suffice. She will not seem out of place, except for her bronze skin. If need be, she will tell them truthfully that she comes from afar.

Serakh follows the sounds of hard labor to the birthing chamber. Three women are in attendance. The oldest, a wizened woman with gnarled hands, looks at her with suspicion and asks, *"Êtes-vous la nourrice?"*

French. The language of the place once known as Gaul. Serakh waits for the gift of mutual understanding to unfold and the woman's words to form meaning. The question becomes, "You are the wet nurse?"

Serakh removes the scarf from her nose and lips, and reveals the youthful face that belies her abundance of age. She smiles, thankful that the old woman does not startle at the color of her skin.

"I am here to do what I can," Serakh says. She sees no harm in letting them think she is a trustworthy soul hired by the husband to breastfeed his baby so that his wife can soon be with child again.

The old woman nods and returns to the task at hand. Serakh steps into the shadows in a corner of the room and watches, eager to learn the purpose of her presence.

Three large waxen candles cast light on a young woman—Dolcette they call her—straining on the birthing chair in the last minutes of what Serakh learns is her first labor. She reminds Serakh of the rabbi's daughter who once accompanied her across the *olam*, a strong-willed girl named Miriam who embroidered the garment that bears the blue thread, a garment that now belongs to another Miriam, one of the many.

The *sâge-femme*, an expert in midwifery, sits on the floor in front of the birthing chair. The sturdy horseshoe-shaped seat supports Dolcette's legs. "Push," she urges. "Bear down and push."

The third woman, with a mole on her cheek, adjusts the glistening amulet that hangs between Dolcette's breasts. She straightens the straw dolls surrounding the chair, and then holds Dolcette's shoulders and whispers in her ear.

Dolcette's face contorts with exertion. She flings curse after curse at the floor, the walls, the ceiling. She cries out for her sisters and mother, who, Serakh learns, live far from Paris and cannot attend to her.

"Push!" The *sâge-femme* reaches between Dolcette's legs.

Dolcette emits a low-pitched growl as the baby is delivered. She arches her back and covers her eyes with her hands. The *sâge-femme* raises the baby for all to see. The woman with the mole whispers a prayer of thanksgiving.

Head, torso, arms, legs, a penis. The *sâge-femme* coos with delight as she hands the baby to the old woman to rub clean with salt, and then to wash and swaddle. The *sâge-femme* delivers the afterbirth intact and smiles. "You will heal well," she says.

Serakh sees in the face of the *sâge-femme* the expectation that Dolcette's husband will pay her generously for her good news.

"You are blessed," the *sâge-femme* croons to Dolcette. "A firstborn son."

"A son?" Dolcette opens her eyes, now wide with terror. She sucks in her breath and shrieks.

The women draw back in surprise. The *sâge-femme* places a cup of broth in Dolcette's hands. "Drink this," she says. "Your mind is clouded with pain. You will feel joyful when your strength returns."

Dolcette hurls the cup across the room.

Serakh rushes to her side. "What is it, child? Speak freely."

Dolcette clutches Serakh's robe. "Who are you?" she whispers, her breath hot and sour.

"Call me Serakh." She wipes Dolcette's fevered forehead with her sleeve. "I am here to help you. Do not be afraid."

The *sâge-femme* approaches with another cup of broth. "Your baby is already pink with health. There is no deformity. This son will be your pride. Listen to your wet nurse. Now we will care for your baby and prepare your bed."

She hands the broth to Serakh. "See that she drinks."

While the others are busy elsewhere, Serakh puts the cup on the floor. She knows better than to waste time on words that will not comfort. "Tell me. I will do what must be done."

Dolcette flattens her lips into a thin line of determination. "Take him. Hide him. Never let my husband near him. Never."

She clutches at the amulet and fixes her eyes on Serakh. "I prayed for a girl. She would have been safe. But now...by all that is holy, I beg you, raise my baby as a Christian or a Jew, only keep him safe."

Serakh's forehead creases in worry and confusion. *Why would this young mother, barely a woman, abandon her firstborn son?*

Dolcette grabs Serakh's hand. "Are you a Jewess?"

Serakh nods. *We were a tribal people, living from harvest to harvest.*

"Then you know of the covenant of sons."

"On the eighth day there will be your baby's circumcision, his *brit milah*. It is an ancient rite."

"Yes, and then. And then." Dolcette rips the amulet from her neck and throws it on the floor. "And then nothing will save him. Nothing! My beloved has made a terrible vow. On the ninth day, Avram will kill our son."

"This cannot be," Serakh says, even as she realizes that she is hearing the reason for her presence in this spot on the *olam*.

Tears flood the agony on Dolcette's face. "My dear Avram is possessed. He is from Mainz!"

Serakh shudders. *Mainz. Blood on the walls. Children*

screaming. A world reeling with horror. Her hands shake as she wipes Dolcette's cheek and kisses her forehead.

The *sâge-femme* walks toward them. "Your bed is ready."

"Your son will be safe," Serakh whispers, handing the broth to Dolcette. "Put your trust in me. I will find help. Do not suffer from fear while I am gone."

As the women lift Dolcette from the birthing chair, Serakh slips a straw doll into her pouch and wonders how best to leave unnoticed. She winces with the painful memory of intertwinings that have not gone as she had hoped. She prays that this time she will not fail.

CHAPTER ONE

D<small>AD SCRUBBED THE SCORCHED</small> roasting pan, leaving me to do the real dirty work. "You get the family together to light the candles, Miriam Hope," he said. "I'll be done here in four minutes."

I stuffed Mom's leftover Jell-O mold into the fridge, growled at an innocent container of turkey giblets, and consoled myself with the happy thought that Thanksgiving vacation was almost over. Twelve hours max before Josh went back to UCLA and life in the Friis household returned to bearable. Not that I was counting the minutes or anything.

I started with the easiest member of the family. Grandpa was napping with Sylvester in their favorite chair in the living room. Forehead kiss for thin, frail human. Scratch behind ear for plump, white-bellied tabby cat.

"Suh-stay p-put," I managed. "W-we'll l-light the c-candles in here."

Grandpa asked about Mom again. I reminded him that she was in Israel buying stuff for her gift shop, and that she'd be back in a few days. I didn't tell him which day. He'd forget anyway. I didn't tell him I was the one who persuaded Mom I was well enough for her to go. Now, four days later, I already regretted it.

Grandpa leaned forward and patted my leg. "Such a fine dinner we had, *sheyna maidl.*" He sprinkled Yiddish on our family like kosher salt, making sure we were Jewish enough despite Dad. *Sheyna maidl.* Pretty girl. Which used to be halfway true, sort of. I touched the bandages hiding the right side of my face. Forget the *sheyna* part now.

Taking a deep breath, I headed down the hall to Josh's bedroom. My folks had made Dagmar sleep there the first week I came home from the hospital so Mom could sleep in Dagmar's bed downstairs with me. I know it's childish, but I felt special with my mother hovering over me, back when I thought I'd heal completely, back before I knew the mutilations might be permanent.

I stood outside Josh's half-opened door. Dagmar was marching back and forth in front of Josh, her paisley skirt brushing the tops of her army surplus boots.

"That is complete bull," she said.

"It is not, and you know it." The usual. My brother and sister could team-teach a graduate seminar in advanced argument.

"You have no sense of responsibility," Josh said. "If this Gabriel guy hadn't found Hope in time, she could have died."

Crap! I clenched my jaw, despite the pain. The last thing I wanted was Josh bringing all this up again—Josh, who hadn't even sent me a get well card. I opened the door and stood there. Undead. "D-dad wants to l-light…"

"The candles. Right." Josh smoothed the crease in his pants. He jerked his head toward my bandages and scowled at Dagmar.

Dagmar rolled her eyes. "Quit it, Josh. She's sixteen already. She's not a kid. How many times do I have to tell you it wasn't my fault?"

How many times do I have to hear Dagmar swear she warned me about the licorice? "Stop!"

Josh shook his head at Dagmar and strode past me toward the living room. Not one word of sympathy. I wasn't exactly expecting any from him—he's not that kind of brother—but still. I rubbed the itchiest part around my ear and wished I could turn the clock back to the instant before I let Dagmar drag me to her Halloween party.

Dagmar retied the chartreuse-and-orange shawl around her

waist, linked arms with me in her show of sisterly solidarity, and escorted me down the hall. "Our brother is an ass," she said. "Don't let him get to you." She smiled. "Gabriel asked about you again. Isn't that sweet? I bet you'd recognize him now."

I shrugged. The sooner everyone stopped talking about that night, the better.

We gathered in front of an enameled copper menorah Mom had imported from Israel on her last trip there. No wonder it hadn't sold. Who would buy a lion with eight candleholders over its back and another candleholder sprouting from a giant cruet of olive oil?

Dad stood behind us in his polite Danish-Lutheran way. Josh lit the *shamash* candle on the cruet and used that candle to light the first candle—lion butt. The start of Hanukkah, the twenty-fifth of *Kislev* on the Hebrew calendar, I'd forgotten which year.

I was in charge of leading the Hanukkah blessings, because blessings sound better sung on key, and because I don't stutter when I sing, which is always cause for celebration. But this time, even with the stitches out and the infection gone, I knew I'd be off. My breath was too shallow, my muscles too tight. The doctors told me I should be able to sing perfectly fine. I didn't believe them.

I started softly in the key of G, afraid I'd mess up. Josh looked at his watch. Dagmar hummed along while she leaned against Grandpa's chair and turned her palms toward the ceiling. My sister takes in auras, she tells me, and apparently Grandpa was giving off the best one.

Sure enough, I flatted on the high E. *If you can't chant three measly Hanukkah blessings, you can kiss your singing career good-bye.*

I bit my lip and watched the candles burn. Even if I convinced Mom I was well enough to go and I came up with half the trip expenses, there was no way I'd get a solo for the Northwest Choral Music Festival. No solo, no chance for a music scholarship.

This year, no one had bothered with Hanukkah gifts, since

money was tight and we'd outgrown Lincoln Logs, Mr. Potato Head, and Madame Alexander dolls. Dad's side of the family believes you never outgrow your need for Christmas presents.

Josh reached for the bowl of chocolate coins. He must have been thinking about Christmas presents from Denmark, too, because he told Dad, "You should definitely buy stock in those Danish building blocks. Lego is a great investment."

Dad put his arm on Josh's shoulder. "I'm investing in you so you can go to graduate school next year."

"We're *watching every penny* because we are *investing* in *you*," Dagmar snapped. "Mom is working *her tail off* in her store because we are *investing* in *you*." So much for peaceful auras.

I shoved a bowl of chocolate coins under Dagmar's nose and gave her a beseeching look. She took a coin, unwrapped the gold foil, and ran her tongue over the chocolate.

Josh cleared his throat and stuffed two chocolate coins in his pants pocket. "Hey, Hope, speaking of money, how's your little dreidel business? I'm telling you, call them *Maidl's* Dreidels. Rhyming sells product."

If I made mud pies, Josh would tell me they'd sell better with pinecones on top.

He took another coin. "How much are you selling them for?"

"Fifty cents for the big ones, twenty-five for the smaller ones," Dagmar answered.

I bit my lip again.

"Not bad," he told me, ignoring Dagmar. "But you should price the smaller ones at thirty cents, same as a gallon of gas. Double that for the larger ones. That's your ideal price point."

Dagmar rolled her eyes. "Gee, thanks, Mr. Economics Major. Do you realize how many nickels and dimes we'd have to carry around if we did that?"

Dad finally deflected the discussion. "How are you feeling today, Ephraim?"

"I had a good nap." Grandpa's voice was thin and raspy. He told Dad everything was fine, which is the kind of lie he tells everybody but me.

I unwrapped a coin for Grandpa and had one myself. Dad

handed Josh the car keys to go cruising downtown. Dagmar announced that she had a meeting at a friend's house near campus. Then Dad told me he wanted to bike to the physics lab.

"You won't mind staying here?" Dad's question sounded more like a statement.

I shook my head. Since Halloween, home still felt like the easiest place to be. No funny looks from total strangers. No questions. Getting Josh and Dagmar out of the house at the same time was a bonus.

"Thanks," he said. "I won't be long. Three hours at most."

Which might mean the middle of the night. Dad lost track of time when he was working. No matter. I could manage. After helping Grandpa into bed and kissing him good night, I retreated downstairs to my half of the bed-and-bath suite that used to be Grandpa's until he couldn't climb the stairs. Dagmar had piled my scarves on her chair. My red wool scarf was missing—no surprise. Scarves topped Dagmar's borrow list. Tied for second place: jewelry and underpants.

I reclaimed my scarves—which I wear a lot now—and stacked my library books on Dagmar's bed. It wouldn't take her long to call the library to renew them. We have an unspoken agreement. Dagmar borrows my stuff, I borrow her voice.

I glanced at Gabriel's get well card, the cheery Hallmark kind with a bluebird and daffodils. He'd put his address and phone number under "Feel better soon" and his signature, but I hadn't had the guts to write back. Calling him was naturally out of the question.

After nearly a month of practice, I'd mastered the art of no-look showering. Careful to avoid the mirror over the bathroom sink, I peeled away the bandages that looped around my ear and down my jawline. I turned my head away from the shower spray, draped a warm wet washcloth over the right side of my face, and washed my hair with no-sting baby shampoo. I patted my face dry and aligned new gauze pads and bandages by feeling the boundary that separated regular skin from welts, puckers, and stitch nicks.

When it was safe to face the mirror, I set my hair in the

rollers I used to share with Dagmar until she let her hair go wild. Until she let everything else go wild, too, including her feelings for guys. She dismissed me as the last of the big-time virgins. Which I don't see as so horrible. At least not for now.

I snuggled into plaid flannel pajamas, bedded down with Jean Plaidy's *The Thistle and the Rose*, and devoured another two chapters about medieval England and somebody else's life. It would have been the perfect escape, except that I missed Sylvester, who wasn't in his usual spot on the corner of my bed. I bobby-pinned the page and headed upstairs, figuring Sylvester might be stuck in Grandpa's room.

Grandpa's door was closed. I heard his usual Tommy Dorsey big band music—and a woman's deep alto voice: "You can wait no longer to fulfill your promise. She is needed elsewhere. A baby's life is at stake. She must be able to come with me if she chooses."

My grandfather was probably playing a record and listening to "*Theatre Five*" on the radio at the same time. You never knew with him these days. At least he remembered to take his medications. Most of the time.

I knocked.

No answer.

The doorknob didn't turn. He'd locked himself in again.

I knocked louder. "Guh-randpa, open the d-door." I put my ear to the wood. All I could hear was music—"Stardust," I think—and that woman's voice, now almost a whisper: "It fills me with great pain to say this, but you must act quickly. You are nearing death, Ephraim."

Death? Ephraim? My heart beat a wild staccato tempo. Ephraim was my grandfather. Ephraim Jacobowitz. I pounded on the door.

"Guh-guh-randpa!"

Sylvester yowled.

Light flashed under the door, blasting my bare feet blue.

CHAPTER TWO

IRACED TO THE KITCHEN for the small, flathead screwdriver I used when Grandpa got into this mess last September. I wiggled the blade into the slot in the doorknob, heard the pop, and rushed in.

No woman. No record playing. No *"Theatre Five."* Tommy Dorsey's band blared on the radio. My grandfather sat on the edge of his bed, wiping his nose with the wrinkled handkerchief that lived in the pocket of the cardigan Grandma Miriam had knitted for him before I was born.

Car headlights glinted off the mirror on Grandpa's dresser. White lights, not blue. Had I really seen blue? And heard a woman's voice?

This must be how they start. I leaned against the door, suddenly dizzy. The doctors had warned me to expect flashbacks after an LSD trip, but they couldn't say when these side effects might start. I'd been lucky so far.

Not anymore. I managed to park the screwdriver on Grandpa's dresser and stumble to the chair next to his bed.

"Here, *sheyna maidl*, for whatever is troubling you, a handkerchief always helps."

The room stopped spinning. I took the handkerchief from Grandpa's outstretched hand. "Are y-you okay? W-was s-someone in here?"

He bobbed his head, which I took to mean yes, but yes to what? I shouldn't have asked him two questions at once.

"My Miriam of blessed memory ironed seven handkerchiefs for me every week, a fresh one for each day, even when she was busy at the print shop." He patted my knee. "She still wonders why so many people call you Hope."

Poor Grandpa, still speaking to his dead wife. I rubbed the back of my neck. I could have explained for the gazillionth time that I go by my middle name because "Hope" doesn't gag me as much as "Miriam" does, and it's hard enough feeling stupid when you talk, but when you can't even say your own name... Instead I asked, "W-was there a w-woman in your room?"

"*Nu?* A man is entitled to company in his own house. We listen to the radio after work. How else do we know what's happening with our boys on the front line?"

Sadness welled up inside. He didn't used to be this way. I touched his hand, a collection of blue bruises under parchment skin. He was back in World War II again. Or World War I. Or Korea. He probably didn't even know about Vietnam.

"Tomorrow after school you'll take me to buy war bonds," he said. "And I am counting on you to take care of my jade plant after I leave." He pointed to the shiny, waxy-leafed mini-tree overwhelming a porcelain pot on his desk. "Let the soil dry out first, and then water it well."

Tears ached in the back of my eyes. "You sh-shouldn't l-lock yourself in. S-s-suppose you got ill or f-fell?"

He scowled. "I never lock my door. Never."

"But j-just now..."

His face beamed. "Yes, just now we were talking about my jade plant. Stay, *sheyna maidl*. I have for you a Hanukkah present."

I tucked my hair behind my left ear and folded my hands in my lap. He stood, steadied himself, and then patted my head. "I have for you a gift from your grandmother, my Miriam of blessed memory."

I nodded. And waited. He stood over me, his hand still on my head. Moisture leaked from his nose. I smoothed the handkerchief and returned it to him.

"A gift," I prompted.

His forehead wrinkled in confusion, then relaxed. "Yes. Now where did I put it when I moved here?"

He hadn't seen it in six years? Why wait so long? "Y-your duh-resser?"

"Smart girl."

After I turned off the radio, we opened all the drawers and rifled through clothes, old papers, and a box of memorabilia. Whatever he was looking for wasn't there. Still, I was feeling better—no more flashes of blue light or strange voices.

I checked under his bed and rescued a faded black sock smothered in dust bunnies. That left Grandpa's desk—nothing there—and then the closet. Grandpa asked me to take down the hatbox on the top shelf.

I put the box on his bed and let him open the lid. He lifted out a gray fedora and stroked the brim, his eyes getting the blank stare that meant he was somewhere else. I concentrated on what had been folded in half under the fedora—a soft woolen bag, creamy white with embroidered flowers. It looked like a feminine version of the black velvet bag Grandpa used for his prayer shawl when he came to services to hear me sing in the temple choir.

The prayer shawl inside was smaller than Grandpa's prayer shawl and made from the same wool as the bag, with a white-on-white pattern. I laid it over his pillows and admired the beautiful embroidery that decorated the top edge—yellow and orange flowers, purple grapes with green vines, and crimson lettering.

"Guh-randpa?" I touched his sleeve.

He stopped stroking the hat brim and looked at me, then at the prayer shawl. A smile creased his face. "You found her *tallis*," he whispered.

He traced the letters on the shawl with an arthritic finger.

$$צֶדֶק צֶדֶק תִּרְדֹּף$$

"The writing is ancient Hebrew script, see? It is a passage from the Torah. *Tzedek, tzedek tirdof.* Justice, justice you shall pursue."

My grandfather refolded the shawl and placed it in my arms as if it were a newborn baby. "Here, *sheyna maidl*, this is my gift to you from your grandmother. She wants you to have it. She says it's time."

Delighted, I swirled the shawl over my head and let it drape across my shoulders down to my knees. The short fringes on the ends and the longer ones at the corners were all white, except for one long thread—a vivid blue—in the left front corner.

I reached for the blue thread.

Grandpa lunged at me, his eyes wild with anger—or terror. He yanked the shawl from my shoulders. "No!"

CHAPTER THREE

WHAT DID I DO wrong? I stood there speechless, my stomach churning.

Grandpa's hands shook as he put my grandmother's prayer shawl back in the bag. "You must not wear this. Never. Don't you let Dagmar wear it, either. I know she borrows clothes from you." He grabbed my wrist. Hard. "This *tallis* will take you away. You hide it. Hide it good!"

"Guh-randpa, you're …you're h-hurting m-me."

He let go of my wrist, muttered something in Yiddish, and started to whimper. I put my arms around him. *When had he gotten this thin?*

Grandpa reached into his cardigan pocket. "For whatever is troubling you, a handkerchief always helps," he told me again, wiping his nose. "A pressed handkerchief is better."

I raised my eyebrows and nodded in agreement.

He looked at my bare feet. "Also slippers. Watch you shouldn't catch cold. Now you must hide your gift. Your mother must never find out."

Really? Why not? I decided to wait to ask my grandfather until he was more coherent, and I humored him by putting the prayer shawl in one of the extra pillowcases we keep in his room.

"S-see," I said. "It l-looks like l-laundry now."

"No one must know of this *tallis* but you," he warned.

I promised I'd keep it safe, reminded him to leave his door unlocked, kissed him good night again, picked up the screw-driver, and told him I'd see him in the morning.

"From your mouth to God's ear," he said.

Sylvester followed me into the kitchen, where I planned to finish the leftover pumpkin pie. Grandpa might think handkerchiefs are best for whatever troubles you, but I go for dessert.

Parking the shawl-stuffed pillowcase on the counter, I walked toward the whatnot drawer to return the screwdriver. An ambulance siren blared outside. Once, and then again. Closer. I tightened my grip on the screwdriver.

The right side of my face began to tingle, then burn. I stared at the screwdriver as the blade grew longer. Tiny teeth sprouted from the tip.

Gasping for air, I tried to drop the screwdriver. The plastic handle fused with my flesh. Blood oozed from my fingertips.

My heart pounded in my ears.

And then the screwdriver turned back into a screwdriver. No teeth. No blood. I flung the damn thing on the floor, grabbed the kitchen counter, and closed my eyes.

Big mistake.

A man's mouth floated in space, a zipper where his lips should be. His lips unzipped, and musical notes flew out of his mouth. The words *stitches* and *ambulance* twirled around his dance-floor tongue. One, two, three. One, two, three.

"No!" I jerked my eyelids open.

One shuddering breath followed another. *This must be a flashback. Instant hell.*

Struggling to gain control, I practiced the diaphragm breathing I'd learned in choral music class. Inhale. Slow release. Inhale. Slow release.

The back door slammed, and I prayed for a miracle. My mother would crush me against her and announce, "Happy Hanukkah, sweetie. I'm home a few days early." I'd settle for Dad. Even Dagmar.

"Cutesy pajamas," Josh said. "They'd go great with bunny slippers. Any pie left? I'm starving."

"I-I…"

He tossed the car keys on the kitchen table and headed for the refrigerator.

I steadied myself against the counter and watched Josh's back as he claimed the pumpkin pie and a carton of milk. Inhale. Slow release.

"Mom should have ordered an extra pie." He took a swig of milk from the carton, then finally turned and studied me like I was some stock market listing. "Hey, kiddo, you look kind of wobbly."

"I-I j-just had a fuh-lash-b-back."

Josh's look shifted into what seemed to promise genuine concern. "A flashback? You mean like a mini-LSD trip?"

I hugged my chest and nodded.

"Is Dagmar here?"

I shook my head.

"She is never here when she should be. Would she even think to leave you instructions or anything? No, of course not. So, now what am I supposed to do?"

I wanted to grab him by his perfectly pressed shirt and yell, "You're supposed to comfort to me, you idiot! You're supposed to tell me everything will be fine." Instead I shook my head again and took another deep breath. The screwdriver next to my bare feet stayed a screwdriver.

"I bet she's out with those nutcases peddling their propaganda on campus. Free speech? That is such bull." He pointed the milk carton at a chair. "You should sit down."

For once in your life you should shut up and hold me. The chair looked too far away. I clung to the counter.

"Okay, kiddo, but don't blame me if you fall on your face." He grabbed a fork from the dish drain and dug into the pie. "Don't you think Mario Savio and his merry band of weirdos are making a big stink out of nothing? I mean, so what if the university declares another twenty-six feet of walkway off-limits to campaign tables and bans political speech on campus? The nutcases can go set up their signs and posters someplace else, right? This whole protest business is a complete crock."

Two seconds of silence.

"D-don't t-t-tell D-Dad," I managed. If he and Mom knew about my flashback, they'd never let me go away to the music festival.

"What? You think Dad is a Savio fan?"

I tapped my head.

"Ah, your fried brain. Dagmar really messed you up this time." Josh took another bite of pie.

I bit my lip.

"So, tell me this. Dagmar says Mario stutters worse than you. And you stutter pretty bad, so he must *really* have a problem. Anyway, Dagmar says this guy doesn't stutter when he's speaking to a crowd. Like it's a miracle or something. How's that possible? Dagmar's bullshitting me, right?"

I glared at Josh. Why bother to explain that I had no idea Mario stuttered and that the students had every right to protest? I might even give up the music festival if I could find the guts to speak out like they were. It took only two steps to reach the pillowcase on the counter. Sylvester and I headed downstairs, leaving the screwdriver on the floor and my ass of a brother to his stupid pie.

I unlatched my window—Dagmar's favorite late-night entry—and told myself the flashback episode lasted only a few seconds. Everything was going to be okay. Maybe that was the only one I'd ever have. Maybe if I had told Josh to hug me and make me a cup of tea or something, he would have. *Who are you kidding? Talk about bullshit.*

I opened the *tallis* bag and spread the prayer shawl across my chair. Grandpa's gift was the one good thing about tonight.

Sylvester arched his back and hissed.

"S-silly cat. Isn't it gorgeous?" The words almost flowed. If only I could pretend everybody was my pet cat. I ran my hands through the long white threads hanging from each corner. And that single blue thread, too.

Sylvester scratched my arm.

"Ow!" I picked him up mother-cat style by the nape of his neck. "W-what's with you tonight, you cuh-razy beast?"

He went limp. I tucked my hand under his bottom. "You're b-banished until you can behave." I put Sylvester in the hall leading to the bathroom and the workroom/garage, and started to close the door.

That's when I heard a woman's voice behind me, coming from the direction of the open window. The voice I'd heard in Grandpa's room.

"Miryam Tikvah, I come in peace."

My hand gripped the doorknob. Air rushed out of my chest. I forgot how to breathe.

I should have run out through the garage. I don't know why I didn't.

I closed the door and turned toward the voice.

CHAPTER FOUR

SHE STOOD BY MY desk, holding out her hands and beckoning me to come closer. She looked about Dagmar's age—bronze skin, gold-flecked hazel eyes highlighted with white eyebrows and nearly invisible eyelashes. No make-up. No jewelry. She wore a floor-length beige wool robe and an ochre headscarf that hid most of her white hair. Maybe she was part of a cult. Maybe she was from some exotic country.

Miryam Tikvah. How could she know my Hebrew name? And how had she opened the window and closed it so quietly? Maybe she wasn't really there. *Oh, God, not another flashback!*

I took a breath and stared at her, waiting for her to start glowing or turn into some bizarre creature.

She didn't change.

Keeping her in my sight, I dug into the pile at the foot of Dagmar's bed and closed my hand around one of Dagmar's clogs. And I let it fly.

She caught the clog a second before it would have slammed into her stomach. Her eyes widened in surprise. "I have done nothing to harm you. I come in peace. Why do you insult me with the throwing of a shoe?"

I felt my shoulders relax. Better to be visited by a stranger than a flashback. "First of all, my name is Hope. Second, I threw the shoe to see if you were really here. And third, get out of my room."

The words gushed out of my mouth without a glitch. Weird.

She sat on my bed, put Dagmar's clog on the floor, folded her hands in her lap, and beamed at me. "Then I, too, shall call you by this name in your place and time. Hope."

I inched closer to the bedroom door, ready to escape. There was something really off about this girl. She was probably one of Dagmar's friends, maybe someone from our temple, which was why she called me Miryam Tikvah. Her voice had a guttural quality to it. Israeli? She was probably stoned or worse— on LSD, which should be illegal in California but isn't. Lysergic acid di-whatever. Since my first and only trip, I'd renamed it Lethal-Suicidal-Deadly.

"I'm going to bed now," I said, pointing to my pajamas. "You'll have to wait for Dagmar outside." No stutter again, which sometimes happens when I am over-the-top angry. But I felt more frightened than angry, and fear usually makes it harder to push the words out. Crazy.

"I am not waiting for your sister, Dagmar. I am waiting for you." She reached toward the prayer shawl.

"Don't touch that," I managed to say loud and clear. Something was really bizarre with my speech. Not that I minded.

The girl put her hands back in her lap. "This is a beautiful gift. I know it well. I, too, bear a gift. A guardian doll." She reached into a small bag that hung from a belt around her waist. "Here," she said, showing me some sort of odd fetish made of yarn and straw. "For you. For Hanukkah."

She put the doll on my desk. When she faced me again, her eyes had hardened. "Hope, we must talk of your grandmother Miriam, daughter of Julius, who has worn this garment. We must talk of the young woman Dolcette. She has great need of you. Please sit by my side. I have much to explain."

I didn't budge. "You were in my grandfather's room, weren't you? I heard you talking to him."

She tapped a finger on her knee, a fast, impatient rhythm. "Your grandfather knows of me. Your grandmother has traveled with me."

I shook my head. "You had no right barging into his room and telling him that he's dying." My throat tightened. This strange girl voiced a truth I didn't want to hear.

I took a breath and continued. "If you don't leave, I'm calling the police." Me? Using the phone? Highly unlikely, but I didn't have to tell her that. I swallowed hard, forcing myself to stay calm.

The girl stared at my rug, her finger frozen mid-tap.

Silence.

Then she stood and smoothed her robe. "This is difficult for you, and I cannot force you. Please know that Dolcette cannot wait long. Once you are intertwined with her, you may leave your here and now and return in an instant, but a day in your time is also a day for Dolcette."

"Who's Dolcette? You're not making any sense."

"Come and see." She stepped closer.

I reached behind my back for the doorknob and eased the door open a crack.

"I have traveled a long way through the *olam* for you. Through every place and all time. Time is boundless for me, but Dolcette needs you now. She has only eight days. Fewer and fewer as the minutes go by."

"I see," I said. And I did. She was definitely tripping on something.

The girl touched the box of dreidels I planned to give to my friends. "May I have one of these Hanukkah tops as a token in exchange for the guardian doll?"

I wanted to shout at her to go away and leave me alone, but I've learned the hard way with Dagmar that when someone's high, you don't shout at them. They could freak, and then you'd really have a problem on your hands.

Instead I said, "Sure. Take two. It's really time for you to leave." I motioned toward the window. Letting her out through the garage would have been easier, but I didn't want her to come any closer.

"I will take only one for Dolcette." She cocked her head and looked at my bandages. "You have an injury?"

"I'm fine."

"Then I shall not fear for your safety when we travel through the *olam*. Now it is time for you to fetch your cat."

"Why?"

"I must leave the way that I came."

Which I figured was through the window. At least that made sense. Maybe she didn't want Sylvester to run after her. Okay, I could play that game.

The instant I turned my back and stepped into the hall, I saw a bluish spark of light reflecting off the wallpaper in front of me. That same blue. Was my brain becoming sensitive to a certain kind of light? Could there be some crazy, post-LSD neural link between seeing blue flashes and speaking like a normal person? That would be a welcome side effect. Bring on the blue! I made a mental note to ask the doctor when Mom and I saw him again.

Sylvester meowed from under my workbench. By the time I coaxed him into my arms and returned to my room, the girl was gone. I latched the window shut. I was not about to let any of Dagmar's friends scare me like that again.

Sylvester attacked the doll. I let him claw it to pieces.

CHAPTER FIVE

FIFTEEN MINUTES LATER, DAGMAR knocked on the window. I helped her climb inside.

Judging from her breath, she was more drunk than high. While she stripped for bed, she showed me the remains of a large chrysanthemum she'd tucked into her cleavage. Her mango-sized breasts jiggled, teasing me that the demi-gods of DNA had bestowed Mom's gorgeous figure, thick black curls, and hazel eyes on my sister. I got stuck with cow-brown eyes, tits the size of Meyer lemons, and the droopy blond hair belonging to Dad's side of the family.

"Feel how soft the petals are, Hopey-Poo," she said, sounding more like nine than nineteen. "Soft as a baby's behind. Soft as my behind." She patted her bare bottom, which is another reason why I don't bring my friends down here, not even Leona. You never know when my sister is going to be sleeping something off, but you can bet she'll be sleeping in the nude.

"Y-you c-came home early." I said, voicing my excuse for the window being latched. I sounded like me again, which was both comforting and a disappointment.

Dagmar flashed her little-girl pout. "No one to play with. My friends are pissed that Mario and some other free speech guys got this expulsion letter from the high mucky-mucks. Everybody and his uncle are glum, glum, glum, and then some. I had to settle for wine, 'cause you don't want to trip when you're surrounded by totally bad karma."

Dagmar smiled at me and recited what she calls her LSD nursery rhyme:

Sing a song of sixpence
A pocketful of rye
Four and twenty blackbirds baked in a pie
When the pie was opened
the birds began to sing.
Oh wasn't that a tasty dish to set before the king.

"Acid is just fungussy rye," she explained to me for the gazillionth time. "It's the fungus among us. A natural high, Hopey-Dope."

I clenched my fist. "You puh-romised that…"

Dagmar hit her forehead with the palm of her hand. "You're right, you're right. You are *so* right. I promised no stashes of the good stuff in our bedroom and no jokes with you about acid until the day after forever."

Then she got that older sister, sympathetic look. "Aren't you supposed to change your bandages every night? Here, let me help you."

I thrust my hands in front of my face. "All d-done," I lied. "D-do you know a g-girl with buh-ronze skin and wh-white eyebrows?"

"What's her name?"

I shook my head. Had she told me? "She b-barged in on Guh-randpa. And and she cuh-limbed in the w-window."

"Wild. And then what?"

"I g-gave her a duh-reidel, and she l-left."

My sister wiggled under the covers and giggled. "Good job, Hope Springs Eternal. We *all* love your dreidels." She sang her crazy version of *I Have a Little Dreidel* off-key, which grated like nails on a blackboard.

I have Hope's little dreidel.
She made it out of wood.
And when I'm high and ready,
I'll spin it and feel good.

So much for Dagmar's promises.

The garage door opened.

"D-Dad's home. Puh-ipe down."

"Ooh, shhhhhh," she told herself. "We mustn't disturb The Great Dane, our famous physicist, while he solves the mysteries of the universe!" She giggled again and stumbled out of bed. I managed to drape my quilt over her as she opened the bedroom door, and I wedged myself in front of her, in case the quilt slipped.

Dagmar flapped the sides of the quilt like a bird in flight. "Hey! How's the universe tonight?" So much for not disturbing Dad.

Dad stopped wiping mud spatters from his bike. He looked up at us and shook his head. "The universe is complicated, Dagmar," he said, his voice flat and tired. No stern lecture this time. I figured he knew Dagmar was naked and soused—two good reasons to avoid a father-daughter confrontation.

"Good night, Miriam Hope. Sleep well."

I smiled my good night.

I guided Dagmar back to bed and put my grandmother's prayer shawl on top of my bookcase, away from sister and cat. I set the alarm for six thirty because of school the next day, and I made sure the window was locked. Sylvester stretched out on the corner of my bed—my feline sentry in case that strange girl came back in the night.

My pillow felt hot. The closed, dark room threatened to smother me. Listening to Dagmar's soft snore, I stared at the ceiling, afraid to shut my eyes.

6:28. I woke from a dreamless night and turned off the alarm two minutes before it was set to ring. Mom says I was born with an alarm clock in my brain. I shuffled to the bathroom, changed the bandages on the Frankenstein half of my face, then turned on the overhead bathroom light and woke Dagmar.

She rolled over and flung an arm in my direction. "What day is it?"

"M-Monday."

"Do I have classes?"

I looked at the calendar, which I keep for both of us,

otherwise Dagmar would never remember her schedule at Berkeley. "Cuh-chemistry l-lab at thuh-ree ten."

"I'll sleep in."

The prayer shawl was still hiding in Grandpa's pillowcase, but Dagmar has a sixth sense for any new clothes on my side of the room. I decided the shawl would be safer in my school locker than left unguarded at home. Besides, I wanted Leona to see it.

I found a note on the kitchen table:

0527.
Driving Josh to airport.
Then going to lab.
Home for dinner.
xo,
Dad

I shook my head and smiled. Being both scientific about the time and valentine-cutesy was so Dad. Grandpa gave me a real hug and kiss, plus oatmeal. "Porridge," he calls it. He's been okay with cooking something simple in the morning. Still, I checked to make sure he'd turned off the stove. He had.

"D-Dagmar is downstairs if you nuh-eed anything," I told him. "I'll buh-ring Chuh-inese home for d-dinner."

He stirred his instant coffee. "Where is Rachel?"

"M-Mom is on a tuh-rip." I reminded him of the Thanksgiving dinner she made for us on Wednesday before she took the early morning flight Thanksgiving Day. "She'll be b-back s-soon. T-tuna fuh-ish or c-corned beef?"

He couldn't decide which one he wanted for lunch, so I made half a sandwich of each. I grabbed an apple and a half-full container of cottage cheese, and raced out the door to meet Leona.

She waved to me as I turned the corner of Roosevelt and strode up Channing toward Grove. From a block away, Leona Nash could double for Audrey Hepburn in *Funny Face*. We were both wearing headscarves, Hepburn style. Up close, Leona's hair is lighter and her eyebrows a little thinner than Audrey's. She's got that pixie look and perfect complexion I would resent, only she's watched out for me since second grade, so resentment isn't on the agenda.

"My Thanksgiving was too horrid for words," she said, her bubbly expression showing me I shouldn't worry. "You know my cousin from Fremont? The one with the Harley? Well, he came up to visit for the weekend, and he brought us salamis for Hanukkah. Salamis, can you believe it? From some deli in Fremont that's supposed to be the best in the galaxy. Our house smells positively putrid now. Hope, I'm telling you, Josh is a complete ratfink, but at least he doesn't smoke cigars and walk around with salamis. How's the…um…the wound?"

"B-better."

She squeezed my arm. "Excellent! I bet your singing's gotten better over Thanksgiving break. You are so lucky the infection didn't damage your vocal cords. You'll sing great without the bandages."

I managed a nod. If I'd shrugged, she'd be all over me with a pep talk I didn't feel like hearing, even from Leona. Six guys from our track team jogged past in their gym shorts. The last guy had these amazing leg muscles, flexing and pumping, flexing and pumping.

Leona must have caught me watching, because she hummed the opening bars of "My Boy Lollipop."

I laughed for the first time in days.

"Can I persuade you to go to the Hanukkah party Saturday night?"

"M-maybe."

"It'll be fun. You haven't gone out with the gang since… um… the accident. Kenny is coming. That new guy. He'll talk your head off, but he's nuts about opera and he's got a great voice. You'll like him."

Nearly everybody talked my head off. I've got a doctorate in listening.

I tightened my scarf.

"Oh, come on. Eric was a jerk. Don't let him put you off guys forever. If Stephen and I weren't going together, I'd go out with Kenny myself."

"M-maybe."

Leona opened the school door for us. "My friend, two may-bes in a row from you mean yes."

I didn't argue. When we got to my locker, I shifted my scarf from my head to my shoulders and decided to wait until our usual after-school nosh at Barston's to show Leona my prayer shawl.

"I have a make-up quiz in geometry, so I'll be late," Leona said. "Meet me over there. See you third period. Hey, did your parents decide about the music festival yet?"

I shook my head.

"Then good luck with Mr. Z."

I needed more than luck.

CHAPTER SIX

A S SOON AS I got to choral music, Mr. Zegarelli summoned me to the piano, and I had to tell him I didn't have my money or permission slip. Leona gave me her ultra-sympathetic look from the alto section.

"Miss Friis," he said, his long, delicate fingers conducting our discussion in front of the whole class, "before you came back to us last week, you missed two-and-a-half weeks of rehearsal due to your unfortunate accident."

My stomach twisted. Leona had told the kids at school that I was in a car accident, and so far no one seemed suspicious. But word gets around. By Christmas break, I might as well have tattooed a message on my forehead: LSD—*the trip that lasts a lifetime.*

"There are other young women in this class who do not have your God-given gift of perfect pitch, Miss Friis, but who are quite capable of singing first soprano in our madrigal group for the festival."

Martha and Francine. Yes, but they could care less about a scholarship to a music conservatory. I needed this solo.

"Surely you are well aware that the permission slips and trip deposits were due to me before Thanksgiving, and yet you have not turned them in. What do you have to say for yourself?"

I didn't want to admit that Mom still worried about my having flashbacks while I was away—and now I understood why—and that Dad insisted I pay for half the expenses—which I hadn't managed to do yet. I concentrated on Mr. Z's polished-mahogany piano bench and wished I could sing the words instead of say them.

"M-my m-m-mother is away," I managed. "C-c-can I l-let y-you know n-next Tuesday?" Mom was coming back on Monday, and I was determined to show her how totally together and mentally sound I was. Maybe I would be by then.

"Miss Friis, look at me when I speak to you. There. That's better. Next Tuesday is December 8. I don't need to remind you that the Portland festival starts January 28. The rest of your classmates at Berkeley High School are counting on us to win."

I bobbed my head in affirmation.

"Have you been practicing all your scales, as I recommended?"

"Y-yes," I whispered.

Two full measures of silence. My face burned with embarrassment.

"You have until next Tuesday."

"Thuh-ank you." I hurried to my seat in the soprano section and pretended to sort pieces in my music folder until my cheeks cooled down.

Mr. Zegarelli lectured the class. "As for the rest of you, do not think that your place in the competition is secure. You will not be allowed to represent Berkeley High School in *any* extracurricular event if you get involved with the student demonstrations at the university in *any* manner. The principal and I will not tolerate any participation in the unrest on campus. Is that clear?"

Someone in the tenor section coughed. Mr. Zegarelli thrust an index finger at the tenors. "Do I make myself clear? Good. Let us begin with 'Now Is the Month of Maying.'"

Now is the month of praying, I thought. I could use a new face and a ton and a half of confidence to sing the way I used to. I could use a miracle.

After school, I called home to check on Grandpa. There was a fifty-fifty chance he would get the phone. No answer. One day, my father and his physics friends might invent something useful, like a way for me to send him a note over the phone without speaking or for Sylvester to answer the phone and send an "all's well" signal.

Bright sun had broken through the clouds, and the afternoon

was glorious. I unbuttoned my coat and listened to the melodies of sparrows and chickadees that avoided our yard thanks to Sylvester. Barston's was packed, but I managed to find an empty two-seater booth wedged into the way back. The coffee shop was filled with so much clatter and chatter that I could ignore it all—no one was talking to me. The Drifters were belting out "Under the Boardwalk," and I could smell the menu: cakes and pies and brownies and cinnamon buns. I leaned against the black vinyl seat and imagined how proud Grandpa would be if I went to the music festival in Portland. He still had family there. Maybe they'd come to the competition.

"What can I get for you?" The waitress twirled her pencil like a miniature baton. With so many customers in the shop, I didn't dare tell her I was waiting for Leona.

I cleared my throat and said, "Hmmm… a hot ch-ch…"

"Hot chocolate," she spat back.

I pursed my lips and dipped my chin once.

"Whipped cream?"

I chin-dipped again.

"Will that be all?"

I cleared my throat. "F-f-for now."

The waitress disappeared into the crowd. I left my book bag and pillow-cased prayer shawl in the booth and went to the ladies' room. One sink, three stalls, a quiet, chilly refuge from the noise outside.

When I got out of the stall, there she was again, that girl, standing by the sink. Caressing my prayer shawl.

Some nerve! I grabbed for the shawl. "Hey, that's mine. Give it back."

That crazy girl must have spun out of my way because the next thing I knew I had collided with the sink, and she was standing by the towel dispenser.

"Hope," she said softly. "A thousand pardons, but it is very hard to find you alone. Dolcette has great need of you, and nearly a whole day has passed. I see that you have brought your garment of fringes to this eating place. I pray that you will trust me."

I leaned against the sink, my heart in triple tempo. Even

Dagmar wouldn't track people down after school, steal their stuff, and follow them into the ladies' room. Unless she was high. Which might be the case with Miss Weirdo.

I stared at the girl and said nothing, hoping the silent treatment would make things easier. It does sometimes with Dagmar.

"My name is Serakh, daughter of Asher," she said. "The One has guided me to you. Dolcette is sick with fear for her newborn son. I have given your top to her as a pledge that you would come."

You could hardly see her white eyelashes.

"A dreidel you call it, with the Hebrew letters that stand for *ness gadol hayah sham.*"

Ness was miracle; *gadol*, great. *Hayah sham* meant happened there. A great miracle happened there, meaning ancient Israel or the temple in Jerusalem The story of Hanukkah. What Jewish kid didn't know that? Half-Jewish anyway.

"Dolcette is waiting for a great miracle. She takes the top as a sign that you will appear. I have been guided to you for the intertwining. I beg you to return to her with me."

I replayed the Hanukkah story in my mind, how Judah Maccabee and the Israelites fought for religious freedom and won back Jerusalem from the Syrians. And how a tiny bit of oil for the Temple light burned miraculously for eight days until the Israelites could make more. There was nothing in the Hanukkah story about a Dolcette.

She folded my prayer shawl and handed it back. "Please. You have only to touch the long blue thread in this fringe and close your eyes against the light."

Not a chance. I kissed the shawl—it seemed like the respectful thing to do to a prayer shawl after it had been dragged into the bathroom—and gave her my fiercest stare.

The girl glanced at the ceiling, then back at me. Her face aligned in a trust-me look that Dagmar uses on me and means anything but.

"I am wearing an extra gown for you under my robes. No one will see the clothing of your place and time. Have no fear. You will not be mistaken for a conjurer or a witch."

47

Stoned. Definitely stoned. I edged away, wondering whether I could slip past her and get out the ladies' room door.

She leaned closer. "I cannot force you, but shall we have a contest? It is the twenty-fifth of *Kislev*, yes?"

I nodded. Today was still technically the twenty-fifth in the Hebrew calendar, the first day of Hanukkah, because days went from sundown to sundown, the way they are counted in the Bible.

"Dolcette also celebrates Hanukkah. If I can take you to her within an instant, you will agree to listen to her story. If I fail, I will not come for you again."

A contest? This girl was getting on my nerves. I opened the stall doors. Empty. The window was nothing but those glass bricks. No way could Serakh win, unless Dolcette was right outside the ladies' room door. In that case, when Dolcette came in, I'd run for it.

"Fine," I said.

Serakh seemed delighted. "Hold tightly to the blue thread and let me touch you," she said softly.

I wrapped the shawl's one blue thread around my fingers. Up close, Serakh smelled like farm animals. Maybe it was the wool. She asked me to close my eyes, but I refused.

"As you wish," she said.

Oh, God! The blue thread strangled my finger. Bright blue light bombarded me. I squeezed my eyes shut and doubled over in pain. My stomach turned upside down. My lungs screamed for air. I was trapped inside a horrid sound-and-light show, drowning in a flood of panic. No, no, no, no…

CHAPTER SEVEN

THE PAIN FINALLY EASED. I could breathe again—just barely. Something rough scratched my back. Another something poked into my thigh. I opened my eyes to forest and fog.

Serakh squatted beside me, propping me against a giant oak tree.

Impossible.

She held my shoulders, keeping me upright.

"Breathe," she said.

I shivered in the icy dampness. "Where am I?"

"Shh…Take a moment to recover." The girl helped me to stand and then slipped a warm woolen caftan over my shoulders and my prayer shawl. Still groggy, I let her stuff my hair under a large, beige linen cap.

"Wipe the pigment from your lips," she ordered, handing me a long brownish-gray rectangular cloth." When I hesitated, she asked, "Shall I do this for you?"

I forced my head from side to side and then rubbed my mouth. The cloth reeked of onions and sour milk.

She rubbed dirt into the lipstick stain, and then tied that putrid cloth under my chin and over the top of the cap. "We must hide the bandages, as they are not of this place and time." Had the caftan and cloth been black, I could have passed for a nun.

I grabbed her hands. "Stop. Wait. Tell me what happened. Tell me where I am. Who are you?"

She didn't try pull away from my grip. "I am Serakh, daughter of Asher, as I have said. We have crossed to a spot on the *olam* that is different from your own. The *olam* stretches to all points in the universe from the beginning of time to the end of days. I beg you to turn away from your fear. You are safe with me."

I had no idea what this crazy girl was talking about, except for the fear part. Which, for some odd reason, was quickly being replaced by curiosity. "Where is Dolcette?"

"A few steps away. Let us walk together. I will help you."

We were closer to civilization than I'd thought. What looked like a forest was only a cluster of a dozen or so trees. A neighborhood of old wooden and stone buildings crowded together several yards away. A chorus of voices echoed from somewhere nearby. Serakh clamped her hand over my mouth, her fingers rough and calloused against my lips. "We must be silent," she whispered in my ear, her breath smelling of olives and lamb, with a hint of decay.

The voices faded. She took her hand away and pointed to my penny loafers. "Can you remove the silver discs on top, lest they attract attention? I will keep these adornments safe in my pouch. Your robes will hide most of your foot covering."

I focused on the dimes I had slipped into the penny slots, dimes for phone calls. For one mad moment, I contemplated finding the pay phones at Barston's and calling Dad. Which is real and which isn't? There's no getting out of your own head.

"We have only to enter the nearest house and you shall see Dolcette."

The wool itched my neck and shoulders. "What?"

"Dolcette," Serakh repeated. "You have vowed that if I showed you Dolcette in an instant, you would talk with her. You see her house, yes? Dolcette lies within. Now that you are dressed in these garments, it is safe to go inside."

I gave Serakh the dimes. Her hand felt solid enough. Real. "This is not happening," I assured myself out loud. "I'm in the ladies' room at Barston's."

"You do not trust your eyes?"

No. Or my nose. Or my ears. My brain is betraying me.

Before I could open my mouth again, Serakh had clutched

my hand and guided me toward the buildings. As we left the trees, I glimpsed a river on my left and a high-arched wooden bridge from the land we were on to the opposite shore. In the distance, on my side of the bridge, a tile roof peeked over the tops of the trees. A manor house? A castle? Impossible.

"Dolcette has given birth to a boy in the first moments of Hanukkah. The women who attend her have gone to the market. Her husband shelters elsewhere until the eighth day of his son's life. This is the perfect hour for you to be here."

"To be where?"

Serakh nodded. "Ah, my apologies. I have not said, Tikvah. Here I shall call you Tikvah, as it will be a familiar name for Dolcette. We are in the Jewish quarter of Paris, by the indulgence of King Philip. The Christian knights have passed, and we are safe for now."

CHAPTER EIGHT

"**P**ARIS? PARIS, FRANCE?" I tugged at Serakh, forcing her to stop. My mind must have conjured up a mad madrigal scene from the Middle Ages, a bizarre 3D version of "Now Is the Month of Maying." Only it felt more like December.

Serakh leaned closer and frowned. "Take care that you are quiet. Stay by my side and say nothing. You will come to understand soon."

Two minutes later, we stood in a kitchen dimly lit by a fire in a stone hearth. Serakh pointed to a copper or brass triangle that hung on the wall near a rough wooden table. The triangle was solid, with eight teaspoon-sized cups on the bottom and another teaspoon-sized cup half way up one side. I'd seen enough Hanukkah objects in Mom's gift shop to know this was the kind of menorah they used centuries ago.

"The first day of Hanukkah," Serakh said. "The women who attend Dolcette will light the oil for the second day at sundown. I have taken you back to the twenty-fifth day of the month of *Kislev* in a distant year, but during the same hour of the holiday that you celebrate in your place and time."

"I can't believe this," I whispered. Still, the table didn't float. The walls didn't turn into cottage cheese. Nothing seemed surreal. Other than the entire situation, of course.

Serakh led me up narrow stone steps and into a cramped bedroom with a low, timbered ceiling. A half-shuttered window on the far wall let in fading light from the late-afternoon sky. The wood-planked floor was bare. An oak bed contained what seemed to be a human form covered in a thick cotton quilt. A large candle burned on a small table, casting light on a blue-and-white ceramic pitcher and bowl, and a small leather pouch.

Serakh bent over a rectangular wooden box on the floor and picked up what looked like a football wrapped like a mummy with a doll's head on top.

"Hold him," she said.

The tiniest human I'd ever seen. My arms automatically formed a cradle as I gazed at his sweet face. Closed eyes, tiny nose, puckered lips barely moving, seemingly sucking on air.

Serakh stood beside me, her face soft and gentle. "Dolcette calls him Mon Trésor. Her husband will name him at the *brit milah* ."

Mon Trésor. After two-and-a-half years of high school French, that was easy enough: "my treasure." *Brit milah* was Hebrew, which I hardly knew except for the regular prayers and pieces for the temple choir. I guessed that it meant the same as a *bris*. Circumcision—the cut that counts for Jewish boys.

The quilt moved, revealing a head with long dark curls escaping from a large linen cap like mine. Serakh whispered and cooed, feeling the forehead of a girl who looked young enough to be at Berkeley High. Her eyelids were puffy, as if she'd been crying, and she smelled of lavender and sweat. Dolcette—who else could she be?—moaned and slowly sat up in bed.

She grabbed Serakh's sleeve. "Oh, Madame, you are back. I have been praying for your return. Quick. Take the baby now while they are away."

She spoke in English, which I suppose made sense in my alternate reality. A part of me struggled to remember that I was still in Barston's.

"There is still time," Serakh said. "This is Tikvah. She is the sister of my husband of blessed memory. She is a worthy young woman, wise in many ways."

Really? I cleared my throat.

Dolcette smiled at me. "Tikvah is the perfect name for a Jewess. You give me hope. Are you also new to Paris?"

Paris again. This looked nothing like the city I'd studied in French class.

"We come from afar," Serakh explained for the both of us.

Mon Trésor let out an amazingly loud wail for such tiny lungs.

"Bring him here," Serakh instructed. "He's ready to nurse."

Serakh took the baby and told Dolcette to loosen the top of her gown.

Dolcette frowned. "But aren't you the wet nurse? Shouldn't you be the one to give my baby sustenance?"

Serakh positioned the baby's head near Dolcette's left breast, which looked too large for her thin arms and chest. "You are the mother. You must learn to feed your child as well, especially in the beginning."

Mon Trésor opened his mouth and lunged at Dolcette's nipple. Serakh gently pulled his lower lip down and eased him away.

"He needs to have the whole nipple in his mouth or you will not nurse well," she told Dolcette. "Let us try again."

Lunge two—as bad, apparently, as the first. Serakh eased him away again. She examined his mouth, then handed the crying bundle back to me and took a small knife from the leather pouch. "No harm will come to your child," she told Dolcette. "I will help him."

Dolcette's whole face exuded trust, the way Grandpa's does while I cut his toenails. Curious, I jiggled the baby and made shushing noises, but he kept fussing.

Serakh poured water from the pitcher over her right hand, and then she cut off a sliver of her right thumbnail. She held the knife over the candle, the short metal blade reflecting the weak fire. With her index finger, she pulled the skin back from the ball of her thumb and touched the blade to her nail. She winced, put the knife down, and told me to sit on the edge of the bed with Mon Trésor facing away from me. "Hold his head steady," she instructed. I didn't dare do otherwise.

Serakh guided her thumbnail under his tongue. His crying arched to a scream for a second, and then she took him in her arms and rocked him. When he quieted, she guided him back toward Dolcette's breast and stuffed nearly the whole nipple into his tiny mouth.

Dolcette gasped and then relaxed into a smile. Mon Trésor's pink hand rested on her breast. His jaw worked hard, and he seemed to be nursing well. Serakh begin to sing softly, starting with a perfect B flat. The melody had a Middle Eastern flavor to it, in a minor key, sad but sweet. She reached under Dolcette's pillow and extracted the dreidel I'd given to her when she'd invaded my bedroom. A flower dreidel, one of my better ones, with a sunflower I'd painted on the side that had the Hebrew letter *S*. At least my brain had made one logical connection in all this craziness.

"Love your new child with an easy heart," she told Dolcette. "The young woman who crafted this token is here with us now."

Dolcette's mouth dropped open. She looked at me as if I were her guardian angel and Supergirl rolled into one.

Serakh kissed Dolcette's forehead. "First you must let the baby nurse." She hummed another melody line and then told us, "The baby was tongue-tied. It is a common problem. The *sâge-femme* should have cut the extra strand of flesh under his tongue when he was born. Now he will feed better and speak better when he gets older."

I stared at my dreidel with its *ness gadol haya sham*. A great miracle happened there. Maybe today I'd get the miracle I'd yearned for since forever. That barbaric act of Serakh's, cutting something in the baby's mouth—maybe that's what I needed. Forget all those speech therapists and exercises. Maybe my tongue just needed to be freed.

I touched Serakh's sleeve. She looked at me, her hazel eyes narrow and questioning. I took a breath.

"What you just did to the baby. With your fingernail. I…um …I was…because in real life, I stutter."

Her face softened. "I understand. Can you do this?" She opened her mouth and rolled the tip of her tongue toward her nose and then toward her chin.

I stuck out my tongue and did the same. It was easy. Can't everyone do that?

"You are not tongue-tied," she said. "You have no such restraint."

My eyes felt full. I bit my lip. *Stupid.* Why did I even get my hopes up?

Serakh put her hand on my left cheek. "Moshe, our great leader, speaks with effort. Still, he is chosen by The One to guide our people from Egypt and make of them a nation."

"That's a story. Nobody believes it."

"It is so." Serakh arched her eyebrows.

I shook my head.

"I know," she said. "I was there."

Enough. I had to get back to reality. I closed my eyes, hoping to open them in Barston's. And I shouted, "Leona!"

CHAPTER NINE

"**L**EE OH NAH?" SERAKH frowned. "I do not understand this phrase."

I spread my arms and twirled in a crazy pirouette. "*You* don't understand? Ha! Imagine *me*."

Serakh caught me in mid-twirl. "The contest is almost over. I will take you back soon. But first we must hear what troubles Dolcette. Help me change her discharge rag while the baby nurses."

I did as I was told. Was there a choice? Afterward, I felt a sudden gratitude toward the person who invented sanitary napkins. Serakh took the baby from Dolcette and patted his back until he burped. "Please now, child, while the others are away, speak from your heart."

Dolcette's lips quivered. Serakh hummed softly. Mon Trésor gurgled. I sat on a stool near Dolcette's bed and waited to hear what my brain was going to make up next.

Dolcette took a breath and began, her eyes darting first to me, then to Serakh, than back to me, as if seeking sanctuary. Finally she said, "Avram is from Mainz."

"This you told me at the hour of birth." Serakh looked grave. "It explains much."

I was clueless.

"Three years ago, my father found Avram wandering in the forest north of the king's realm and brought him to safety in Paris. Avram told us that he had been buying rye from the farmers east of the Rhine for those terrible days. When he returned to Mainz, he discovered that everyone in his family was dead. His friends—dead. The great rabbi. Hundreds of Jews. All dead. Those Jews whom the Christian knights had spared sacrificed themselves and their children so as not to fall into blasphemy and sin. They honored the name of the Holy One, blessed be He, and were taken immediately to Heaven to sit at His feet."

Wait. Whoa. Stop right there. Even in my wildest dreams…

Serakh must have seen the shock on my face, because she touched my knee and shook her head. "We will speak of this later," she whispered to me. "Let Dolcette finish." Then she helped Mon Trésor to settle on Dolcette's other breast. "Your father found Avram," she prompted.

"Yes. Papa and I had come to Paris for Papa's business and to find a husband for me. I had warm feelings for Avram from the beginning. He was lost in sadness and grief, but I felt sure he would recover."

Dolcette gripped the covers and stared into space. I watched Mon Trésor nurse, falling more and more in love with him by the second.

Serakh's eyes filled with tears. "But Avram did not?"

"He was such a kind man, so quiet. He rarely spoke of Mainz. Papa gave him the bakery business as my dowry. We married, and Papa returned to Falaise to be with Mama. Avram continued to make trips north to the grain farmers by the Rhine. He prefers their rye, though he sells little to the community here in Paris. When he came back on the evening before *Rosh Chodesh Kislev*, he brought me the news that the Christian knights had captured Jerusalem from the Saracens."

I nodded, doing a quick calculation. Since *rosh chodesh* means the start of a new month, and Hanukkah always begins on *Kislev* 25, Avram must have returned nearly four weeks ago. I had just come home from the hospital then.

Dolcette stroked the top of her baby's head and said nothing. I watched Mon Trésor working his little jaw muscles as if his life depended on it. Which, I then realized, it did.

Dolcette took a deep breath and continued, her voice tight and strained. "Avram told me that the Christian armies burned the great synagogue with many Jews trapped inside. Then they exiled all Jews from Jerusalem. He believes this tragedy is his fault."

"A sad time," Serakh said. "Jerusalem is a holy place that should belong to all peoples of the earth."

I touched the baby's tiny fingers. "But how could Avram be responsible?"

Dolcette's lips quivered. "I told him the same, day after day. He would not listen. Avram told me that he had a vision, a fearsome one. Avram made a vow to name our firstborn son Ysaak and to send him to Heaven. By the blood of our son, the Jewish people would be restored to their rightful place in the Holy City."

Unbelievable. Jews didn't sacrifice their children. Wasn't that the lesson from Abraham and Isaac in the Bible?

Serakh shot me a warning look. I bit my lip.

Dolcette touched a wisp of Mon Trésor's fine black hair. "I told Avram no, we are simple, humble Jews, not prophets. I told him no, we will have a girl. See, I am carrying high, not low. When I eat garlic, the smell does not seep out through the pores of my skin. Avram prayed it would be so."

I shook my head. How could I have ever dreamed this up?

Dolcette grabbed Serakh's arm. "Now you see there is no hope here. Only until the *brit milah* is my baby safe. Take him now!"

Serakh stroked Dolcette's hand. "Cast your fears aside. Tikvah and I will find a way. Your son will grow to manhood and honor you in your old age."

Dolcette's eyes drilled into mine, searching for reassurance.

"Tikvah, tell Dolcette that you will not let this come to pass."

"I'm sure everything will be all right," I said, trying to sound convincing. What else do you tell a dreamed-up character desperate to save her child?

Dolcette wiped a tear from her cheek and kissed my hand.

"Now let us tend to you and your little one," Serakh said. "Tikvah and I must leave soon, but we will return with the answer." She rubbed Dolcette's feet while I watched the baby nurse and wondered how all this could seem so real.

The lines in Dolcette's face eased, and her shoulders inched downward. "Let me help you with your travels," she said. "I have a penny coin of silver from the lands the Duke of Normandy has conquered. A merchant in Falaise gave it to my mother. She assures me that the silver is genuine. Please take the coin from my pouch."

It looked more like a dime than a penny—a shiny sliver of silver with a man's face on one side and a cross and squiggles on the other. Since I didn't have a pouch, I slipped the coin into the empty slot in my penny loafers.

Serakh put Mon Trésor across Dolcette's lap and told her to tap on his back until he burped. Then Serakh replaced the soiled rag between his legs with a clean diaper and wrapped him again. Mon Trésor was nearly asleep when I put him back in the cradle. So was Dolcette.

Serakh kissed Dolcette's forehead and blew out the candle. As soon as we closed the bedroom door, she whispered, "Learn what you can about Avram and the events of Mainz, and then do what you must."

"This is completely ridiculous."

Serakh's eyes narrowed. "No. This is true. The One has guided me to you, so I feel certain you will find a way. There must be knowledge that comes of your place and time or of a special skill that you possess. Let us return to the trees. You will give me my robes, wind the blue thread around your finger, and close your eyes against the flash. It will not be as bad this time."

She lied.

CHAPTER TEN

I WOULD HAVE SCREAMED IF I could have forced my mouth to work. What difference does it make whether you feel hit by a ten-ton truck or an eleven-ton truck? The next thing I knew, I was back in the ladies' room at Barston's, slumped against Serakh.

"Breathe," she commanded, just like the last time.

I sucked in air, my head throbbing.

She waited until I could stand on my own and then said, "Here are your two silver discs."

"Dimes," I managed to mutter.

"Are not flat metal circles called discs?"

"Never mind." I stuffed them into my skirt pocket, too dizzy to bend down and put them in my penny loafers.

I straightened my cardigan and blouse and pulled up my knee-highs. Serakh stood next to me by the mirror. My face was nearly as pale as my bandages. My left eye twitched.

"Soon you will leave this room," she said softly. "I will not follow. But we will meet again for the sake of Dolcette and her baby. I trust that you will help her. I will visit you again when you find the answer."

I took another deep breath, my head pounding. I clutched my prayer shawl as she guided me to the door. "You go to the tables and I will travel from this room. Do not be afraid."

I stumbled out to the booth where I'd left all of my things.

"Perfect timing," Leona said, gesturing to the two hot chocolates, one slice of apple pie, and two forks the waitress must have just brought. Her smile vanished. "Hope, what's wrong? Are you okay?"

I dropped into the seat across from Leona and bit back tears. "Did something happen at school today?"

"I-I…S-so weird. There w-was this girl. In in the l-ladies' room. And then I had a fuh-lashback or s-s-omething."

"What!"

I winced. Half of Barston's could hear her.

"Sorry." Leona ratcheted down the volume. "What happened? Did you faint? You could have gone totally berserk in there! We have to tell your dad. Or go to the doctor. I thought you said you haven't had any flashbacks. I could so totally kill Dagmar."

I shook my head. All of this was absolutely incredible. The Beatles were singing "I Saw Her Standing There," and if it wasn't such a scary coincidence, I might have managed a smile.

Leona started shredding her napkin. "This is an awful time for your mother to be in Israel."

"L-last week I was f-fine." *What's happening to me now?*

"Do you want me to call my mom to take you home? Do I look funny? Like the wrong color or something?"

Leona seemed ready to wave her hand in front of my face and ask me how many fingers she was holding up. Still, she meant well. I stared at the prayer shawl bunched in my lap and concentrated on breathing. I was freaked enough already. Telling her the truth—whatever that was—was more than I could handle. She was my best friend. She'd forgive me.

I rubbed my temples. "Y-you have a buh-rown s-s-spot on your n-n-nose."

Leona gasped. Then she rubbed the tiny birthmark over her left nostril. "Very funny. Come on, you know what I mean. I'm worried. You can't fool me. I know you're upset."

I shrugged and picked up my fork. The apple pie tasted like mush. My heart still hammered in my chest. Leona shook her head and took a sip of hot chocolate. "Tell me what happened in the ladies' room."

"R-really, I d-don't w-w-ant to talk about it." Which was so true. What could I say? That a psychedelic girl from who knows where had turned the ladies' room into a living tableau of some

Renaissance horror show? Or worse, that LSD was taking over my brain? I tucked my feelings away until I could sort them out later.

Leona's napkin was now complete confetti. "Okay, but I'm walking you home in case you get sick or something. Deal?

"D-deal." I smoothed the prayer shawl, folded it neatly, and showed it to Leona. She cooed over the embroidery and asked me a ton of questions. I answered mostly with nods and shrugs. I kept thinking about Serakh, and Dolcette, and Mon Trésor, wondering why everything still felt so real. No. It didn't happen. It couldn't have happened.

The waitress gave us her we-need-the-table look. Leona and I split the bill, as usual. I put my shawl in its bag and collected my books.

"I'm buh-ringing in Chuh-inese for d-dinner," I said, trying to pretend that everything was normal.

"Great idea! You love Chinese. From Hunan Garden?"

"Um-hmm."

"There's a new place on Shattuck. House of Chen. My dad says they have better food than Hunan Garden, although you know him. He could eat a mule and think it's filet mignon."

A genuine smile graced my face, until I looked down at my penny loafers and saw that silver coin.

Waves of blood whooshed against my eardrums. My body turned to marble and my eyes refused to move.

"Hope, speak to me! Should I call an ambulance? Hope?"

The marble cracked. Inch by inch I turned toward the voice.

Leona was crouching next to me, her face clouded with concern. "You were staring at the floor and suddenly you went sort of catatonic."

"I n-n-need air."

Leona parked me on a bench in front of Barston's. After I convinced her I felt better—which I sort of did—she went back inside to pay the bill and collect our things. As soon as she left, I pulled out the coin and studied it in the palm of my hand. A figment of your imagination doesn't weigh anything. A flashback doesn't fit in your penny loafers. Whatever happened in the ladies' room wasn't the same as the Mr.-Zipper-Mouth-screwdriver flashback I had in the kitchen.

I slipped the coin into my pocket, stuck the dimes in their usual slots, and stared at the sidewalk.

Leona appeared with our things. "Is your dad home?"

I shrugged. You never knew when my father would be off somewhere, figuring out what Einstein meant.

"What's his phone number at the lab?"

I filled my lungs and shook my head. "I-I'm okay. Honest. I j-j-ust got d-dizzy. I'm d-due for m-m-my p-period."

Leona rolled her eyes. Still, she sat next to me quietly for a couple of minutes, while I cobbled myself back together. Dad and Einstein. Maybe there really was such a thing as a time warp, or whatever they called it. Physicists aren't crazy—at least my father wasn't. Flaky sometimes, but not crazy. Maybe Serakh took me through some sort of time warp. Outlandish. But not impossible.

As we walked to House of Chen, Leona agreed not to tell her folks about what happened. Her mom might tell my mom, and then I'd never get permission to go to the music festival. She chatted about Mr. Zegarelli's warning to stay away from the student demonstrations on campus.

"My dad's really upset," she continued. "I mean, suppose they come after the administration? Suppose they decide to block the entrance to Sproul Hall so my dad can't get to work? Is Dagmar involved?"

I shrugged. My sister hung out with the hippies and drug-gies, and maybe they were a part of this. But from what I saw in the newspapers, the protestors dressed as straight-up as my business-major brother.

Leona offered to order the Chinese food for me, and I let her. Then she walked me home. "Call me tonight," she said. Besides checking in with my grandfather, the call to her is the only one I don't mind making.

I put the food in the fridge, leaned against the counter, and scratched at the edge of my bandage. I counted my inhalations. And when I got to ten, I clenched my fist and shut my eyes.

Nothing. No flashbacks. No zipper mouths, no screwdrivers with teeth. No girls with bronze skin or newborn babies. I counted to ten again and let my eyes open to my own kitchen in my own time. And that coin.

The
Second
Day

PARIS
26 Kislev 4860
ANNO DOMINI 1099, FESTIVAL EVE AND
FEAST DAY FOR SAINT ABRA OF POITIERS
Sunset, Sunday, December 11–
Sunset, Monday December 12

BERKELEY
26 Kislev 5725
Sunset, Monday, November 30, 1964–
Sunset, Tuesday, December 1, 1964

CHAPTER ELEVEN

I TRIED TO CALM MY nerves and sort out my thoughts while I picked at my moo goo gai pan—the mushrooms slick and slippery in my mouth. The coin was real. I could still feel it in my pocket. Therefore Serakh must be was real, right? Time warps could be…real? Maybe. If I thought like a physicist.

"You are feeling ill, *sheyna maidl?*"

I touched Grandpa's hand and I sipped my tea. "N-not hungry."

His forehead wrinkled in concern.

"The p-penicillin. Fuh-rom the c-car a-accident," I said, using the white lie that Mom decided would be easier for her father to handle.

Grandpa took another bite of his lo mein and folded his napkin. "I'm not hungry tonight, either. I'll go to bed early."

He hoisted his thin frame from his chair and leaned against the table, unsteady. As I got up to help, he raised his hand to stop me. "No, no, I can make it on my own."

Shuffling down the hall toward the bathroom, my grandfather seemed to have shrunken into himself since breakfast, as if he'd added ten years to the seventy-six he'd already lived. He looked paler, his eyes more watery, his speech slower.

Walking by his side, I longed to tell him about Serakh. Nothing about a time warp—that was barely believable—but maybe Grandpa knew something about her. After all, Serakh said she had met him and my grandmother Miriam, and she knew about the prayer shawl.

I took a gamble. "I s-saw that g-girl who v-visited you l-last n-night."

"What girl?"

"Sh-she has buh-ronze skin and wh-white hair. Her n-name is S-Serakh."

My grandfather stopped shuffling. He touched his chest, his hand shaking. He muttered something in Polish or Yiddish and slumped against the wall.

"Guh-randpa!" I grabbed him under his arms. Color returned to his cheeks. I remembered to breathe. We stood together while he recovered his strength. He patted my cheek, the way he's done since I was a little girl.

"I am fine," he whispered.

I didn't believe him.

We walked hand-in-hand to his bed. I got him a glass of water. He took a sip, then pushed the glass away. "I should never have given you that *tallis*. Never. She'll take you away like she did my Miriam.

I sat next to him on the bed. "N-no one t-took Guh-randma away," I explained as gently as I could. "She d-died about a f-few weeks b-before I was born."

He shook his head. "My Miriam told me so many times. Finally I believed her. She made me promise that the child named for her would get her *tallis*."

"D-did she know S-Serakh?"

"Who?"

"The-the g-girl who c-came to your r-room l-last night."

"I was alone in my room all night."

I bit my lip, and then I kissed his cheek. No way could my grandfather give me a coherent story until the morning, and maybe not even then.

I put the half-filled glass on his end table, laid out his pajamas, and sat next to him again. A thin stream trickled from Grandpa's nose. He waved away the tissue I handed him and dug into his cardigan for that wrinkled handkerchief I'd forgotten to replace with a fresh one this morning. And then he wept, long and loud. I stroked his back, and then I put my arms around him.

Sadness pulled at me. Mom had postponed her trip by a

couple of weeks to take care of me, and now it was my turn to take care of Grandpa. I wished she'd cancelled the trip entirely so she could be home with her father. He needed her, and I was making a mess of it.

After he'd cried himself dry, he took my face in his hands and kissed my forehead. I managed a smile, because he likes that, and I put my lips to his cheek. I blew him another kiss as I closed the bedroom door.

The house was quiet. Too quiet. I wished anybody else were home—even Josh. I put Sylvester outside for his pre-bed feline adventures, cleaned up the kitchen, collected the prayer shawl and my schoolbooks, and nearly walked past the menorah in the living room.

With Grandpa asleep, I might have skipped lighting the candles, and I didn't need to be reminded how so-so my singing was. But that ridiculous lion seemed lonely. Without bothering to turn on the light, I put two candles in his butt end and the *shamash* candle in the cruet. I lit the *shamash*, used it to light the other two, and sang the blessings. This time I filled my lungs and did a half-decent job.

Each of the blessings started with the same stock phrase I'd sung a million times at temple without thinking: *Baruch atah Adonai, Eloheinu Melech ha-olam*. Blessed are You, Lord, our God, King of the universe. *Ha-olam*. The universe. And *olam* was more than that. At services I sang prayers that included *l'olam*. Forevermore.

I stared at the flames. *Through every place and all time*, Serakh had explained. The *olam*—as if she'd stepped out of the ancient Hebrew prayers. My mind wandered to that metal triangle with tiny cups of oil. Hanukkah at Dolcette's. *I will show you Dolcette in an instant*, Serakh told me. And she did. And she said I would see her again.

A door creaked. I felt someone behind me. I shivered, suddenly afraid. And that's when Dagmar said, "You having a séance here in the dark?"

My shoulders relaxed. I grabbed a breath.

She flicked on the light, plopped herself on the couch, and

finger-combed her hair. "Is that Chinese food I smell? I'm starved. Got any left?"

"Uh-huh." Dagmar fills a room, and that's exactly what I needed just then.

"You're the best. Is Dad home yet?"

I shook my head.

She glanced at the menorah. "Happy Hanukkah, Hope for the World. Come sit with me in the kitchen," she said, as she walked away. "I've got a bunch to tell you."

I rubbed the back of my neck and watched melting wax drizzle over the lion's butt. Sylvester yowled outside. I glanced out the living room window into the darkness. My own reflection shimmered, backlit by a heart-stopping flash of blue.

Serakh! I had to see her again. Frightened or not, I had to have answers. I raced to the front door.

CHAPTER TWELVE

THE NIGHT WIND BROUGHT a damp chill off the Bay. Lights from the house next door cast shadows around our lilac bushes, deepening the darkness.

Another blue flash. My body twitched as if an electric shock had passed through me. Had she come and gone? Was it because Dagmar was home? Determination drowned out fear. I had to understand what was happening to me.

"S-Serakh, are are y-you still here?"

The lilac bush rustled. Sylvester scrambled onto my shoulder, digging his claws into my sweater.

"Ow! W-what's with you? D-did you see her?"

Why am I asking? Of course he has. And if he's come out of hiding, she must be gone.

Sylvester nested in my lap while I sat in the kitchen and half-listened to Dagmar. I curled my fingers around that silver coin and stared out the window.

Dagmar slurped wonton soup from Dad's coffee mug. "I heard it straight from one of my connections who hangs out with the free speech kids. They're organizing a huge rally Wednesday in front of Sproul Hall, and I mean huge. Now's your chance. Forget school tomorrow. Stay home and paint dreidels. I'll help. You've still got a supply of plain ones, right?"

I dipped my chin in the affirmative.

"We'll do that sales-team thing like we did at the street fair in Alameda. The Jewish kids will buy your dreidels as Hanukkah gifts. The non-Jewish kids, too. I'll give my spiel about that miracle story with the flask of oil. Everybody likes miracles. Everybody likes tops. We made a mint last week."

"S-seven d-dollars." Not exactly a mint. I cracked open the fortune cookie I hadn't had at dinner. The tiny message inside read: *Good things come to those who wait.* I wondered when I'd see Serakh again. Was she a good thing?

"We'll make lots more at the rally. Don't you need money for your music competition in Seattle?"

"P-Portland. B-but I c-can't go if if I juh-oin the puh-rotest. School r-rules."

Dagmar took another slurp. "C'mon, Hopeless. They'll never catch you with all those kids around. And just in case they do, I'll explain that you were helping me with sales. My friends really dig your dreidels. The Great Dane will be so impressed with how much money you make that he's bound to convince Mom to let you go." Dagmar hugged the mug against her impressive cleavage. She stretched a contagious grin from one hoop earring to another.

I leaned back in my chair. I still had twelve dozen large, unpainted wooden dreidels and another twelve dozen smaller ones. If we sold all the big ones for fifty cents each and the smaller ones for twenty-five cents, that would be seventy-two dollars plus thirty-six dollars, or about a hundred dollars. Dagmar would take her usual twenty percent, which was only fair, as she did the talking. I could nearly double my music festival fund. And if I stayed home, I could keep an eye on Grandpa.

I cleared my throat. "I-I never p-painted so m-many at once. They m-might not dry in time."

Dagmar took one more and wiped her mouth with the back of her hand. "That's why God created hairdryers. You do the painting, I'll be in charge of the drying. Paint lots of birds on them. Birds and flowers. Art!"

Dagmar announced that she was going to soak in our bathtub downstairs, and left. I rinsed out her mug before the gunk inside congealed, and I left it in the sink.

Restless, I called Leona, who almost always puts me in a good mood. I told her I felt fine, and she agreed again to keep quiet about what happened at Barston's. Then I told her about going to the rally.

Two beats of silence. "Don't do it. Dagmar is dragging you into trouble again. You should have heard my dad at dinner tonight. This whole protest thing is getting out of hand, like it did in October. I'm telling you, they're going to call in the police. What if they catch you? Mr. Z is bound to find out."

I wrapped the phone cord around my finger. "M-maybe I'll p-paint the duh-reidels and g-g-give them to D-Dagmar to s-sell."

"Great idea! Hey, I have to go. My mom wants me to wrap Hanukkah presents. Good luck with the painting. See you Wednesday."

Sylvester followed me downstairs.

Dagmar came out of the bathroom just as I put my prayer shawl on top of my bookshelf. She was towel drying her hair and belting out, "You Don't Own Me," and I was sure her new-clothes sensor was shut down.

I LET MYSELF SLEEP until 8:30. Dagmar was in her usual spot, scrunched at the end of her bed, her pillow over her head. I reached down and extracted that coin from its hiding place between my mattress and mattress pad. The silver soon felt warm from the heat of my palm, the way silver does. Nothing magical. Sitting on my bed, I hugged my knees and tried to understand everything that had happened to me since Sunday night. I might as well have tried to sing underwater. Forget it. I was no good at fathoming the unfathomable.

I flung off the covers, put the coin back in its hiding place, and woke Dagmar, so she could call the school attendance office to tell them I'd be out sick. Then I got into dungarees and a paint-stained T-shirt and went upstairs.

Grandpa seemed better, although he wanted breakfast in his room. Dad had finished the rest of the Chinese food, washed his plate and the mug Dagmar used, and folded the dish towel in exact thirds. His on-the-phone voice drifted in from the den, so I left him a note on the kitchen counter explaining that I wasn't feeling well and had decided to stay home from school.

Dagmar wandered off, promising to be back soon. Sylvester curled up on my bed. I left the door to the upstairs open, in case Grandpa needed me, and I took a can of root beer and a bag of pretzels to the corner of the garage that doubles as my workroom. Mom parks on the street, so there's enough space on our old kitchen table and shelves for my paint supplies and a family-pack of Juicy Fruit gum.

Sunshine swept through the open window on the other side of the garage. I balanced the record player Dagmar and I share on a box of Mom's office supplies and set three of my favorite LPs on the spindle. Perfect. Singing along with English madrigals from *The Triumphs of Oriana*, I put a base coat on the first two dozen dreidels and set them on a rack I'd made from chicken wire fencing. My vocalizing sounded halfway decent. Madrigals are like speaking, only better, with their crisp melodic lines. If I were still going to speech therapy, I would recommend madrigals as a vocal exercise.

> *All creatures now are merry minded,*
> *The shepherd's daughters playing...*

Dad's voice yanked me back from Ye Merrie Olde England. "Good morning."

He sat on the top stair, his coffee cup in his hand, his chin stubbly, and his blond hair—a shade lighter than mine—crying out for a shower and shampoo.

I turned off the record player and put my singing on hold. "G-good m-morning." I wondered whether Dad was concentrating on some problem in the lab, or whether he enjoyed slobbing out when Mom wasn't around.

"You must be feeling better if you are working on your dreidels."

I let my smile answer for me.

"Excellent. I'll be home until 2:35. Then I have a graduate seminar—assuming any students will come to class today—and then I'll check on things at the lab."

Which meant he'd probably work late again. "How's Guh-randpa?"

"Napping. Any idea where Dagmar is?"

I shrugged. Dad took another sip of coffee. Dr. Henrik Friis, eminent physicist, leading expert on the secrets of the universe. I walked partway up the stairs, my heart doing double-time. "D-Dad?"

"Hmmm… What's up?"

Say it! "D-do you th-think t-t-ime is… um…fuh-lexible?"

He cocked his head. "That came out of the clear blue."

I bit my lip and asked again with my eyes.

"Well, the short answer is yes. Time certainly isn't linear, the way most people think. The universe is more complicated than that. Why do you ask?"

I picked at a fleck of yellow paint on my fingernail. No way could I tell him about Serakh, and blue flashes, and Dolcette. Even if he didn't drag me to the doctor right away—and who would blame him?—he'd certainly nix any chance of my going to the music festival. "J-just c-curious," I said.

We let it go at that.

I HUMMED SOFTLY AND went back to painting. About a half-hour later, Sylvester yowled. The back of my neck tingled. I knew what I'd see when I looked up.

Serakh sat at the top of the stairs, where my father had been. She was eating a cucumber.

She pointed the cucumber at a rip in her robe. "Your cat has the heart of a tiger."

I stared at her for a full three beats, waiting for a wave of fear that never came. Chomping on a cuke, for Heaven's sake. How unthreatening is that?

"Your grandmother had such a cooling box. It is very useful. Do not worry. I was careful to close the door to the box after I removed the cucumber, and I did not disturb anyone in the house." She held out the cucumber. "Would you like a bite?"

"No thanks," I said, as if this were a normal conversation with a normal person. I chose to believe it was.

She walked down the stairs. I stayed put.

"You ate cucumbers with my grandmother?"

"I have never lost my fondness for them. A pity they are not in season in Dolcette's time and place.

She stood an arm's length away, solid, sensible. Her eyes were clear and focused. She seemed to be under the influence of nothing stronger than herbal tea.

"What's really happening to me? Who are you?"

Loosening her headscarf, she let her thick white braid cascade down her back to her waist. "I am one with an abundance of years and a passion for cucumbers."

"I'm serious."

She straightened her shoulders. "I, too, am serious. Who I am does not matter. You are the one who matters. You are of the line of Miriams since the first Miryam, who found water in the desert on our long journey from Egypt. Your grandmother Miriam once stood before Moshe to pursue justice at the river Jordan. Now you bear her name and her birthright—the blue thread—and you are intertwined with Dolcette. You are worthy."

Worthy? I'd been called sweet, or responsible, or talented, but never worthy. And every time I was with her, I spoke like a normal person. My kind of miracle. Whatever made that happen, I wanted more.

"Dolcette needs you. Perhaps if you see her again, you will discover what we must do to save her baby. You have only to wear your garment of fringes and touch the blue thread as before."

"This is completely crazy."

She popped the last of the cucumber in her mouth and wiped her hands on her robe. "Yes, this I have heard from other Miriams, even from your grandmother at first. But Dolcette cannot wait. She is terrified for her child. Trust me. You will return to this very spot on the *olam*." Serakh's face relaxed into a smile. "Only your brave and ferocious cat will know I have been here."

"My grandmother stood before Moses?" I knew Serakh

would say yes, just as she'd told me that it was true that Moses stuttered.

"The universe is complicated," I told myself as I covered the jar of modeling paint, soaked my paintbrush in solvent, and headed for my shawl.

CHAPTER THIRTEEN

THIS TIME IT REALLY was easier to make the crossing. And this time I smelled fresh bread. We were back in that same grove of trees at the edge of that same group of houses by the river. I don't know why I was more excited than afraid. Maybe the aroma of baking bread is always inviting. Maybe the place felt more familiar. Does repetition do that to you, like going to the same haunted house two nights in a row?

The tree I rested against felt warm in the midmorning sun. A horse whinnied. A man shouted, and another man answered him. Church bells pealed. Notre Dame?

Again the robe over my prayer shawl and regular clothes. Again the linen cap with my hair tucked underneath and a scarf to hide my bandages. When I'd caught my breath, I reached down and collected the dimes from my penny loafers to give to Serakh.

She smoothed my robe. "We are going to meet Avram, so you can judge what best to do. You will understand the words of every person that you hear, as you did with Dolcette, because you are with me. Your words will flow in the magic of blended language."

I stared at her. "Blended what? Is that why I don't stutter around you? Because I'm not really talking? But I feel my lips move."

"I do not know why this happens. You form the words in your mind and perhaps on your lips. I translate them into that which is meaningful. It is a useful skill."

"Useful? It's an outrageously amazing skill!"

"Come, our time grows shorter." Serakh's forehead creased with determination. No more easy-going banter about eating cucumbers. Now I had work to do. But what?

Picking our way around a dead rat, several foul-smelling puddles, and a maggot-infested glob of who-knows-what, we reached a low stone building with no door. Two bearded men stood inside near a rounded brick oven that looked like it belonged in a pizza parlor. The older, gray-haired man was kneading dough on a flat wooden pallet. He wore a flour-dusted tunic that came to his knees and a pair of baggy leggings. The younger man, with his back to us, was taller and more muscular, with dark brown hair, and a leather vest over his tunic.

"Good day to you, gentlemen," Serakh said. "We are new to Paris. Is this the oven for the Jews?"

Jewish ovens? My brain zipped forward to 1964 and the new ads for Levy's rye bread. Dad at the kitchen table, showing Mom the ad in *The New York Times* with the slogan, "You Don't Have to Be Jewish to Love Levy's" and the American Indian eating a rye sandwich. Dad joking, "You don't have to be Jewish to love Rachel." Mom laughing and then getting her love-you-so-much look, and taking Dad's free hand in both of hers.

The older man grunted, not bothering to look up. The younger one turned and stepped forward. Except for his short, reddish brown beard, he could have been Paul McCartney, straight off the Beatles' plane from England. Hazel eyes, curly eyelashes. He was drop-dead gorgeous.

"How may I be of service?" Tenor voice as pleasing as his face. "I am Avram of Mainz."

Impossible. Baby killers don't look like this..

"Avert your eyes," Serakh hissed in my ear. "He must not think we are brazen women."

I blinked. Paul McCartney of Mainz stared at me. I couldn't help it. I stared back.

Serakh stepped between us. "Kind sir," she said, "I inquire about the hours when my sister-in-law and I might bake our loaves, and about the oven fee."

Pretending to pick at a soiled spot on my sleeve, I hid a smile at our invented relationship. Avram stroked his chin and stood silently. Serakh waited.

Finally he said, "And where do you buy your flour, eggs, and yeast?"

Serakh stood taller, as if slightly offended by the question. "From the Jews, certainly. Else how could I be assured of their purity for bread? I buy parsnips and cabbage, and a bit of cloth, from any good farmer's wife, Jewish or not, as we all must earn a living together."

I waited for Avram to say something against Christians, since they had attacked Mainz. But he seemed to ignore Serakh's last sentence. Or maybe he agreed with her.

"I supply the purest flour, good dame," he said. "My wheat and barley are the best in Paris. My rye I personally transport from farmers in the north. I sell my flour in the market on Thursdays. The yeast you may buy from any of the sellers there. The freshest eggs come from the farm owned by my father-in-law, Rav Judah of Falaise."

"Thank you for your kind advice. I will visit your stall next Thursday."

"And I will offer you the use of this oven." Avram glanced at me with a friendly, open face. I reminded myself that you can't judge a book by its cover. I longed to let my eyes linger over that cover. Instead, I looked at the floor.

"I am a widow," Serakh said. "And so is my sister-in-law. She is slow, poor dear, and understands very little. We are two women struggling alone."

Thanks for nothing! I coughed. Serakh cleared her throat.

"My oven is free to widows and orphans," he said.

Serakh curtsied. She nudged me, and I did the same. "You are most gracious," she said. "I will put raisins in my first loaf and give it to you and your wife in honor of your newborn son. You are blessed."

The old man muttered, "That's what I tell him, but all he does is frown and turn away. You would think his wife bore him twin daughters with withered arms and club feet."

Avram's face hardened. "Enough, Shmuel. Tend to your work."

Serakh stepped back, dragging me with her. "I meant no offense, good sir."

Avram smashed his lips together. He walked toward the oven. "Good day," he said over his shoulder. I thought I heard a quaver in his voice.

"Good day," Serakh said.

"Good day," I repeated, relishing my fluid speech. "And thank you."

Serakh took my elbow and led me down the narrow alley. "He shows no sign of illness, no pox or palsy. I fear he is enthralled by the inclination to do evil and does not know it. What shall we do?"

I spread out my arms and exhaled my frustration. "I have no idea."

"It pains me to hear this."

"I'm sorry," I said. And I was. But what could I have learned since yesterday?

She tented her hands and brought them to her lips. We stood together in silence. Then she said, "Have you come to trust me? Do you believe now in the intertwining?"

I closed my eyes and counted to ten, the way I had when I first met Serakh. I opened them to find I was still in the Jewish neighborhood of Paris sometime in the Middle Ages. No flashback or hallucination or dream or wild concoction of brain chemistry. *Time is flexible. The universe is complicated.* "Yes," I said.

Serakh smiled. "Good. Then you will discover what needs to be done. Now let us visit with Dolcette. She has need of us."

I followed Serakh along a narrow winding alley, stepping as carefully as I could from one clean, dry patch of dirt to another. The buildings on either side leaned into toward each other, almost touching, cutting off warmth and hiding the sunlight.

Dolcette's kitchen door was unbolted. When no one answered Serakh's knock, we stepped inside and when up to Dolcette's bedroom. Her door was closed. Serakh knocked again.

The door opened halfway and two women motioned for us to step inside. Neither of them seemed happy to see us. The older one could have been Dolcette's grandmother, with a gaunt face and arthritic fingers. The younger one, maybe Dagmar's age, had thick black eyebrows and a large mole near her left eye. The older woman shut the door, blocking our exit, her eyes darting from us to a large wooden bucket a few feet away.

Dolcette sat in bed with Mon Trésor, wrapped in a tight bundle, sleeping against her chest. She glared at us as if she were the evil twin of the girl I'd met the last time.

"I cannot trust you," she said, her voice shaky, her eyes filled with fear. "Do not come any closer."

CHAPTER FOURTEEN

S ERAKH SEEMED AS CONFUSED as I was. I mouthed "Avram?"
She dipped her chin in approval.

"We have just come from Avram at the bakery," I told
Dolcette. "Your husband sends his best."

"Turn away from them, child," the old woman commanded.
"Do not look into their eyes."

"Tante Rose, I won't know the truth unless I see their faces."

Tante? Aunt in French. So, not her grandmother. Was the
other woman her cousin?

Serakh spread her arms out, palms up. "We mean you no
harm, Dolcette. We are here only to help you. Surely you have
known this from the moment of your child's birth."

"Ha!" The older woman thrust an arthritic finger at Serakh.
"You appeared at the birthing. You came again—with your sister
witch—at the very hour we left poor Dolcette alone. You cast a
spell on her newborn. Why else does he sleep so deeply and suckle
so lustily? You told Dolcette that you are the wet nurse Avram
hired. You lie! Celeste, tell us what happened this morning."

The woman with the mole wrung her hands, her voice barely
above a whisper. "I spoke with Master Avram this morning,"
she said. "He asked after my mistress and the baby, as he will
not see them before the *brit milah*. He told me that he did not
hire a wet nurse."

Serakh clenched her fist. She faced Tante Rose. "When we
met at the birthing, I did not claim to be the wet nurse. It was
you who thought me so. You accuse us falsely. There is no spell.
We have handled the child with care."

Tante Rose reached for a bucket by the door. "You are here once more to cast another spell. Be gone!" She threw the bucket's watery contents at Serakh.

I thought, for one crazy instant, of Dorothy spilling that pail of water on the wicked witch in the *Wizard of Oz* movie. I half-expected Serakh to cry out, "I'm melting!" But she just stood there, her robe soaked, her eyes blazing.

"Foolish woman," she said. "Tikvah and I will return when Dolcette is in wiser company than yours." Serakh yanked off her headscarf and used it to wipe her face. Her long white braid tumbled down across her shoulders.

Dolcette gasped. She seemed to study Serakh's face for the first time, as if she hadn't noticed the white eyebrows and white eyelashes before.

"She's not a witch," I said, sweeping my hands up over my head. "She's... She's an angel!" Why not? They believed anything in the Middle Ages.

"Blasphemer! Spawn of the devil!" Tante Rose blocked the door. "We will destroy you."

Celeste grabbed my waist.

As I squirmed out of her grasp, the embroidered prayer shawl that Grandpa gave me fell on the floor.

"Tante Rose, look," Dolcette shouted. "It's Mama's *tallis*!"

I hugged my shawl to my chest. "No. Absolutely not. This belonged to my grandmother."

Serakh put a protective arm around my shoulder. "Trust me again," she whispered. Then she turned toward Dolcette. "Your mother has sent us to see to your welfare," she announced. "This garment of fringes is her token."

What?

Mon Trésor whimpered. Dolcette kissed his forehead and rocked him gently. He made sucking sounds with his tiny lips, and then grew quiet again. Celeste took the baby and retreated to a corner of the room.

"Your mother would not have done such a thing," Tante Rose said.

Dolcette held up her hand for silence. "I need to think."

Tante Rose smacked her lips. "Young mothers do not need to think. They need to rest and listen to their elders." She glared at me. "How did you get this *tallis* from Madame Miriam?"

Miriam. My grandmother's name. Miriam Josefsohn Jacobowitz.

"She has come by the garment honestly," Serakh said. No lie there. "She wears it under her robes to keep it safe in our travels. Miriam bat Shlomo of Troyes would have wanted it so."

"You do know my mother then," Dolcette said.

"Most certainly," Serakh said, answering for one of us. I had no idea who this other Miriam was. My grandmother would have been Miriam, daughter of Julius, of Portland.

Tante Rose looked skeptical. "Soon we shall get the truth. Rav Judah and Madame Miriam are coming for the *brit milah*. They have already started on their travels. It's a long way from…" She stared at me, waiting for an answer.

Serakh coughed. Our eyes met. She mouthed "Troyes." But that didn't sound right. I remembered what Avram had just told us at the bakery—Rav Judah with the fresh eggs.

"Falaise," I said.

Serakh's eyebrows danced with surprise. Dolcette smiled. So did Celeste. Tante Rose positively snorted.

My shoulders relaxed. "A lovely woman," I added. "I look forward to seeing her again." It felt good to hear my words flow smoothly, even while I was lying through my teeth.

"And so you shall," Tante Rose said, making it sound more like a challenge than an invitation.

Dolcette leaned back against her pillow. "I have such a craving for broth," she said.

An odd remark, but Tante Rose seemed pleased. "Excellent. Finally you have an appetite. Celeste, stay here with these… guests. I can manage on my own in the kitchen."

Four beats after Tante Rose left, Dolcette asked Celeste to put the baby in his cradle. While Celeste's back was turned, Dolcette nodded at us and put her finger to her lips. Then she gripped her abdomen and moaned.

Celeste rushed to her side. Dolcette grimaced in pain.

Serakh turned away from them and covered her mouth, but her eyes were smiling.

"Oh, my poor mistress," Celeste said. "I will fetch your aunt."

Dolcette shook her head. "No, no, she is busy with the broth. Celeste, my dear, please run to Madame Juliane for willow bark and ask Tante Rose to make me her healing tea."

Celeste looked doubtful. Dolcette moaned again.

In another three beats, Celeste was gone. Serakh closed the bedroom door. Dolcette's eyes were riveted on mine. "You have spoken with my mother?"

I looked at Serakh, hoping she'd answer for us now.

"We have been to the bakery," Serakh said, repeating what I'd told Dolcette earlier. "We've spoken with your husband Avram."

"He seemed very sad," I added, taking up the story from there. "Has he said anything more to you about his vow?"

Dolcette frowned in confusion. "My husband wouldn't think to enter this room so soon after our baby's birth, with me in an unclean state. I won't see Avram until the day of the *brit milah*, and maybe not even then. How can I face him, knowing what he plans to do?" Her shoulders twitched.

My mistake. "Of course," I said. "I understand. Can't Celeste and Tante Rose help you?"

"They refuse to listen to me. They think I am possessed by the evil spirit of Lilith, despite the amulets we have used to guard against her. I sleep with a knife under my pillow to protect the baby from Lilith, but who will protect him from his own father?"

"What about your rabbi?"

Another frown.

I bit my lip. Wrong again. This community would consider Dolcette unclean for every man, especially a rabbi. "Serakh and I could go to see him on your behalf."

"Perhaps," Serakh said, with a look I took to mean I was making a complete mess of this. Surely the rabbi wouldn't defend Avram's actions. No, I refused to believe that was possible.

She straightened Dolcette's quilt and patted her hand. "Is your grandfather well enough to travel to the *brit milah*? Rav

Shlomo is such a wise and tolerant scholar. He has written that those Jews who were forced to convert after the great tragedy in the Rhineland should be welcomed back into the community if they wish."

Dolcette shook her head. He wasn't coming? She didn't trust him to save Mon Trésor? I started to ask Dolcette when the door creaked open.

Celeste returned with a cup of broth and a vicious slap mark on her cheek. I clenched my jaw.

"Tante Rose has gone for the willow bark," Celeste mumbled. "She told me not to leave your room again."

Serakh straightened her shoulders and cleared her throat. "We do not wish to trouble Tante Rose," she announced. "We will visit again when Madame Miriam arrives. I promise you."

"Pray, stay with us longer," Dolcette said. "We have so much to discuss."

Serakh's voice grew serious. "We must go."

Dolcette didn't argue. Celeste led us downstairs. We curtsied good-bye and headed for the trees by the river.

CHAPTER FIFTEEN

W<small>E MUST HAVE SURPRISED</small> the dickens out of Sylvester. This time he crouched under my desk. I curled up in bed, my muscles cramped and my lungs struggling for air. Serakh stayed with me until I recovered enough to ask about the prayer shawl.

"How can this belong to my grandmother and Dolcette's mother? They lived centuries apart. It doesn't make sense." *As if everything else did.*

Serakh caressed the embroidery. "Do you know what these words mean?"

"My grandfather told me. *Tzedek tzedek tirdof.* Pursue justice."

"A fine man, your grandfather, although he did not wish your grandmother to travel with me. This you will not believe. Dolcette's mother is the person your grandfather would know as the daughter of Rashi. She is another Miriam. She embroidered this very garment, which has passed from Miriam to Miriam over the generations."

I hugged my pillow and let my eyes rest on the poster of Monet's water lilies decorating my wall. Rashi was a Jewish scholar from the Middle Ages. The time period fit with Dolcette. Of course, this was all true because I was hearing it from a person who materializes and dematerializes in a blue flash. Just as I do.

Sure. Right. A giggle erupted from my chest. And another and another.

Serakh creased her forehead. "What is the humor?"

I couldn't stop. "I mean…look at the two of us…and you…you of all people…magical you…you're telling me it's hard to believe…"

GIGGLES ARE CONTAGIOUS. SERAKH's deep alto laughter filled the bedroom. Even Sylvester lightened up, crawling out from under the desk, although his tail still twitched. I felt my muscles relax and my body unwind.

Suddenly Serakh put her hands over my mouth. "Someone is coming. I must go. Find the answer. I will pray for you."

I turned my face to the wall and covered my head with my pillow to avoid the flash. Sylvester yowled again. Then silence. I put my head on my pillow and pretended to be asleep, waiting for Dad or Dagmar to appear. The clock ticked. One minute. Two. Was Serakh's hearing that much better than mine? I took another breath. Exhausted, my body demanded sleep. I lost count of the minutes.

I woke up to Dagmar jostling my shoulders. "Get up, get up. You've been dead to the world for a million years."

I blinked.

She dangled something like a bottle of nose drops in front of my face. "Patchouli oil," she said, her face beaming with pleasure. "It's perfect for your dreidels."

I sat up and rolled my shoulders. It was still morning, a little after eleven. I'd slept less than an hour.

"Trust me on this. We'll rub a drop on each dreidel and everybody will want one." Dagmar waltzed around the room with the bottle. "Colors and smells all spinning and whirling together. Colors turning into smells, smells changing into tastes and shapes and sounds. Patchouli dreidels—the beautiful mind-stretching experience."

My mind had had enough stretching for one day. Still, I took an aspirin and got to work. It felt good to do something I understood.

Patchouli smells okay if you like musk. Dagmar blasted my creations with hot air and listened to twenty minutes of madrigals before she gave me the madrigals-drive-me-crazy look. I put on my new *Joan Baez/5* album, and she bobbed her head to most of it, except my favorite, the aria by Villa-Lobos: "Bachianas Brasileiras No. 5."

We switched to Peter, Paul, and Mary's *In Concert*. Which

was fine by me. Dagmar thrust the hair dryer in the air and belted out the PP&M cover of Bob Dylan's "The Times They Are a-Changin'." Dagmar's voice kept going flat. I hummed along, trying to keep her on key. She has the breath control of a rabbit in heat—or me when I'm not at least trying to sing.

When I went upstairs for lunch, Grandpa was still in his pajamas and had hardly touched breakfast. "Your father insisted on giving me my pills, which do nothing, I tell you. But I refuse to get dressed. Who is coming to see me?"

I cajoled my grandfather into eating two small cubes of cheese and drinking half a glass of diluted orange juice. I brought him the handbell Mom gave us when we were at home sick and might need her. He patted my knee and assured me he was fine. Which he clearly wasn't.

"He l-looks p-pale," I told Dagmar, when I came downstairs later, leaving open the door to the main floor.

She took a handful of chocolate chip cookies from the box I'd brought down. "Is his breathing labored? Does he have the sweats? Is he shivering?"

I shook my head. None of the above.

"Then he's just tired today, Nurse Hope. Old people get tired. There's nothing to worry about."

I decided to believe her.

Dagmar snagged Dad when he came for his bike. "Henrik, two minutes of your time." She's the only American I know who calls him by his Danish name instead of Henry.

Dad rubbed his newly shaved chin and checked his watch. "I can give you six minutes."

Dagmar showed him my dreidels drying in their chicken wire cradles. "Look what Miriam Hope made. Aren't they beautiful?"

The Miriam Hope bit was for Dad's benefit. He prefers that to Hope.

"We *so* want to sell them tomorrow during the Joan Baez concert. This means so much to us."

What concert?

Dagmar clasped her hands in a dramatic prayer pose. "Can't

your teaching assistants and lab assistants take over for one een-sy-teensy day? Just this once while Rachel is gone? We'll make a tuna casserole for you and leave it in the fridge."

Dad looked at me, his eyes soft. "You've taken excellent care of your grandfather, especially with your mom away. Normally I would say yes."

"She did a ton of homework before Thanksgiving. She's caught up in all her classes now," Dagmar said. "One short day won't hurt, Henrik. Just this once. A concert in the fresh air would be therapeutic, don't you think?"

I frowned and stared at the floor. Just because Dagmar calls the library for me doesn't mean she can act like I'm not in the room.

"Is this true about being caught up, Miriam Hope? You missed nearly three weeks of school."

"I-I have a p-paper d-due in h-history. I'll g-go to choral m-music in the m-morning. I w-won't m-miss that."

Dad smiled. "Of course not. You still have your heart set on a singing career." More of a question than a statement.

I shrugged.

"At the slightest sign that you don't feel well, please come straight home."

I nodded.

Dagmar flung her arms around him. "You're the best!" As he biked down Roosevelt, she called after him, "Don't wait up for us tomorrow night. We might be late."

I gave Dagmar the tell-me-more look.

She ran her fingers through her curls. "Baez is singing at the rally tomorrow, didn't I tell you? And they're talking about occupying Sproul Hall afterward, which is perfect for us. A cap-tive audience for your dreidels. Plus, you don't have to worry about Grandpa because The Great Dane will be home."

Occupying Sproul? My stomach lurched. Being on the pub-lic plaza was one thing. Occupying the administration building was going too far. "B-but I t-told you. S-school r-rules."

Dagmar squeezed my shoulders. "I know, I know. That dumb rule about going to the music festival. Listen, if you don't want to stay, I'll sell the dreidels for you. But Baez will be there. It'll be a blast. And Gabriel's been asking about you. I keep telling him you're all right, but he wants to see for himself."

"I-I'll th-think about it." The last thing I needed was to get involved with one of Dagmar's druggie friends. I didn't remember Gabriel from the Halloween party or the hospital. At least I didn't think I remembered him. A voice, maybe.

"We'll meet at Sather Gate after choral music class, which is when?"

"Th-third p-period."

"Which ends when?"

"E-eleven forty." You'd think my sister graduated from Berkeley High in the '50s instead of last June.

"I'll bring the dreidels. I'll take care of everything. Except the tuna casserole. You'll make it, won't you?"

I was wondering when she'd get around to that. I nodded.

"Yes! I am so jazzed." She waltzed to the bathroom. I got back to painting.

Exhausted after ten dozen large dreidels, I decided to forget the small ones. Dagmar skipped out for dinner as usual, promising to bring back pizza.

Grandpa was still napping at 5:30, so I got a Hostess cupcake—I believe in dessert before dinner—and poked around in our *World Book Encyclopedia*. It was an old set from 1951, but serviceable. I scribbled notes on every topic that seemed connected to Avram and his bakery, and my time with Serakh in Paris. I felt like I was back in the sixth grade, but it was a start.

Mainz. Large trading center in Western Germany. On left bank of the Rhine River. One of the oldest German cities.

Crusades. Military expeditions to take back the Holy Land. Started with Pope Urban II in France. Several campaigns. First crusade 1096–1099. Crusaders captured Jerusalem in 1099. Islamic forces later recaptured city.

Rashi. *RAH- shee.* (1040?–1105) French-Jewish writer. Born in Troyes, France. Real name Rabbi Solomon ben Isaac. Most noted works were commentaries on the Bible and Talmud.

Rye. Hardiest of the small grains. One of the most important plants of northern Europe. Rye flour used to make black bread eaten by many in northern Europe. Fungus that grows on rye gives it the disease ergot. Poisonous to humans and animals. If used properly, has high medicinal value.

Ergot. *UR-got*. Parasitic fungus. Commonly infects rye. Causes disease called ergotism, common among people who ate bread from infected rye grain. Symptoms often gangrene and convulsions. Also known as Saint Anthony's fire or erysipelas.

I found nothing useful on coins, or what happened to the Jews during the Crusades, and nothing about horror or bloodshed in Mainz, except that the city got bombed in World War II. The Nazis probably sent the Mainz Jews—if there were any by then—to concentration camps, but that was centuries after Avram's time. If Dolcette's grandfather was Rashi and he was still alive when I saw her, then it made sense—magical sense anyway—that I traveled to Paris at the end of the First Crusade.

I doodled on the page, trying to connect the topics in some logical manner. No good. I remembered the dot-to-dot coloring book Dagmar took to the Halloween party, even though it had nothing to do with her costume—she had been dressed as some sort of fairy princess.

Dagmar had insisted that I shouldn't sit home and waste my Marcel Marceau mime costume just because Leona had the flu and couldn't go with me to the party at Leona's friend's house. There I was on a Saturday night, all dressed up as Bip in whiteface, ready to smile and play mute—the perfect costume for me. I'd told my sister that I didn't mind staying home, but she was all "this will be so much fun." The next thing I knew I was out the door. Stupid me.

Doodle. Doodle. Connect the dots. Rye. Rotten rye. Saint Anthony's fire. Dagmar called LSD "rotten rye," but was she right? I went back to the World Book. Nothing on LSD.

I rubbed my forehead. What was I missing? What was wrong with Avram? He looked perfectly healthy. Except that he planned to kill his son.

The
Third
Day

PARIS
27 Kislev 4860
ANNO DOMINI 1099, FESTIVAL EVE AND
FEAST DAY FOR SAINT LUCIE OF SYRACUSE
Sunset, Monday, December 12–
Sunset, Tuesday, December 13

BERKELEY
27 Kislev 5725
Sunset, Tuesday, December 1, 1964–
Sunset, Wednesday, December 2, 1964

CHAPTER SIXTEEN

I TURNED ON THE LIGHT in the hall and opened Grandpa's door. The room could use an airing. Sylvester rubbed against my leg.

Grandpa was lying in bed in the dark. "Rachel?" His voice seemed forced, raspy.

"It's H-Hope, Guh-randpa. T-time for d-dinner."

"I'm not hungry, *sheyna maidl.*"

"Y-you *have* t-t-o eat s-something." Taking his cold hand in both of mine, I went for his Hanukkah favorite—the potato pancakes Mom had made and frozen before she left. "*L-latkes* and s-sour cuh-ream?"

"For *latkes* and a glass of wine I will move these old bones. But I eat in my pajamas. Starting tomorrow I eat in my bedroom until Rachel comes home. Deal?"

"D-deal."

After I gave him a drink of water, he seemed more alert and together. He walked on his own to the living room, where I lit the menorah for us and sang the blessings.

I decided to make two tuna casseroles and heated the water to cook the elbow macaroni. We ate together in comfortable silence (*latkes* for me, too, with salad and a hard-boiled egg).

Afterward, Grandpa sipped his wine and watched me collect the box of macaroni, a bag of frozen peas, two cans of tuna, and a can of cream-of-mushroom soup. "What is this sadness?"

"J-just t-t-tired." Which was true. While my mind raced in triple time, trying to connect the dots, my body ached with fatigue.

"You cannot fool your old grandpa."

I shrugged.

He hummed a simple melody in a minor key, a tune I seemed to have always known.

"Nu? Tell me your troubles."

I got up from the table and walked toward the stove. "N-nothing. I-I'm a l-little sad. I-I'm r-reading about the J-J-Jews in Germany a l-l-long time ago."

Grandpa rubbed the stubble on his chin. "That's why I came here, to this country. Germans you cannot trust. And Russians, no better."

It only took a moment to dump the macaroni in the boiling water, but by the time I looked back, my grandfather was rocking slightly, his eyes seeming to look inward.

"'Beat the Jews,' they shouted. It was summer in my beautiful Bialystok. 1906. Another pogrom. This one was the worst I ever saw. They slashed Chayim from ear to ear. Chayim, who worked in the textile mills, a loving husband to my sister, the father of her children. He twitched and gurgled, blood everywhere, and still they spat in his face and stole his shoes. They left him to rot."

I rushed to the table and put my hand on his shoulder. "Th-that's h-horrible, Guh-randpa."

It was as if I weren't there. He finished half a glass of wine in three gulps. "When night came, our people would take his body to prepare it for burial. Then it would be too late. So I stole a meat cleaver from the kosher butcher and desecrated Chayim, may God forgive me. I chopped off two of his fingers to get his gold wedding ring. I sewed the ring into the waistband of my trousers and I never told Rivka. Chayim's ring bought a third-class train ticket to Gdansk for Rivka and me and Rivka's children. I worked and stole, and starved, to bring us all to New York. Your grandmother's Uncle Hermann of blessed memory offered me a job in the print shop, and the Industrial Removal Office paid for our train fare from New York to Portland."

I wiped spittle from the side of his mouth. "I-I am s-so s-sorry."

His eyes focused on me again. He stopped rocking and shrugged, his bony shoulders lifting his pajama top. "*Ach!* I would do it again, wouldn't you, *sheyna maidl?* To save a life? I met my Miriam of blessed memory in Portland. Nothing is always one hundred percent horrible. Nu? You don't agree?"

"Don't agree about what?" Dad framed the kitchen doorway, his book bag over his shoulder and one pant leg still clamped against his shin from his bike ride.

Before I could say anything, Grandpa asked, "Where is Rachel?"

"She's still in Israel buying items for her gift shop. Today is Tuesday, Ephraim. She'll be back this coming Monday. Six more days."

"Call her, Henry." Grandpa's hand tapped the kitchen table. "Tell her to come home now."

Dad studied Grandpa the way I imagine he would an alpha particle. "I'll do my best," he said, his voice inflected with sadness. He helped Grandpa to bed while I got the tuna casseroles ready to bake.

When he came back, Dad wore a worried look that must have matched my own. I glanced at the telephone.

He glanced at the kitchen clock. "It's 4:57 in the morning in Haifa. I'll call the international operator tomorrow at 10 a.m. our time, but please don't get your hopes up. You know how your mom is. Somebody tells her about an artist on some kibbutz, and she wanders off to places that don't have reliable phone service. Grandpa will be fine until your mom gets home."

I bit my lip and put the casseroles in the oven. *As Grandpa would say, from your mouth to God's ear.*

He peeled a banana and offered me half. I shook my head. "Things are heating up on campus, Miriam Hope. The students are angry about the university's plan to expel Mario Savio and several other free speech leaders. Don't let Dagmar drag you into doing something foolish again."

I shook my head and slapped the stove with a potholder. "I-I didn't know it had eh-LSD. I-I th-thought it was j-just l-l-licorice."

His smile was thin, his face tired. "Yes, we've gone over this with you and Dagmar more times than I can count. In theoretical physics, we could travel backwards and undo that whole horrible night. Believe me, if I could build you a time machine, I would."

I closed my eyes and leaned against the kitchen counter. *Daddy, meet Serakh, my human time machine. Serakh, this is my father, Henry Friis.*

"I...uh...s-since I'm on c-campus...D-do you know p-professors in the h-h-history duh-partment? F-for the M-M-Middle Ages?"

"Is this for your history paper?"

I lied with a bob of my head. What could I say? It's for a trip across the *olam*?

Dad didn't ask for details. "Try Professor Cavanaugh. She's an expert in that field, I think. We're on faculty committees together. Nice woman. Friendly."

I promised myself I'd see this professor after the rally and learn what I could about Mainz. Maybe that's what Serakh needed me to do.

WEDNESDAY MORNING DAWNED COOL and crisp, the perfect day for a rally. I put the bag of dreidels next to my sleeping sister and dressed in my pink long-sleeved oxford blouse and gray tweed skirt. Grandpa was still asleep, too. Dad was listening to someone on the kitchen phone. He mouthed "international operator" and smiled a good-bye.

On our way to school, I reminded Leona about my plans for the rally. She raised her eyebrows in disapproval.

"I thought you were going to let Dagmar sell the dreidels."

"I-I want to hear J-Joan Baez. P-plus I have t-t-to do r-research on c-c-ampus."

"Well, if there's any trouble at all, you go straight to my dad in the financial aid office. It's on the third floor of Sproul Hall."

I shifted my books to my other hip. "Th-the r-rally's outside. I'll s-sell a bundle of duh-reidels."

"And suppose someone sees you at the rally and tells Mr. Z.? He'll never let you sing at the music festival. You'll lose your chance to wow the judges. Don't you have your heart set on winning that music scholarship? It's too risky."

"N-no one will s-see me. I n-need the m-money."

Leona stopped and faced me. "I don't want anything else to happen to you, Miriam Hope Friis." She glanced at my bandages. "I'm serious."

You'd think I was marching off to Vietnam.

Leona's anxiety nagged at me through homeroom. I spent history class wondering what Dagmar would do if I didn't show up. During English, I decided that I could trust her to sell the dreidels and give me my share. Or most of my share, anyway.

But suppose she meets some guy at the rally and gets stoned for the rest of the day and forgets about the dreidels?

I strode into my choral music class determined to sneak out to the rally afterward. Cash was always tight in the Friis family when Mom was buying inventory, and I needed money for the trip. End of story. Still, I blew two full measures in "Now Is the Month of Maying." Mr. Zegarelli's hands stopped in mid-conducting.

"S-sorry," I said.

He tapped his baton on the music stand and scowled. "Let us start again, from the top of page 6, letter B. Miss Larson and Miss Wolfe, please sing with Miss Friis this time."

Martha and Francine grabbed their copies of "Now Is the Month of Maying" and rushed to stand on either side of me. Their smiles weren't exactly rapacious, but everyone knew they wanted to share my soprano parts for the competition. I concentrated on the music and did a decent job on the rest of the piece.

After class, I stuffed my books in my locker and convinced myself that no one would notice me skipping the rest of school. Clutching my purse, coat, scarf, and empty book bag, I walked to the front door. No hall monitors. Perfect. I emptied my brain of what-if-they-stopped-me excuses and headed down Allston toward campus. The sun warmed my face, promising a huge turnout.

By the time I got to the entrance at Bancroft and Telegraph, the Campanile was chiming noon. A zillion kids covered Sproul Plaza. I practically gasped for air as I wove through the crowd to get to Sather Gate.

And there she was—Dagmar—wild black curls, army boots, peasant dress with a thick woolen vest, our bag of dreidels—and... *Crap!* Draped around her hips and knotted at her waist was my prayer shawl.

CHAPTER SEVENTEEN

AGMAR WAVED AT ME, then put her hands in the air and twirled. "The perfect sales outfit," she said, as I got closer. "This is the most gorgeous prayer shawl I've ever seen. Totally Jewish, totally hip. You've been holding out on me." She crushed me to her in a patchouli-smothered hug.

I shoved clenched fists in my coat pockets and shook my head. "This was Guh-randma's. N-no one is supposed to w-wear it. Guh-randpa would have a fit." I didn't mention that I was about to have a fit.

"Grandpa's not here." Said with a little two-step and another twirl.

I shook my head again. "I-I m-mean it, Dag-m-mar."

She stopped twirling and gave me her I'm-disappointed-in-you look.

The prayer shawl was my lifeline to Serakh. I had to stand my ground this time. "M-m-m-mine." I held out my hand.

She rolled her eyes. "You're the boss." Which is so not true. She handed me the shawl, and I slipped it into my book bag. My shoulder twitched. Maybe Leona was right. Maybe this was a bad idea.

"So, Hope Against Hope, let's get us the big bucks. Like Josh the Capitalist Wonder Brother says, know your customers. I'll give you the short version, okay?"

I was tempted to remind Dagmar of her rants that guys like Josh are the scum of the Earth. I was tempted to remind her that I already knew all about the protests on campus because they had happened a few blocks from Berkeley High, and I couldn't help but hear about them. The two-day sit-in with the police car in October had even made *The New York Times,* which Mom and Dad read religiously. I was tempted to say that my sister spent more time stoned off campus than she spent in class on campus. Instead I said, "Okay."

Dagmar, I knew, was not to be deterred. She counted on her fingers, starting with her thumb. "First the high mucky-mucks banned students from distributing political stuff anywhere on Cal's campus, even in their usual old place at the Bancroft-Telegraph entrance. Mario Savio and a bunch of kids started the free speech movement to protest the ban."

Cal. She used Berkeley's nickname for its football team, like this was some sort of arch-rivalry between the students and the administration. The professors seemed to be somewhere in between, with my father leaning toward the students' side.

She grabbed her index finger. "So now they plan to kick Mario out of school. The FSM kids say they'll demonstrate big time if that happens and the ban on political activity stays. And last night the Academic Senate sided with the high mucky-mucks and told everyone not to come here today."

She raised her middle finger in triumph at the hundreds of people surrounding us. "This is the result. Got it?"

I nodded.

Dagmar plowed our way to a bench. She stood on top of it, and yelled, "Buy your hand-crafted, miracle-of-freedom, liberty tops here. It's for a worthy cause."

I looked up at her. "W-what w-worthy cause?"

"You," she said, giving me the wide-eyed Bambi look. "We're supporting your future singing career."

I couldn't help but grin.

We worked the crowd, as Josh would say, with Dagmar doing the talking, while I smiled, the mute but talented artist. Six dollars later, we stopped when Joan Baez stepped up to the microphone, strummed a chord on her guitar, and began to sing. She stood in front of an American flag, in a thicket of reporters. Her long straight hair, as dark as Dagmar's, fell across her turtleneck and sweater. She looked stunning in her dark skirt, black high boots, and fishnet stockings. She treated us to "Blowin' in the Wind," and "All My Trials," and "The Times They Are a-Changin'," sunlight glinting off the large cross hanging from her neck, and her glorious voice vibrating across Sproul Plaza. Joan Baez was twenty-three, but I bet she had been great at sixteen, too. If I sang half as well as Baez, every music conservatory in the country would want me.

Josh was right about one thing. When Mario spoke, it would take a stutterer like me to detect the slight hesitation in his voice. Maybe Mario could manage public speaking like I could manage singing. Maybe he didn't have a brother who used to make him do stuttering interpretations of Porky Pig in front of his friends.

"There is a time when the operation of the machine becomes so odious, makes you so sick at heart, that you can't take part," Mario said. "You can't even tacitly take part, and you've got to put your bodies upon the gears and upon the wheels, upon the levers, upon all the apparatus and you've got to make it stop. And you've got to indicate to the people who run it, to the people who own it, that unless you're free, the machines will be prevented from working at all."

I wondered if Leona's father thought he was a gear in the university machinery. Mr. Nash, Number One Cog. After the cheers died down, Mario headed for the front doors of Sproul Hall. Then everyone started to follow him. He could have been the Pied Piper of Hamlin.

No. That wasn't it. I felt somehow that what Mario said rang true. Talking wasn't enough. For me, talking was hardly worth the effort. Sometimes you just have to act. Hundreds and hundreds of people—even some professors—walked toward Sproul Hall. They seemed to be in an almost festive mood, as if they were joining a party inside.

Baez sang "We Shall Overcome." She said something about going in with love in our hearts and how we would succeed. Succeed? Was this my fight? I hadn't thought so when I'd cut school after Choral Music. Now I wasn't sure. Dagmar and I were swept up in the crowd. And then I was inside the building, and the "we" who were overcoming included me.

The crush of bodies nearly smothered me. It was impossible to turn around and go out—too many people—but I needed breathing space. "L-let's f-find Mr. Nash," I told Dagmar. I un-buttoned my coat. "H-he's on the third fuh-loor."

"Chatty Cathy's dad works here? Yeah, right, I forgot."

I should have defended Leona, not that Dagmar would have listened. Instead I pictured my friend with a pull-string in her back and a smiley doll face, and I laughed. "M-maybe he'll b-buy a duh-reidel."

"Sure, what the hell. I'll snag a chair in his office and rest awhile."

By the time we got upstairs, the third-floor hallway was filled with students sitting on both sides. Most of the offices seemed to be closed and dark, but there was a light coming from under the door for financial aid.

The older woman behind the front desk glared at Dagmar. "This office is off-limits to protestors. If you don't leave immedi-ately, I will call campus security."

It was my turn to take charge, because Dagmar's sense of propriety has been on vacation since President Kennedy's as-sassination. "W-we c-came to s-see Mr. N-Nash," I managed to say. "I-I'm fuh-riends w-with his d-daughter."

The woman pursed her lips and patted the bun at the base of her neck. "Well, why didn't you say so in the first place? Mr. Nash is through the first door on your left."

Mr. Nash came around from behind his desk. "Hope, I see you had the good sense to check in with me. Leona said you might come." He glanced at my sister. "You two girls aren't planning to stay much longer, are you?"

"As long as it takes," Dagmar answered before I could get a word in edgewise.

Mr. Nash gave me the earnest, worried look that Leona in-herited. "The Chancellor and the Dean of Students are prepared to call in the police to stop this occupation. Perhaps even the highway patrol. They are consulting with Governor Brown. You really should leave."

"We're we're j-just here to s-sell duh-reidels," I managed, pointing to the bag.

Mr. Nash arched an eyebrow. "That's what Leona told me. For the music festival in Portland?"

"You'll buy a dreidel, won't you...sir?" Dagmar's voice dripped with sweetness. "They're only a dollar."

Twice the price? Unfair. I bit my lip.

Before I mustered up the nerve to contradict Dagmar, Mr. Nash handed me a ten-dollar bill. "I'll take ten," he told me. "That's probably all you'd get from the students here this afternoon. I'd leave the building now, before the situation gets out of hand."

I mangled two whole sentences thanking him.

"Take your sister home," Mr. Nash told Dagmar. "She's not even a student here."

"Of course," Dagmar said in that tone she uses with our parents when she's about to do the opposite.

After we left Mr. Nash's office, I grabbed Dagmar's arm. "A-a d-dollar each?"

She beamed. "Why not? He can afford it. The Nashes have two cars and a poodle."

I shook my head. There was no winning this argument. "L-let's go," I said.

"In a little while. Captive audience, remember? Mr. Nash is so wrong about how many kids in Sproul will buy our liberty tops. And he's in the finance office, can you believe it? Mario's right. The people running Cal are totally screwed up."

Dagmar wanted to drag me up to the fourth floor, but we compromised on selling dreidels from the third floor down, and then leaving. I got four more dollars—less Dagmar's twenty percent—on the way to the stairs.

The second floor was just as crowded as the first. There wasn't an empty space on either side of the hall, except the entrance to the bathrooms. Dagmar waved to a cute guy sitting by a window at our end of the hall. He was eating an apple and reading a textbook on organic chemistry.

"Hey, Gabriel," she shouted. "Look who I have here."

He looked up, his eyes an intense blue, his curly brown hair cut short on the sides but left long across his forehead, a scar running from his full, wide mouth to the base of his nose.

"Hope!"

Gabriel's deep baritone voice gouged a hole in my brain. No! Desperate to stay in control, I forced my eyelids to stay open. As I turned to Dagmar, her head shrank to the size of a tennis ball.

CHAPTER EIGHTEEN

"WHAT'S WRONG? YOU LOOK like death." Dagmar's voice was alarmingly loud coming from such a tiny mouth.

My own mouth refused to open. Impossibly heavy, my eyelids thunked shut. Red lights flashed. Sirens screamed. That deep baritone voice thrummed in my head. His mouth unzipped, and words flew out. *Hang. On. Mime. Girl.*

"No!" My eyes jerked open. I tripped over something. Dagmar caught me in mid-fall. Her head was its regular size.

"H-he...I-I...I-I..."

"See, I knew you'd recognize him. Gabey-Baby got us to Alta Bates Hospital. He stayed in the emergency room the whole time, I think. Not that I remember all that much, but he was there when Mom and Dad came."

I shivered, despite the heat from all those bodies, and shook my head.

"Come on. He's been asking about you for ages. The least you can do is thank him. He won't bite."

"Y-your h-head shuh-rank...and then...and...and..."

"Just now?"

I nodded.

"Oh, Hopey-Dope, were you scared? Yes?" Dagmar hugged me, a sisterly comfort that felt sincere this time. "They'll come and go. Relax. Let them happen. If you get uptight, they'll get worse. Sometimes they're awesome. Like *Alice in Wonderland*. Take a deep breath, and let's go see the man himself, and later I'll take you home, okay?"

I rubbed the back of my neck.

Gabriel waved to us and spoke to two guys sitting next to him. They got up and wound their way toward us. "Gabe's saving those spots for you," one of them said. "Prime location. Snag them now."

Dagmar guided me to him. He closed his organic chemistry book, stuffed his apple core into a brown paper bag, and held out his hand. "Gabriel Altman," he said. "Pleased to meet you now that your mind is no longer blown. You look great."

"She's just had a flashback," Dagmar announced for half of Sproul Hall to hear.

I covered my burning cheeks with my hands and looked away, but I didn't dare close my eyes.

"Ouch. Hey, I'm really sorry, Hope. Are you okay?"

I shrugged.

Dagmar's voice pierced the air again. "Don't you give me that look, Mr. Holier than Thou. Acid isn't any different than pot."

I uncovered my face and managed a smile. No need to make a scene. That zigzag scar pulled at his upper lip and flattened one nostril slightly. When my bandages came off, people would gape at my face, too.

"Cleft palate," he said. "You should have seen me before surgery."

"I-I d-d-didn't m-m-mean to stare".

"No worries. It happens all the time. People are curious, that's all. I'm surprised you're here. Dagmar didn't tell me you were into civil rights."

"She's not." Dagmar wedged past me to sit next to Gabriel. I thought I saw him frown, but I could have been wrong. Dagmar gets every guy she wants—at least that's what she tells me.

"We're selling her hand-crafted, miracle-of-freedom, liberty tops to the assorted assembly," she said. "She's desperate for money to go to a music festival in Portland where she'll become famous, win a scholarship to the San Francisco Conservatory of Music, and live happily ever after."

Gabriel leaned across Dagmar, "How much are the tops, Hope?"

"Fifty cents each." Dagmar thrust the bag of dreidels under his nose. "For you, forty."

I reached into the bag and gave him one. "F-Free," I said. It was the least I could do for getting me to the hospital on Halloween. I slipped another dreidel into my skirt pocket to keep for Grandpa. Then I gave Dagmar the let's-leave look.

She ignored me. "So, Gabey-Baby, I've got selling to do. Hope should stay here with you for a few minutes. I want her to be safe. She might need minding."

I gritted my teeth. This wasn't part of our deal, but I didn't feel strong enough to go up against Dagmar.

"Sure," he said. He took a deck of cards from the back pocket of his chinos. "I figured the occupation would last a while. Do you play gin rummy?"

At least I won't have to talk much. I nodded.

"What nice Jewish kid hasn't learned gin from his—or her—grandparents?" He raised his eyebrows with that I'm-a-member-of-the-tribe look. "A penny a point?"

I dipped my chin in the affirmative.

Two games later, I led by thirty-nine cents. Gabriel didn't say much, and I said even less. His hands were large, with long fingers, perfect for the piano. We used his organic chemistry book as a card table. He didn't seem like someone who would have been at the Halloween party—he was too straight-looking. Too nice. And clearly he wasn't into LSD. Finally I got up the nerve to ask, "D-do you…um…are are you p-part of D-Dagmar's cuh-rowd?"

Gabriel picked up the ten of spades and put down a five of clubs. "I don't do drugs, if that's what you mean," he said, rearranging his cards. "Except for marijuana, and not much of that. A couple friends from Core were at the party, and I stopped by to see if they wanted to come to the midnight showing of *Psycho.* That's when I found you on the kitchen floor. Someone told me you were Dagmar's sister, so I took Dagmar with me in the ambulance."

I willed myself to focus on the cards and on how my new pantyhose itched. Here and now and nothing else. "C-Core?" I knew what it meant, but I had to switch the subject away from Halloween.

"Congress of Racial Equality." Gabriel waved his cards as he spoke. He had two jacks. "The frat boys say it stands for Commune of Radical Eggheads. You know, we're all communists, right? Standing up for civil rights is un-American—that sort of garbage. You'd think Senator McCarthy was still alive and blacklisting loyal citizens who believe in justice for all. It stinks."

His eyebrows crinkled. I gave him my tell-me-more look, my head cocked slightly, my eyes welcoming and lips in a soft smile.

"Core belongs on campus. Jack Weinberg was manning a Core table on Sproul Plaza when the police arrested him in October. Do you remember that?"

I nodded. Who could forget the newspaper picture of that lone police car surrounded by hundreds of students? "D-did you speak thuh-en?"

"Yup. I took off my shoes and stood on the car roof and had my three minutes to talk to the crowd. Dozens of us did. I lost count after the first twelve hours."

I wondered what I would have said if I had the nerve. Here were all these kids speaking up about the right to express their views on campus, and I could barely get a sentence out without feeling ridiculous. Any way you looked at it, it didn't seem fair. I put down the jack of clubs I was saving and let Gabriel win the game.

"Jeez, it's hot." Gabriel pulled off his V-neck sweater. Dampness stained the underarms of his shirtsleeves, but he didn't smell bad. No, not at all. His shirt could have used ironing. He rolled his sweater into a pillow and offered it to me as a backrest. "Want to play another game?"

"Okay," I said. No stutter for a change. I imagined Serakh standing next to me, working her magic on my speech, making it easier to get to know this guy who was sitting so close that I could see the tiny shaving nick on the underside of his chin.

"I-I'm not l-like D-Dagmar," I said, arranging the cards he dealt me.

"I see that."

I bit my lip. Under-endowed me with my mini-breasts. Is that what he meant?

"So was that stuff about the music conservatory true?"

"S-sorta." I waded through that awkward moment when someone expects you to say more, and you don't. Gabriel didn't seem to mind. He didn't talk over me or around me. He didn't rush to kill the silence.

A few minutes later, I put my ace of hearts facedown on his book. "G-gin."

"You're bankrupting me!"

We shared a Baby Ruth that Gabriel pulled from his bag. I liked the way his hair fell over his forehead when he looked down. His shoes were scuffed. He had tiny ears.

Dagmar came back with five dollars and fifty cents in dreidel money—so I forgave her for breaking our deal. Not that I felt deserted. She was right. Gabriel made me feel safe. And a little unsafe. Which felt good, too. Very good.

Someone announced that the FSM kids were sending out for food. Probably pizza. I thought of my dull tuna casseroles and hoped that Grandpa wasn't upset that I was away. Dagmar had told Dad we'd be out past dinner.

Gabriel asked us to keep his place while he went to the bathroom.

"I gotta pee, too, Hopeless," Dagmar announced. "Can you hold the fort?"

She didn't expect an answer. I put Gabriel's organic chemistry book on my lap and stretched out next to his book bag. No one bothered me, and the constant noise was almost soothing. I relaxed against my own book bag, which was filled with my prayer shawl, and finally dared to let my eyes close. What floated in front of my eyelids this time was Mon Trésor, his tiny fist on Dolcette's breast.

I looked at my watch. Too late to go to Prof. Cavanaugh's office. She'd have to be first on my list tomorrow after school.

Gabriel's baritone woke me with, "I'll mind your stuff, if you need to use the ladies' room. Dagmar's wandered off again."

I brushed my hair in the bathroom, smoothed my blouse,

and put on lipstick. As the sky darkened and we played another game of gin, Gabriel told me about his sit-in the previous March at the Sheraton Palace Hotel. "There were hundreds of us, like in here, only more comfortable, because we were in the lobby. Eventually the hotel owners agreed to hire blacks on the same basis as whites."

He touched my bare arm, just below where I'd rolled up my sleeves. "I figure they'll arrest us here, too, like they did at the hotel, but it's not the end of the world, Hope. Don't let them drag you down the stairs, though. Your rear end will ache for weeks." His fingers slid along my skin, setting the little hairs there into a frenzy. "I'll make sure you're okay."

The **Fourth** Day

PARIS
28 Kislev 4860
ANNO DOMINI 1099, FESTIVAL EVE AND
FEAST DAY FOR SAINT NICASIUS OF RHEIMS
Sunset, Tuesday, December 13–
Sunset, Wednesday, December 14

BERKELEY
28 Kislev 5725
Sunset, Wednesday, December 2, 1964–
Sunset, Thursday, December 3, 1964

CHAPTER NINETEEN

W E ATE PEANUT BUTTER sandwiches—no pizza after all—while Gabriel studied his organic chemistry book and highlighted parts of it with these funny, new yellow markers. I looked at the illustrations in his biology book and wondered whether he was in pre-med. Dagmar went on selling sprees—at least that's what she told us—and always returned with more money.

I cat-napped against Gabriel's shoulder and listened to him turn the pages in his book and mumble to himself. At one point I thought I heard him say, "Oh, my, such good apple pie, sweet as sugar."

I sat up and stretched. "A-apple pie?"

Gabriel took a strand of hair that had plastered itself to my cheek and guided it back behind my unbandaged ear. "Oh, my, such good apple pie, sweet as sugar. It's a mnemonic for the dicarboxylic acids. A memory aid."

"Eh-every g-good boy duh-serves f-fudge." I smiled.

"Yup. Lines on the treble clef. My parents wanted me to play the trumpet—Gabriel blow your horn—they have a weird sense of humor. I took up the cello instead. I still play sometimes."

I imagined singing while he bowed the strings. "A-Are you puh-re m-med?"

"Pharmaceutical research. Like the cure for cancer. I'm a chem major with a minor in biology."

We were silent together. He cleared his throat and caressed the front of his organic chemistry book. "My favorite mnemonic is the one for remembering the orbital names for electrons: 'Sober people don't find good in killing.' It sounds like it has to do with politics."

"S-sober...what?"

"Sober people don't find good in killing. It's a great line, don't you think? I wish it were true. Look at Vietnam. Or Mississippi. Or even California. When I...hey, did I say something wrong?"

Thoughts clunked into place inside my head. Maybe whatever happened at Mainz wasn't the only reason Avram vowed to kill his son. Maybe he wasn't sober. Not drunk, but high. Accidentally high. Maybe I'd been playing gin rummy on top of the book that held the answer.

I shifted toward Gabriel, my hand accidentally landing on his chest. "T-tell m-me about r-rotten r-rye. D-Dagmar s-says eh-LSD is...I m-mean..." What do I mean?

Gabriel frowned. "You're not listening to Dagmar, are you? Hope, that night at the party you missed doing some very serious damage to yourself by a few centimeters. LSD can drive you around the bend."

Exactly. "Yes! I m-mean, n-n-no. It's it's n-not about m-me. C-Can rye m-make you cuh-razy?"

I put my hand back in my lap and waited. Six beats of silence, while he seemed to be thinking. Then he said, "Have you heard of ergot?"

I bobbed my chin. Thank you, *World Book Encyclopedia*.

"I'm no expert, but the ergot fungus contains a chemical compound that's linked to lysergic acid." Gabriel thumped his organic chemistry book. "Comes in handy sometimes. Do you know about Saint Anthony's fire?"

"G-gangrene."

"Well, yes, that's the blood vessel part. But I think there is a neurological component. And, um..." Gabriel looked up at a guy who was now standing in front of us. "Hey, Ken. How's it going?"

"It's good. All good. The free speech kids are meeting with Core at command central. You ought to be there, man."

"Now?"

"Now. We've been looking for you."

"Ken, this is Hope Friis," Gabriel said. "Dagmar's sister."

Ken's eyes widened.

Gabriel coughed. "But not like Dagmar."

The two guys exchanged a look that made me feel embarrassed for my sister, and instantly uneasy sitting so close to Gabriel.

Ken smiled. "Kenneth Collingswood. Nice to meet you."

Go away, Ken. I smiled back and shook his hand.

As Gabriel got up, Ken said, "You'd better bring your things. It's gonna be a long meeting."

Much as I wanted him to, Gabriel didn't argue. "Hope, it was great seeing you. Let's meet again. If you can't find Dagmar soon, just leave, okay?"

"Okay." I watched the two of them navigate their way through the crowd lining the hall. *So this is Gabriel, the Hallmark card guy, the kind, sweet guy who is…what? Sleeping with my sister? Sharing her with Ken? No.* I stared at the ceiling and imagined Gabriel in the lineup on an episode of "To Tell the Truth." I was on the celebrity panel, and the TV announcer was saying, "Will the real Gabriel Altman please stand up."

And that's when I could have kicked myself for not asking Gabriel to borrow his organic chemistry book. Crossing my arms over my chest, I tried to remember everything the encyclopedia had said about Saint Anthony's fire. Which wasn't much. I needed Gabriel's book.

Then a group of kids started to sing:

Announcements, announcements, announcements.
A horrible way to die, a horrible way to die,
A horrible death, to be talked to death
A horrible way to die.

Two official-looking kids with FSM armbands had stationed themselves in the middle of the hall. I stopped thinking about the organic chemistry book for a minute. The boy wore a jacket and tie, and the girl had on an A-line skirt and crisp white blouse. Except for their black armbands, they looked exactly like my group of friends.

The FSM girl held up her hands and asked us to quiet down. She waited until the song was over and the laughter petered out. Then she said, "All members of the administration have left the building and the police have locked all the doors. They are letting people out now, but no one can enter the building."

The hall erupted in grumbling and chatter. Dagmar was coming out of the ladies' room with two other girls. Excellent timing.

The girl next to me put her hand on my shoulder. "Hey, don't worry. It's not like the police are charging up the stairs. We can leave whenever we want to."

The FSM leaders held their hands up for silence again. When there was barely a buzz left in the hallway, the FSM guy took off his glasses and rubbed the lenses with his handkerchief. He cleared his throat, rolled his shoulders back, and cleared his throat a second time. "We have it on good authority now that Governor Brown will be taking repressive measures," he said.

The hallway splintered into catcalls, boos, and mini-conversations.

A guy across the corridor from me said, "Repressive? What the hell for? We've done nothing wrong."

"Idiot," the girl next to me muttered. "We're occupying the friggin' building. We've practically stopped the university from functioning. We're trespassing and damaging property, and violating who knows what else. Of course, the friggin' governor is pissed. We're totally out of control."

Dagmar was climbing over legs and book bags on her way to me.

"I need your attention!" The noise level petered to mezzo-piano so the FSM guy could speak. "In light of these developments, the FSM Steering Committee has decided on the following action," he said. "We urge everyone under the age of eighteen and every non-citizen to leave this building immediately. We urge individuals on probation or parole to leave. We urge women with young children to leave. Those of us who remain should expect to be arrested and sent to prison."

"Holy shit," the girl next to me muttered again. We were in perfect harmony.

CHAPTER TWENTY

Enough. I collected my things and threaded my way to Dagmar. "Let's g-go! I-I h-have to l-leave."

She put her arm around me. "Don't worry, Hope Springs Eternal. The night is young. Nobody's going to arrest anybody. Trust me. There's totally good karma happening."

My sister's karma detection system missed the knot in my stomach. "B-but G-Gabriel s-said…"

"He's a sweetie, don't you think? Too repressed, but I'm working on him. Tell you what. Let's sit by the stairs. At the first sign of trouble, we'll go."

I rubbed my forehead. If I left Sproul Hall, the police wouldn't let me back inside. I'd lose any chance of finding Gabriel, his organic chemistry book, and maybe more about Saint Anthony's fire. But if I stayed in Sproul and the police arrested me, Mr. Zegarelli was bound to find out. Even if the police didn't come, how could I reach Serakh to tell her about the rotten rye? No way would she appear in a blue flash in front of hundreds of kids in a crowded building. Or would she?

By the time we got to the stairs, Dagmar had sold dreidels to a history professor and two of his teaching assistants. We settled in a place I imagined had been recently vacated by a seventeen-year-old, pot-smoking, paroled non-citizen with young children. The guy next to Dagmar offered us a couple of Tootsie rolls. He and Dagmar got to talking—no surprise—while I leaned against the wall, sucked on the gooey chocolate caramel, and weighed my options. Maybe this was where I was supposed to be. Maybe the knowledge I'd get from Gabriel was precisely what we needed for Avram.

Plus the longer I stayed, the more money we made. Did I have enough for the music festival to leave now? Maybe I could stay with my cousins in Portland instead of at the hotel with the rest of the chorus. But then I'd have to get involved with family stuff, and they'd ask me a ton of questions. I'd have to talk. A lot.

I felt a tap on my shoulder.

"We missed the Charlie Chaplin movie," Dagmar said. "But there's going to be a Hanukkah service downstairs. The perfect sales opportunity."

She had a point. The police wouldn't raid a religious service, would they? And Gabriel might be there, since he was Jewish. One last activity and then I was leaving. Definitely. With or without Dagmar.

The service had already started. No Gabriel. Dozens of kids were gathered around a guy somebody said was a teaching assistant named Michael. He lit the candles on the kind of simple rectangular menorah that Mom sold to parents to send to their kids in college. I imagined Dad lighting the lion menorah for Grandpa. He would have, if Grandpa wanted him to, just like the way he took Grandpa to services so Grandpa could hear me sing.

Michael chanted the blessings on key and retold the Hanukkah story, making it sound like the Maccabees would have occupied Sproul Hall, too, in the name of liberty and justice.

"Hanukkah is the affirmation of the struggle for freedom," he said.

And that made sense. Gabriel would have approved.

Someone belted out the first measures of "Artza Alinu," an Israeli song I barely understood, but with a dynamite beat. Dagmar grabbed my hand and reached for another girl with the other. We sang and danced down the hall and clapped and stomped our feet to "Artza Alinu" and then "Hava Nagila," until my palms were sweaty and the room felt like a sauna. After being cooped up for hours, the exercise felt great.

The dance line finally broke apart, and kids started singing "HaTikvah," Israel's unofficial national anthem.

Dagmar draped her arm over my shoulder. "They're playing your song," she said, way louder than she should. A guy looked at us.

"HaTikvah is my sister's song." Dagmar told him. "HaTikvah means 'the hope,' and my sister's real name is Tikvah. She calls herself Hope." Dagmar conveniently didn't mention the Miriam part, or that Tikvah was only my Hebrew name. "She was born on the very same day Israel became a state. Think of the karma!"

The guy looked at me like I was a piece of living history. "That's wild. Do you go to Cal?"

I bit my lip.

"Tikvah is a junior at Berkeley High, but I'm a freshman here." Dagmar pressed the palm of her hand into her cleavage by way of formal introduction. "Dagmar Friis. Our father teaches in the physics department. We're half Danish. You know the Danes saved tons of Jews from the concentration camps. That's why our mother fell in love with him, even though he's Lutheran."

She made it sound like we were part Holocaust survivors, part pastry. I was looking for an escape route, when a girl with an FSM armband interrupted us.

"We have more snacks on the second and fourth floors," she announced. "There's a lecture in Room 410 on Gandhi and non-violence, and a fresh supply of toilet paper in the bathrooms."

Dagmar stood on a chair and waved to the group. "We still have a few of our special, hand-painted freedom dreidels left. Make this a Hanukkah to remember. It's for a worthy cause."

Warmth flooded my cheeks. Still, we made six more sales in the next three minutes.

"I-I'm g-going home," I told Dagmar.

"Oh, it's much too late for that," she said, reneging on her promise not to argue when I said I wanted to leave. Nothing new there. "Dad wouldn't want us wandering around this late. Besides, it's a long walk home. Relax. We're perfectly safe here. It's like a pajama party." She held up the bag of money. "Plus we're making a mint. And you can go to school right from here. The nurse's room has toothpaste, and you can brush with your fingers."

Dagmar would know.

"Tell you what," she continued, drowning me in words. "You take a nap here while I check out what's happening. I'll be back in two shakes of a lamb's tail. Oh, and here's a key to Mr. Nash's office."

"What!"

"I borrowed a key from the secretary's desk. No big deal. In case there was trouble. Which is why I'm giving it to you, because I dragged you here, right?"

She beamed. "I watch out for you, Hopey-Dope. Always have. Always will."

And she walked away.

I clutched the key and watched Dagmar sidle up to the guy she'd told the Tikvah story to. She slid her arm around his waist, and she didn't look back.

I stood there, feeling like an idiot, deciding what to do. There'd be scads of people outside Sproul, including the police and reporters. What if someone took a picture of me, and Mr. Zegarelli saw it? But then, I had a quiet office to myself right here in Sproul. A safe place?

I started up the stairs. Just as I reached the third floor, someone yelled, "The cops are inside! They're starting on the fourth floor."

The hall exploded with noise. Shouts, songs, curses, prayers. Kids scrambling to leave, kids linking arms, determined to stay. I shoved and bumped my way to Mr. Nash's office.

Don't panic. Don't panic. Heart pounding, I stood in front of Mr. Nash's door. Nobody seemed to notice me. I put the key in the lock, leaned against the door, and then I was in. I locked the door behind me.

I walked to the window, the light from campus guiding my steps along the carpeting. I had to act fast, before the police found me. I flung my coat and purse on a chair, pulled my prayer shawl from my book bag, and whispered Serakh's name.

Nothing.

"C-come," I commanded.

Nothing.

"Puh-lease."

I paced in front of the window. She'd always popped up out of nowhere before. How was I supposed to reach her? What was I doing wrong?

Someone knocked. The doorknob turned slightly and caught in the lock. I heard a man say, "I'm tellin' you I heard voices, Charlie. Get somebody up here with a master key. If these wackos get into the business files, there's gonna be hell to pay."

My shoulders twitched. My neck throbbed. If they opened the door, should I hide behind my prayer shawl and mumble in Hebrew? I could pretend I was praying. Would they let me go?

Someone pounded on the door. "Open up. Police."

I pulled the prayer shawl over my head and grabbed all four corners and closed my eyes. "For the baby's sake, come," I whispered.

I heard the man say, "No, I swear I heard something inside. Have you got a shiv? I'm gonna jimmy the lock...So? We'll tell 'em the wackos did it."

And then a familiar voice behind me. "How wise that you have brought your garment of fringes."

Relief nearly bowled me over. I flung the shawl over my shoulders and reached for the blue thread. Serakh rushed to my side. As I closed my eyes again, I heard the lock click and a man's voice. "Holy Mother of God, Charlie! Did you see that?"

CHAPTER TWENTY-ONE

"I HAVE TO SEE AVRAM," I told Serakh, as soon as my head cleared and I could stand on my own. Muddy slush seeped through my penny loafers. Paris slush. I shivered in what felt like early morning air.

I took the dreidel I'd saved for Grandpa out of my pocket. "There's this guy I know who's studying organic chemistry, and he told me a mnemonic for orbital something-or-others. 'Sober people don't find good in killing.' So I thought, Bingo! That's it. Avram thought he saw a vision, but he was really sick from a rye fungus. The kind of sick where your brain gets scrambled. Maybe I'm totally wrong, but if I show him this dreidel and talk to him I might be able to find out."

Serakh cocked her head and cleared her throat.

I must have sounded like Chatty Cathy. "What I mean is, I think I know what's wrong with Avram."

"You wish to go to the bakery?"

"Absolutely. And spend as much time with Avram there as we can."

"Then we shall get dough from Dolcette's kitchen."

The door was open. Serakh didn't bother to knock. The kitchen smell of oatmeal and yeast. Celeste was stirring something in the cauldron.

"Good morning," Serakh said.

Celeste nearly dropped the wooden ladle in the fire. "Good morning," she replied, polite but wary. "Tante Rose is at the market, buying a goose for Rav Judah and Madame Miriam."

"Is Dolcette's mother here?" I asked.

"She is expected on the morrow. May I serve you a goblet of cider?"

"You are indeed kind," Serakh said, walking toward the wooden table. She looked at me and then at the table. I followed her focus. A large ball of dough peeked out from under a damp cloth. "But we are on our way to the market as well. May we ease your tasks by bringing this loaf to the master's oven?"

Serakh didn't have to ask again. Celeste, it seemed, trusted us that much. Or she wanted us out of the house. Either way, we left for the bakery with the bread-to-be.

Shmuel presided over the oven, but I could see Avram bent over a book of leather-bound parchment in the back of the bakery. He seemed to be stroking the parchment, studying it with an intensity that reminded me of Dagmar when she'd come home still out of it, rubbing a square of velvet. A flashback?

After Serakh and I waded through pleasantries with Shmuel, Serakh put Celeste's loaf in the oven. We sat on the bench while Shmuel muttered, and fussed, and threw flour on pallets, and wiped his nose with the back of his hand. Serakh tapped on a pallet. "You look like one who knows where to buy the best cider in Paris," she said. "Might I ask your advice?"

Shmuel mumbled something, his cheeks wrinkling into a smile. Soon he and Serakh were leaning toward each other in a conversation I realized was meant to distract Shmuel. I walked toward Avram, keeping Serakh in my sight. Would the language tie hold?

When I was about two feet away from Avram's back, I coughed. I coughed again. "Excuse me, monsieur," I whispered.

Avram finally swiveled toward me on his stool, blinked, and gave me a questioning look.

I held out my hand the way I used to do when I fed deer at the children's petting zoo. The dreidel nestled like corn kernels in my palm. "My sister-in-law and I would like to give a gift to you and your family. For the gracious use of your oven." I hoped that sounded formal enough and I wasn't speaking gibberish.

He seemed to shake himself awake.

"It is a top," I said. "For Hanukkah."

Avram stared at the dreidel. "Where did you get this?" His

voice was soft and intense. "In all of my travels, I have never seen such an object."

I took a breath. Serakh was close enough for me to communicate with Avram. "I made it," I said, which wasn't entirely true. I hadn't done the carving. I showed him the letters and bluebird and three tiny daisies. "See? The letters are for *ness gadol hayah sham*. A great miracle happened there. It's for a game."

"Yes, I know of this game. Here we use knucklebones." Avram frowned. "Where are you from?"

"The west," I said. No lie there. "Shall I show you? This spins very well."

Avram closed the ledger book and swept a clean spot on his dusty desk with the sleeve of his tunic. Grasping the dreidel's stem with his thumb and index finger, he managed to give it a good spin. The dreidel landed on the side with a daisy and the letter *nun* facing up. The way I learned it, *nun* meant you took nothing and you got nothing. *Nun* stood for *nes*. Miracle.

"I believe in miracles," I whispered, hoping that he did, too. Wasn't that what the Middle Ages were all about—knights, and saints, and wars, and miracles?

Avram grunted.

I cleared my throat, searching for the right words. "Perhaps this has happened to you, kind sir," I started. "Sometimes, after I have had something to...eat...on very rare times...as I am making my dreidels..."

"Yes?"

I concentrated on the dreidel, afraid to look at Avram. I shivered at the memory of my own flashbacks, when the screwdriver changed shape, and words danced, and walls melted. I suddenly remembered how, at the Halloween party, the four bowls of candy on the kitchen table formed a barbershop quartet.

"At very special times, I get lost in the intricacies of my birds and flowers," I said. "I fall into the world of my dreidel. I can taste the colors and hear the wood. Time stretches and I..."

His hand brushed against mine. I lifted my chin. His eyes were wide. Wonder? Fear? Recognition. "I, too, have..."

"Mademoiselle with the blond curls peeking through your

cap—do you also like cider?" Shmuel's voice boomed behind me.

Avram coughed. The dreidel disappeared into the pouch on his belt. I backed away, as Avram stood and stepped toward Serakh. "Your loaf must be ready, Madame. Shmuel, check the oven."

End of conversation, but that was enough. Avram had hallucinations, just like I did when I was tripping on LSD. I felt it in my gut.

"There's a link," I explained to Serakh after we left with the loaf for Celeste. "I'm sure of it now. It's got to do with the chemicals that are in LSD and ergot, which is a fungus that sometimes grows on rye."

"So he is sick?"

"Sort of. Avram ate rotten rye—maybe back in Germany—and he had some kind of hallucination that convinced him he has to kill Mon Trésor. Or something like that. Anyway, I'm on the right track."

"Can you cure him?"

I raised the muddy hem of my robe and navigated my way around what remained of a mangled cat. "Cure Avram? I'm not sure there is a cure, really. We'll just have to see that he doesn't eat the rye fungus again and hope that the flashbacks aren't too bad. They are supposed to fade with time. We'll keep the baby safe until then."

"How long will that be?"

Downwind of the cat, I gagged on the smell, and shook my head. When we turned up another alley, Serakh asked again. "How long?"

"No one knows. LSD is horrible. You're never sure what will happen. I'll try to find out how often Avram gets hallucinations. We'll bring another loaf to the bakery tomorrow."

Serakh gave me the loaf, put both her hands on my shoulders, and brought her face within inches of mine. "There must be more that we can do. If Dolcette's baby were yours, would you live each day in fear that your husband's illness might return?"

The bread felt warm and solid again my chest. Like Mon Trésor. "No," I whispered. "Of course not." My stomach twisted.

"There are only four more days until the *brit milah*. After that, the baby is in mortal danger. He will never be safe until you have cured his father. Of my many travels, this is one of the most difficult. We do not have much time."

Really? "But I go back and forth in an instant. It's all magic. I should have all the time in the world. I mean, when I figure out what is wrong with Avram and how to cure him, can't we go back to…um…where we left off?"

Serakh spread her hands in a gesture of helplessness. "Magic, as you call it, has rules. I cannot change them. During the intertwining, the days that pass in your time and place are as the days in Dolcette's time and place. What you learn nine or ten days from now might be too late."

Think! Something was off. What was it? We walked in silence for a few minutes. Then it clicked.

I stopped by a water trough, with no one to hear us but a mangy-looking horse. "The magic works differently here, right?"

Serakh frowned in confusion.

"What I mean is a day in my time is a day in Dolcette's time. But I can be here for hours and hours and still go back to the same exact minute when I left Berkeley."

"Yes, this is so. Within the same part of the day. There are complications."

"But basically that's how it works."

"Basically."

I nodded, a smile creasing my cheeks. "So then when we are done here I can still see Dr. Cavanaugh tomorrow. You'll take me back to…no. Don't take me back to Sproul Hall. Can you take me home instead?"

Serakh wrinkled her forehead. "Return to a place that is different from the place we left?"

"Exactly. Please. It's important. I'm not supposed to be at Sproul. I could get into trouble at my school, and then they won't let me go to a music competition."

She shook her head. "No one has asked this of me before. I do not know if I am capable."

Crows circled overhead. "No one has asked me to save a baby before," I whispered. "I haven't the slightest clue how."

CHAPTER TWENTY-TWO

CELESTE THANKED US FOR the freshly baked bread and told us that Dolcette wanted to see us. "The rabbi's wife is coming to visit this very morning," she announced with pride as she wiped the table with a clean rag. "I have wrapped the baby in the finest linen and sprinkled lavender on Dolcette's bed. We will have dried plums and walnuts."

The rabbi's wife. I felt my shoulders relax. She'd be the perfect ally to save Mon Trésor.

When we reached her bedroom, Dolcette was arguing with Tante Rose. "They are my guests. I insist that they be with me when I talk to Madame Léa."

Tante Rose's face flushed with anger.

"Good morning to you," Serakh said. "What an honor to be here. I bring news from the bakery that Avram of Mainz is well."

Ten points for diplomacy. "Yes," I added. "We are eager to meet the esteemed wife of your venerable rabbi." *Venerable* rolled against my teeth and lips and came forth in elegant perfection.

Tante Rose pursed her lips.

Dolcette practically snorted. "She is a bitter old..."

Serakh coughed.

Dolcette smoothed her blanket and sighed. "And she has influence. Word has come that Papa's wagon suffered a broken wheel on the road, and there will be a delay of some days. I wanted Mama by my side when we spoke to the rabbi's wife, but I dare not wait any longer."

"This is most unfortunate," Serakh said. And I saw that she meant it. She put Mon Trésor in my arms, and I rocked him.

He looked up at me with clear blue eyes, and I couldn't help but entertain him with my favorite medieval madrigal.

Now is the month of Maying
When merry lads are playing.
Fa la la la la la la…

Mon Trésor seemed to like the madrigal. Either that or he was totally bored, because he fell asleep. I put him back in his cradle.

Dolcette had it right. Bitter and old were perfect adjectives for the plump woman Tante Rose escorted upstairs. Even though her matching light blue headscarf, robe, and purse were spotless, she spent the first five minutes complaining about her maidservant. "The girl cannot use a smoothing board properly," she said. "Look at these wrinkles."

Celeste appeared with a bowl of prunes and walnuts. Tante Rose ushered the rabbi's wife to the one good chair in the room and set the bowl on a small table beside her. I wondered if Celeste had the good sense to have sampled the goodies in the kitchen.

"You need not stay if you are busy, Tante Rose," Dolcette said. "Or if you wish to rest in your room."

Tante Rose folded her arms across her chest. "Celeste and I will stay."

Celeste gave a submissive curtsey.

Silence. Then we started on the usual ageless topics—weather and health. Small talk—although speaking normally was a big deal for me, not a small one. Finally Dolcette looked at Serakh, as if for permission.

Serakh nodded.

Dolcette began. "There is a matter of grave importance, Madame Léa," she said. "My beloved husband Avram has made a terrible vow."

Slowly, painfully, she revealed what Serakh and I already knew. I expected the other three women to cry out in anger, or horror, or grief. I was wrong.

Tante Rose did close her eyes and shake her head. Celeste gasped once and covered her face with her apron, although I had a feeling that Dolcette had already told her most of the story. Madame Léa looked grim.

"Surely there must be something I can do to save my child," Dolcette said, her voice shaky, her hands clasping and unclasping each other.

Madame Léa sighed. "Such is the will of the Holy One, blessed be He. We must not question His judgment."

What! "That's impossible," I said, looking to Serakh for support. "God doesn't want sacrifices. He wants us to make this world a better place, not to kill our children to send them to Heaven."

Madame Léa stood bolt upright, nearly knocking over the bowl of goodies. Red blotches erupted on her face. "I have never heard such blasphemy from a Jewess. Do you not remember Hannah and her seven sons?"

The rabbi's wife launched into a tirade about a character that I barely remembered from Religious School. This was part of the Hanukkah story I hadn't even heard about until last year's confirmation class. Madame Léa spat out gruesome details of how enemy soldiers tortured Hannah's sons to death one by one during the time of the Maccabees. After each son, the soldiers offered to stop if Hannah instructed her next child to renounce his Judaism.

"But, no," Madame Léa continued, her hands slashing the air. "Hannah told her sons to be steadfast in their faith. She sent them to the Holy One, blessed be He. She told them that when they met our father Abraham in Heaven they were to say that he was willing to sacrifice one son, but that their righteous mother had sacrificed seven. While the lights of the menorah are burning, women do no work, in honor of Hannah."

Eyes blazing, the rabbi's wife gripped Dolcette's chin. "This is the courage of Jewish women. This is the path for women of valor. Dolcette, you must be strong, like Hannah."

Waves of nausea rippled through me. This was wrong. All wrong. "But the Hannah story makes no sense here," I said. "No one is trying to convert this baby or his family. He's perfectly safe in Paris. The Crusaders have gone."

Madame Léa rounded on me. "How dare you contradict the word of the Holy One, blessed be He! Avram is a pious Jew. He has seen a vision, like Moses and the burning bush. Perhaps Avram will bring about the redemption of our people. Who are you to question?"

"I have every right to question," I told her, my voice rising. "A baby's life is at stake."

Tante Rose scowled. "Conjurers," she hissed.

Serakh clamped her hand on my shoulder. "My sister-in-law means no harm, Madame Léa," she said. "Tikvah is merely overwrought with grief. She and I have helped these two good women to care for Dolcette's baby since his birth. We are devoted to our faith. Let no word she has uttered be mistaken for blasphemy."

Her lips grazed my ear. "Show you are contrite," she whispered.

I stared at the tips of my loafers and swallowed.

"You will find another way," Serakh whispered.

I swallowed again. "My apologies," I told the floor. After that, I was grit-my-teeth civil. Once I managed a smile. A thin one, but good enough to satisfy Serakh. She was in charge. I felt like I was watching the *Titanic* sink.

Fifteen minutes later, Celeste and Tante Rose escorted Madame Léa downstairs. Serakh lifted Mon Trésor from his cradle and changed what passed for a diaper. "Do not be afraid," she told Dolcette as she got him ready to nurse. "If you are consumed by worry, your milk will dry up in your breasts, and your son will lose his nourishment."

I stood by the door, listening for footsteps on the stairs. "Can't we arrange to have Avram sent away somewhere?"

Dolcette wiped her eyes with the back of her hand, took her baby, and started to cry again. "No, I could not bear it. I yearn for Avram even now. I begged Papa to arrange our marriage. The heat of our unions sparked the life force of the seed within me."

The look on Dolcette's face reminded me of the times my mom and dad eyed each other with so much love that I was jealous. *Will I ever find someone like that?*

"If Avram loves you this much," I said, "then maybe we can persuade him, for your sake, to change his mind."

She patted Mon Trésor. "He has tried. When Avram returned from the Rhineland and told me of his vow, I beseeched him to test the truth of his vision. He applied every remedy the herbalist could devise to balance his humors. Leeches, hot baths, purgatives. He fasted and he prayed. Madame Juliane, the herbalist's wife, told me to give him betony harvested on the feast day for Saint Denis, and I did. Nothing helped. He still believed the vision to be true. He said that the messenger in the vision was an avenging angel. Two days before my confinement to the birthing chair he fell on his knees before me, and we wept."

I shook my head. Angels—if they existed—were the gossamer-winged variety who protected you. They adorned Christmas cards and my old *Little Golden Book of the Bible*. They didn't tell you to kill your child.

"Dolcette, you believe in miracles," Serakh said. A statement, not a question.

"As I believe the sun will rise and set."

"Then do not lose your faith. You will witness your miracle."

By the time we left Dolcette, Serakh had managed to reassure her. Dolcette seemed almost calm.

I was anything but. "This is impossible," I told Serakh as we walked toward the grove of trees. "How can we compete with an angel?"

CHAPTER TWENTY-THREE

AFTERWARD, I SPRAWLED ON my bedroom carpet, with Serakh lying beside me. "You did it," I told her.

She moaned. "Yes, but with great difficulty."

"I don't understand."

"I, too, do not understand. It is the way of The One." She took a long, shuddering breath.

"The One. That's another name for God, right? Well, I have a bone to pick with The One."

She creased her forehead. "A bone?"

"I mean I have a disagreement with God about the way the world should work." Understatement of the year.

She managed a weak smile. "This is natural. Always we are in conversation with The One. Even I, since I was in my first youth. Now, turn away, lie on your bed, and rest. Your mind holds the answer for Avram."

SOME TIME LATER, SYLVESTER rumbled near my neck. And then my alarm went off. Six-thirty. I pounded the ringer into submission and sleepwalked to the bathroom.

When I came back, I poked the lump on Dagmar's bed. All clothes, no Dagmar. I retreated under my covers. Another ten minutes wouldn't hurt.

Dad's voice dragged me out of sleep. "Miriam Hope, wake up. Are you sick? Where is Dagmar?"

I opened my eyes to full sunlight and a worried face. "Dad?"

He ran his fingers through his hair. "Leona just phoned

from school. You never met her this morning. She was afraid you got stuck in Sproul Hall. Her father said he saw you and Dagmar yesterday afternoon. What happened after that?"

"Wh-what t-t-time is it?"

Dad checked his watch. "10:27."

Rats. Too late for choral music, the one class I couldn't afford to miss.

"When did you get home last night?" He shook his head. "I never should have let you go to that Baez concert."

"W-we stuh-ayed on c-c-campus for dinner," I said, stepping carefully from truth to truth. "We w-went to a Hannukah s-service at Sproul and…and…w-we got s-separated. I c-came home."

I wasn't particularly worried about Dagmar. She has a way of making things turn out the way she wants them to. But I wondered what happened to Gabriel. I hoped the police hadn't dragged him down the stairs.

"You're okay?"

I nodded.

"I'm sorry, but I absolutely have to get to the lab to monitor an experiment. It's chaos on campus today. If there are picket lines, I'm going to have to cross them, much as I'd rather not. Research is research. Your grandpa is still sleeping. He should be fine, but I don't think he should be home alone for the entire day. Since you've already missed half of school, could you stay home with him until I get back?"

I nodded again. "M-Mom?"

"I left a message at her hotel. The police are still arresting the demonstrators who occupied Sproul Hall last night. Dagmar might be one of them. Call me if you hear from her or you need anything."

Later, I stood in the shower, offering my back and shoulders the hottest water I could manage. Exhausted, I climbed into sweats and hauled myself upstairs to Grandpa's room.

His breathing had an overtone of a gurgle—what Mom calls a rale. I opened the blinds partway to let in the sunshine. He needed to get up and eat something. Judging from the sour odor, I needed to change his pajamas and the linens on his bed again.

His eyelids fluttered. He finally focused on me. "Miriam?"

I nodded, not knowing if he meant my grandmother or me. "I'll g-get fuh-resh p-pajamas."

He grabbed my wrist, his grip firmer than I'd felt it since he gave up his apartment and moved in with us. "Help me. The box under the bed."

He let me clean him up first, and then sat in his chair sipping water while I took care of the bed. I refused to get the box until he had his pills, crackers, and diluted orange juice. Sylvester joined us for a cracker crumb extravaganza. Then I took the tray back to the kitchen and retrieved the box.

"I want you should have this," he said, opening the top. An old leather album nestled inside, musty with age. "She had a samples album in Portland, for the print shop. She made it in 1912, before she left for California."

I sat cross-legged on the floor next to his chair. "Th-this is from n-nineteen tuh-welve?"

His head shook slowly. "Who knows what happened to that album when they sold the store. This one is later, from our print shop. Double-J Printers. Better than Josefsohn and Jacobowitz. More American. She was so American, my Miriam of blessed memory. So determined that everything should be fair and just." He patted the top of my head. "Like you. I want you should take it to your room for safekeeping."

"We'll l-look at it at d-dinner," I said.

He closed his eyes and smiled. "Yes," he whispered.

I helped him back into bed, with Sylvester and the radio to keep him company. He told me he wanted to nap until his next meal, which he insisted should consist of a small turkey sand-wich with mustard on whole wheat—he hated rye—and a dill pickle, and a radish, and a large bowl of chocolate pudding.

Satisfied that my grandfather felt good enough to think about food, I told him that I might be gone for an hour—two at the most.

"Enjoy," he mumbled, already half asleep.

I stood in the doorway and watched until he turned on his side and started to snore. He was fed and clean and in command of his faculties, and I had to see that history professor. I had to get answers. Mon Trésor's life was at stake.

I raced downstairs, shoved the album under my bed, extracted the silver coin from my mattress, and started looking for my purse. That's when I realized I'd left it at Sproul Hall. In Mr. Nash's office. With my coat. Stupid, stupid, stupid.

I pounded the desk. Not only did I have no money and no coat, but I might as well have left a note for the police. Dear Sirs, I, Miriam Hope Friis, a junior at Berkeley High School, do hereby confess that I unlawfully occupied Sproul Hall in defiance of Mr. Zegarelli's orders and have thus forfeited all rights to go to the super-important high school music festival in Portland.

I huffed, and paced, and snapped two pencils in half. Then I started thinking again. I couldn't do anything about my things at Sproul yet—Dad said they were still arresting kids there. But I could get to the history building from the other side of campus, and I had to see Professor Cavanaugh. I'd take the spare keys from the kitchen and borrow a coat and some money from Dagmar.

Why Dagmar kept Josh's old fisherman's sweater in the back of her closet is beyond me, but it fit well enough and would keep me warm. Searching the pockets in her clothes, I unearthed a tortoise-shell comb, a cat's-eye marble, three foil packets of condoms even though she's on the pill, two nickels, a key to who knows what, assorted candy wrappers, and—yes!—a crumpled five-dollar bill.

A kid's dot-to-dot coloring book fell from the shelf on top of her closet. The same coloring book my fairy princess sister took with us to the Halloween party. When I went to put it back, a plain manila envelope slipped from the coloring book to the floor. Someone had scrawled, "Connect the dots!" across the envelope.

My jaw tightened. Something felt wrong. Sitting on the floor, I undid the little bow-tie clasp on the envelope and pulled out a rectangular piece of blotting paper in a purple-and-gold paisley pattern with perforated squares. Four of the perforated squares were missing. Four doses of LSD.

She promised me! From the moment I got home from the hospital. No more LSD doses in our room.

I pounded my fist on the floor. This time, I was going to do something about my sister and her natural high, fungussy rye. I wasn't sure what yet, so I stashed the dot-to-dot coloring book back on the top of the closet and hid the envelope and LSD blotting paper in my grandmother's album. No way was my sister going to touch those damn doses again.

CHAPTER TWENTY-FOUR

THE DEPARTMENT OF HISTORY bulletin board listed a Joan Cavanaugh in Room 206. I took a breath, climbed the stairs, leaned against the wall outside her office, and practiced saying "Mainz." Because Mainz was the key. I was still muttering to myself, when someone said, "May I help you?"

I turned to see a tall, thin woman about my mom's age standing by the open office door. She had on a navy blue blouse, gray flannel slacks instead of the skirt I would have expected, and a no-nonsense face.

I touched my lips and cleared my throat.

"Come on in. Are you one of my students?" Her voice had a pleasant lilt to it. Second soprano, maybe alto.

I shook my head.

She raised her eyebrows. "Are you going to a Renaissance Fair?"

I shook my head again.

"Excellent!" She waved her hand toward her office. Then she extracted a packet of chewing gum from her pocket and offered me one. "I'm trying to give up smoking. Chewing helps."

I took a stick.

She did, too. "Most of the students who show up at office hours want to know what to wear to a Renaissance Fair," she said, guiding me to the chair facing her desk. "I send them to the theater department." She took her regular seat behind her desk and put on the academic face I've seen Dad wear with his students. "So, now, what's on your mind?"

Mainz stuck in my throat, so I started with Dolcette's coin. I handed it to Professor Cavanaugh, licked my lips, and managed to ask her about it.

She turned it over several times. "William the Conqueror. This is an excellent replica of coins minted in England after the Norman invasion. Late eleventh century. I've never seen one this shiny. Where did you get it?"

I had an urge to tell the professor that the coin came in a Cracker Jack box, which would sound more credible than the truth. Instead I said, "A g-gift."

"Very nice." She gave me the coin. "Is that all you wanted to ask about?"

Nod yes and walk out the door. I took a breath.

"Was there anything else?"

I stared at the floor. *Say it! Now!*

"M-M-M-Mainz." My cheeks burned.

"Mainz?"

I jerked my head. Yes.

"Mainz, the archbishopric and free imperial city of the Holy Roman Empire. It's interesting you should ask about Mainz. I wrote my dissertation on the interrelationship between economic conditions and religious fervor as regards the Rhineland peasantry in the eleventh century. You've come to the right place. By the way, what's your name?"

"Hope Fuh-riis."

"Henry Friis's daughter? From the physics department?"

I nodded.

"Did he send you to me?"

I nodded again.

"Well, Hope, what do you want to know about Mainz?" She waited. And smiled. And chewed her gum.

"W-were there…um…J-Jews?"

She tented her fingers. "Certainly from the beginning of the eleventh century, maybe earlier. By then Jews had migrated into the Rhineland, in the Rhine River region of West Germany today. Cologne had Jews, as did the city of Worms. And Speyer. And a few others. The larger Jewish communities in Europe at that time were in Spain, Italy, and southern France. There was a Jewish community in Paris as well."

I put the coin in my pocket and stared at a black-and-gray ceramic bowl of paper clips on Professor Cavanaugh's desk.

The clock ticked off eight seconds. She cleared her throat once, but said nothing. Verbal ball in my court.

"D-did they b-b-bake buh-read?"

"You mean separate from their Christian neighbors?"

Another nod.

"Definitely. Is this for a paper?"

"S-sort of."

She let it go at that. "The Jews had separate ovens and supervised the baking of bread. There were separate kosher vintners and butchers. Although the Jews paid taxes to the secular authority—the king or prince—they governed themselves as an autonomous community. That was common for Jewish communities in much of Western Europe."

The clock ticked off eleven seconds. I licked my lips. And coughed.

"There are no stupid questions." Professor Cavanaugh sounded like she'd told this to her students a thousand times.

I concentrated on the paper clips. "D-did they ever k-k-kill their ch-ch-children?"

Tick. Tick. Tick. Tick. "D-during the Cuh-ru-s-sades?"

"Oh, my, Hope, do you really want to hear all this?" Her voice softened, now almost a whisper.

I nodded.

Tick. Tick.

"As I recall the phrase used by the Jewish community was *kiddush ha-Shem*, which is Hebrew for 'sanctifying the Name.' Martyrdom to preserve the honor of God. We unearthed chronicles about this in the late nineteenth century. I am sorry. This must be very disturbing for you. What would you like to know?"

Nothing! And everything. I stared at the floor. A sigh erupted from my chest.

I felt a hand on my shoulder. "I canceled class today. The

students are on strike, so no one would have come anyway. There's plenty of time. No rush."

Tick. Tick.

"Henry is raising you in the Jewish faith, as I recall."

Another nod. I shifted my gaze to the swirls of wood grain on Professor Cavanaugh's desk.

"*Kiddush ha-Shem* was one of the horrors of the First Crusade," she said. "It was a sudden response to sudden terror. You have to put the incident in context. Everything in history is context, Hope. That's key. The Jews of that region had never been attacked so viciously before."

"S-so it r-r-really happened."

"Sad to say, yes. I have a few of the primary sources."

"I-I'd l-l-like to s-s-see them."

Tick.

"Are you sure?"

I forced myself to look at her face. Her deep brown eyes bored into mine. I didn't look away.

"Yes," I whispered.

Professor Cavanaugh extracted a notebook from the bottom shelf of her bookcase. "Wait here, please. I'll be back in a minute. The history department just got one of those new photocopiers. They're a godsend."

The office smelled of Earl Grey tea and chalk. A neatly stacked pile of papers guarded one side of her desk, and a notepad and three identical ballpoint pens held court on the other. In between stood a silver-framed photo of two corgi puppies.

Professor Cavanaugh cleared her throat. "Context," she reminded me, coming back to sit behind her desk again. "Do you know anything about the First Crusade? How it started in France?"

"P-P-Paris?"

"Clermont, in southern France. After Pope Urban II's speech, Peter the Hermit and his followers marched north through France, including Paris, but the Jews there essentially bribed Peter to leave them alone. Peter's group wasn't primarily responsible for what happened in Mainz and other places in the Rhineland.

Those atrocities were committed by Count Emicho, Godfrey of Bouillon, and other knights, for their own economic gain.

She handed me a piece of paper. "This comes from Albert of Aix-la-Chapelle—or Aachen. The same place. He was a Christian chronicler of the First Crusade. It's a translation from Latin. I'd like you to skim it here in case you have any questions."

> [The Crusader Emicho] and the rest of his band...attacked the Jews in the hall with arrows and lances...Breaking the bolts and doors, they killed the Jews, about seven hundred in number, who, in vain resisted the force and attack of so many thousands. They killed the women, also, and with their swords pierced tender children of whatever age and sex. The Jews, seeing that their Christian enemies were attacking them and their children...likewise fell upon one another, brother, children, wives, and sisters, and thus they perished at each other's hands...rather than to be killed by the weapons of the uncircumcised.

When I looked up again, fighting nausea, Professor Cavanugh handed me another piece of paper. "And here are quotes from a Jewish source, Soloman bar Samson. They are similar to ones from another Jewish chronicler, Mainz Anonymous."

> The women there girded their loins with strength and slew their sons and their daughters and then themselves. Many men, too, plucked up courage and killed their wives, their sons, their infants. The tender and delicate mother slaughtered the babe she had played with...The maidens and the young brides and grooms...in a loud voice cried: "Look and see, O our God, what we do for the sanctification of Thy great name...

> Inquire now and look about, was there ever such an abundant sacrifice as this since the days of the

primeval Adam? Were there ever eleven hundred of-
ferings on one day, each one of them like the sacrifice
of Isaac, the son of Abraham?

Inhale. Slow release. Inhale. Slow release. Professor
Cavanaugh gave me a glass of water. I slipped the chewing gum
against the inside of my cheek, sipped the water, and listened to
her mini-lecture.

"I don't recall that the Jewish communities along the
Rhine or elsewhere in Northern Europe ever did this again.
Unfortunately, this one instance might have formed the basis
for the blood libel against Jews in the later medieval period. The
people of the early medieval period in Europe were extremely
religious. In general, the Christians and Jews, and the Muslims
and Jews, co-existed rather well. But this was a highly unstable
time, economically and politically. Alliances shifted after the
Norman Conquest, and the era witnessed the initial stirring of a
mercantile class in Northern Europe. Do you see what I mean?"

I nodded.

"Even nature played a role. The spring of 1096 was unusually
wet, resulting in a spike in ergotism among the peasants."

"F-from r-rotten r-rye."

Professor Cavanaugh smiled, as if I were her star student.
"Yes. Precisely. Basically, it comes from eating grain infested
with the ergot fungus. Usually rye, which was the main diet of
the peasants. Some peasants ate three pounds of rye bread a
day."

Tick.

"Saint Anthony's fire? Yes, I see you've heard of that, too.
So you know it's associated with gangrene. But another strain
resulted in convulsive ergotism, which affected the brain not
unlike an LSD trip. Recent evidence indicates that convulsive
ergotism was more prevalent on the northern and eastern side
of the Rhine than elsewhere. Some poor soul suffering from
convulsive ergotism might be revered as a saintly visionary or
killed as a witch."

The neurological component. That's what Gabriel was going

to tell me. I clutched my glass and struggled to put into words what zipped through my brain. Did the Jews of Mainz do what they did because of a rye fungus? Maybe the Crusaders were high, too.

Professor Cavanaugh seemed to read my mind. "You're wondering about the role of convulsive ergotism in the events at Mainz?

I arched my eyebrows.

"There seems to be no evidence that the Jewish community in Mainz suffered from this disease. Many of them were from the burgeoning mercantile class, and thus economically better off than the peasants. Their diets were better. More wheat bread, less rye. More protein, fewer grains. Of course no one knows whether any of the peasant followers of the Crusader knights might have had ergotism."

End of mini-lecture. Professor Cavanaugh touched my sleeve. "Hope, you must not judge those people by today's standards. They lived in different times. And some Jews did decide to save their families by accepting conversion. As for the others, a few hundred apparently, they believed that Heaven was waiting for them and their loved ones. We have to forgive these poor souls, don't you think?"

I stared at the silver picture frame and imagined Mon Trésor playing with those two puppies. "No," I whispered.

Tick. Tick.

Professor Cavanaugh handed me her business card. "This also has my home phone number, in case you have any more questions. Or you just want to talk."

I put the card in my pocket, shook her hand, mangled my thank you, collected the papers, and escaped. Forget Sproul Hall. I couldn't deal with Mainz and Dagmar in the same afternoon. I headed home.

GRANDPA WAS STILL SLEEPING, with Sylvester curled at his feet. I left the door open a bit and went downstairs. I folded my arms over my desk and buried my head on top, waiting for tears that refused to come. Instead I kept thinking about Avram. He came from that time and place. He'd tried to "cure" himself of his horrible vow, and that had failed. Why couldn't he accept that he'd survived the attack on Mainz and build a new life in Paris? How could I ever persuade him that he was wrong about his personal *kiddush Ha-Shem?* How could his God be so different from mine?

CHAPTER TWENTY-FIVE

THE DOORBELL RANG. I rushed upstairs, worried that it might be the police, looking for Dagmar. Or for me.

"Ta-da!" Leona struck a dramatic pose, and then thrust an I. Magnin bag at me. "Your coat and purse," she announced triumphantly. "My dad brought them to me at lunch."

Instant relief. I hugged Leona, bag and all. As we headed for the kitchen, I steered the conversation to the safe topic of an after-school snack. Leona opted for instant coffee with a squirt of chocolate syrup. I got a glass of milk, because I felt too jittery already, and I moved the cookie jar to the center of the table.

"At lunch time, the police were still making arrests." Leona stirred her coffee. "Can you believe it? There must have been a thousand kids in Sproul Hall. Well, you would know, because you were there. Oh, Hope, I was *so* scared when you didn't show up for school today. I called your father, but he didn't know anything, so mum's the word about your leaving your coat and purse. How come the police didn't arrest you? Or did they and they let you go already? Does your dad know? Where's Dagmar? I could strangle her."

I shrugged and smiled. Too many questions to answer at once.

"Lucky for you, the police cordoned off my dad's office and asked him to check his files. When he found your things, he said they belonged to someone who had visited him before the demonstration. Yay, Dad! Plus he brought me ten of your dreidels. Did you sell a ton?"

I nodded and sipped milk to be sociable, my appetite having vaporized after my visit to Professor Cavanaugh.

"I swore my father to secrecy, so I don't think you'll have to worry about Mr. Z. finding out and banning you from the competition. Unless someone else saw you. When did you leave?"

"L-last night."

Leona extracted a vanilla crème cookie from the jar and shifted into giving me a rundown of the latest news at Berkeley High. She was easy to listen to, an antidote to Avram and Mainz. Still, after a couple of minutes, I had to stop to get dinner for Grandpa. I looked at the clock.

"That late?" Leona slurped the last of her coffee and gave me a quick hug. "See you tomorrow."

I rubbed the back of my neck and stood on the front porch in the winter twilight. Time for Grandpa's evening pills. I wondered whether Mom had gotten the message Dad had left for her at the hotel in Haifa, and whether she was coming home early. It was already Thursday, and she was due back on Monday—only a few days to go.

The damn phone rang. I stared at the instrument of my personal torture and bit my lip. This time I had to answer it. Mom could be on the other end. Ring four. Ring five. I filled my lungs with air, hummed, and picked up the receiver. "H-h-h-ello?"

"Hey, *Nudler*, it's Dad." My jaw relaxed. "Noodles" in Danish. My favorite nickname. His voice bordered on the triumphant. Things must be going well at the lab. "How are things at home?"

"F-fine."

"Any word from your mom?"

"N-no."

"How about Dagmar?"

"N-no."

"Well, I was just checking in. I'll be another hour here, at least, so you and Grandpa eat without me. I'll get home as soon as I can."

We didn't chat for long. Dad knows I hate the phone. I like to think that I'm third on his top favorites list, after the mysteries of the universe and my mother.

I made Grandpa's turkey sandwich the way he liked it and put a dill pickle and a radish on the plate. I added a double-sized portion of chocolate pudding with a small dish of marshmallow cream on the side. He'd told me once that there was no such thing as marshmallow cream in "the old country," and it was one more thing he thanked America for. Safety, freedom, and marshmallow cream.

Balancing the tray, I waltzed down the hall and stuck my foot in the partially opened door.

The Fifth Day

PARIS
29 Kislev 4860
ANNO DOMINI 1099, FESTIVAL EVE AND
FEAST DAY FOR SAINT MAXIMIN OF VERDUN
Sunset, Wednesday, December 14–
Sunset, Thursday, December 15

BERKELEY
29 Kislev 5725
Sunset, Thursday, December 3, 1964–
Sunset, Friday, December 4, 1964

CHAPTER TWENTY-SIX

GRANDPA WAS SITTING UP in bed, reading yesterday's *San Francisco Chronicle*. He had slicked back his hair and, judging from three tiny pieces of blood-stained toilet paper on his cheeks, he'd shaved.

"I was just thinking about chocolate pudding." His eyes, which seemed to have sunk deeper into their sockets since this morning, were gleaming. "And marshmallow cream. A minor miracle. Is it still Hanukkah?"

Chin-dip in the affirmative. I put the dinner tray on his dresser.

"Help me to the living room and let us celebrate."

After hearing the Madame Léa's horror story about Hannah and her seven sons, I didn't feel like facing our menorah. Hanukkah was supposed to be about freedom, not *kiddush Ha-Shem*. But I didn't say anything to Grandpa.

Sylvester joined us. I lit six candles for the five nights and sang the blessings.

"Sing them again," Grandpa said. "I love to hear you sing. Psalm 150 you sing so well in the choir. Such a melody. You know I go to services just to hear you sing?"

I sang the blessings again.

"And Psalm 150?"

I wasn't ready. I'd ruin it. The Lewandowski arrangement we sang at temple had a wicked range. If I had the slightest chance of singing it properly, I'd have to take off my bandages, and I didn't want anybody, let alone Grandpa, to see what was underneath. "I-I'm too tired, Guh-randpa," I told him. "A-another t-time, okay?"

Sadness flickered across his face, and I almost changed my mind. "Of course," he said. "Another time." He kissed my cheek. "Did I give you Miriam's album? Good. And her *tallis* you have?"

I nodded.

"Good. Good. You keep that *tallis*, but don't you wear it."

We watched the candles burn. He asked for a glass of schnapps, as if this were a special occasion, and I poured him a jigger over ice, the way he liked it. The candles sputtered. I walked him back to bed. He told me he wanted to eat alone, kissed me good night, and touched the bandaged side of my face. "It's getting better?"

I nodded again.

"Good," he repeated. "I love you, *sheyna maidl*.

"L-love you, t-too, Guh-randpa."

His fingers lingered on my cheek. "Just so you shouldn't worry, I watered the jade plant today."

Sylvester refused to leave Grandpa's room, so I left the door open again slightly. You never know with cats. He could change his mind in the middle of the night.

THE NEXT MORNING, DAGMAR was still gone. I wasn't worried. She was probably in a safe place—jail. Someone else was watching out for her. I figured they didn't allow drinking or LSD trips in there, and they'd give her meals and a bed. Knowing Dagmar, she'd be the star of the show. She was probably selling our "freedom tops" to the inmates.

Plus, if Gabriel was with Dagmar, he'd watch out for her. I put my fingers to my lips. Gabriel. I wanted him to call me and tell me that he and Dagmar were okay. No, that wasn't what I was thinking, not really. I wanted him to call me and ask me out.

No phone calls. I hummed the soprano part of "Now Is the Month of Maying" and got ready for school. The morning was chilly, with the marine layer still rolling in from the Bay. I wore my bright red pullover and a flowered headscarf in counterpoint to the gray skies.

Dad stood by the kitchen counter with a cup of coffee and the newspaper. "Dagmar's not downstairs, is she?"

I shook my head.

"I was afraid of that." He kissed my forehead and showed me a picture in the paper of Sproul Plaza. Dozens of students stood in the foreground, their backs to the camera. In the background, police were lined up shoulder-to-shoulder in front of Sproul Hall. "Now the question is, was your sister in the crowd in front of the building or the crowd inside. If she stayed outside, the police wouldn't have bothered her. It says here that they only arrested the 796 students that occupied Sproul Hall after it officially closed. I haven't heard anything about Dagmar either way. Have you?"

"N-no." I didn't tell him that the police were already in Sproul when I…left. Dagmar didn't stand a chance.

"She drives me crazy, your sister. She always lands on her feet and never feels the consequences of her actions. The rest of us do the worrying, your mom most of all."

"D-did you h-hear fuh-rom M-Mom?" I put an English muffin in the toaster for Grandpa, and got out a bowl of Cheerios for myself.

"Yes, finally. At 1:07 this morning. She's decided to cut her trip short. She's catching an El Al flight from Tel Aviv through Paris today, and I've booked her on an American Airlines Astrojet from New York to San Francisco tomorrow afternoon. Dagmar had better be home by then. Do you have anything planned after school today?"

I shook my head.

"Great. Then I'll stay here to keep an eye on your grandfather and make some phone calls to see if I can find Dagmar. I'm sure the administration has the names of those 796 students. Some of the faculty collected bail money; I'll get in touch with them. If I haven't found out anything definitive by the time you get home from school, I'll bike to campus." He handed me Grandpa's strawberry jelly. "When your mother comes home, everything will be back to normal."

Normal. Blue flashes and trips to medieval Paris. Some normal.

I left the toasted English muffin on a plate in the kitchen—Grandpa likes it crisp and room temperature—and walked down the hall to say good morning to him before I left for school. As I reached his door, tightness gripped my chest. I smoothed my blouse, and took a breath. Something felt off-kilter.

Sylvester sat like a sphinx next to Grandpa's bed. I opened the blinds partway, and that's when I knew.

CHAPTER TWENTY-SEVEN

Y FEET REFUSED TO move. Then suddenly I was racing to the kitchen. Dad must have read my face, because he put down his coffee and newspaper, and we rushed to Grandpa's room.

I stood there, my tongue useless, my mouth opening and closing, opening and closing. I couldn't breathe. I couldn't…I couldn't…And then a strange, high-pitched sound spilled out of me.

Dad enveloped me in his arms. He said words that barely registered. A box of tissues materialized in my hands. I didn't need them. I couldn't cry.

I'd heard somewhere that people who die in their sleep look peaceful. They don't. They look dead. They look empty. I couldn't kiss the face of empty. Instead I held the hand of the emptiness where Ephraim Jacobowitz had been. Then Sylvester rubbed against my leg, and Dad guided me back to the kitchen.

More words, but these I managed to understand. "I have to make some calls now. It's going to be a long and difficult day. I want you to eat something, and then let's get you downstairs to your room."

Time fractured and blurred. Crystal shards pressed against the back of my eyes. I sat on my bed and hugged myself and rocked and rocked.

Funeral directors come faster than you'd think. I scrambled upstairs. Dad was laying out Grandpa's best suit and a navy tie.

I blocked the bedroom door. "Stop!"

Dad's cheeks were blotchy. He cleared his throat, and put

his arm on my shoulder. "Miriam Hope, please. There is nothing we can do for your grandpa now. He lived a good life."

"I-I...his h-handkerchief. I have to puh-ress a fuh-resh one. Guh-randma M-M-Miriam..."

Dad nodded. "I'll tell them to wait."

And they did.

DEATH IS ABOUT TELEPHONE calls. Dad made them. Dad answered them. Afraid to stop and let grief engulf me, I vacuumed the living room rug, wiped down the kitchen table and counters, and put fresh towels and cutesy soaps in the guest bathroom. I couldn't sit still. There would be company coming, although I didn't know when exactly. More talking and more phone calls. Home would be a horrible place. Finally, when I couldn't stand one more second inside, I told Dad I'd go looking for Dagmar.

A picket line blocked the entrance on Bancroft and Telegraph. The students were carrying hand-painted signs. Don't Cross Picket Line. Multiversity On Strike. Gov. Brown—Enemy No. 1. I took a deep breath and walked up to a girl carrying a sign that read Liberty and Justice for All.

Before I had a chance to explain, some idiot man behind me shouted at her, "Go back to Russia, where you belong." The girl said nothing—which would have been my tactic—and kept walking the picket line.

I followed her for a few steps. "Puh-lease," I said. "I-I have to f-f-ind m-my sister. And and G-Gabriel Altm-m-man."

She reached over and brought me through the line. "Sorry," she said. "I didn't realize you were one of us."

Sproul Plaza was jammed. I pushed through the crowd, searching for Dagmar. A guy with a Youth for Goldwater T-shirt stood next to a guy wearing a Young Socialist Alliance armband. Both were waving the same hand-painted signs. Speak Up for America. A girl by Sather Gate held a sign that read Cal Coed: Do Not Fold, Spindle, Or Mutilate. Free Speech For All.

I stood on a bench and managed to see Dagmar, several

yards away, sitting on Gabriel's shoulders and thrusting her fist in the air. She and Gabriel and dozens of other people wore large white V's taped to their clothes.

V for victory? V for violated? A woman standing next to me must have seen me staring at Dagmar, because she said, "That poor girl was one of the students beaten and brutalized, and released on bail."

Dagmar didn't look beaten to me. She practically glowed. I pushed through the crowd and waved at my sister. She smiled and thumped Gabriel's head. He helped her get down, and they waded toward me.

"I was worried about you," Gabriel said. "It looks like you got home okay."

Before I could wedge two words in edgewise, Dagmar enveloped me in a beer-and-patchouli-soaked hug. "Yay! I told Gabey-Baby you'd be fine. You are so clever. I bet you unlocked Mr. Nash's office with the key I gave you and climbed out the back window. Do you still have the key?"

I shook my head. *How can I tell her gently? Where do I start?* "D-Dad..."

"No key? Too bad. And don't start on me about Dad, okay? Gabriel's lawyer is going to represent me pro bono at the arraignment. Our Father Who Art in the Physics Lab doesn't have to get involved."

I took a breath. "W-we h-have to go h-home. N-now. Guh-randpa..."

"In a little bit. First I have to stand in solidarity. And, who knows, maybe make a connection. Then it's home, home, home to soak in the tub. Drown the lice. You wouldn't believe the toilets they have there. Putrid! I dared them to strip-search me. That got them to back off."

Dagmar extracted the cloth bag that nestled in her cleavage. She waved the bag in my face. "Your dreidel money was a lifesaver. And it went for a good cause. I was frugal, totally frugal. Honest. And I'll pay you back. They reduced the bail to sixty-eight dollars for me, and I had to help out Gabriel here. Plus this guy Charlie was in a bind. You know, we've practically closed down the university. Even the labor union is behind us. And then the high mucky mucks have the nerve to publically condemn the demonstration, after what they did, sending in the police. They're all total vermin."

"Shut up, Dagmar," Gabriel said. "Can't you see your sister wants to tell you something?"

Her eyes drilled into mine. "What? You're not going to nag at me about the money, are you? After I saved you from the ravages of prison?"

I drilled back, determined to say what needed saying. "Guh-randpa is dead."

Dagmar stared at me, silent. Then she folded in on herself, as if I'd punched her in the stomach.

"Oh, God," she said. "Not Grandpa. No."

Her head drifted from side to side. Gabriel wrapped his arm around her and then reached for me. "I am so very sorry," he whispered, his breath warm and vaguely pepperminty. "May his memory be a blessing."

We three huddled together in our own private world. I ached to be with Grandpa again in his bedroom, listening to his stories and playing gin rummy. But then Gabriel felt so close, and suddenly all I wanted was for him to hold me forever.

Later, Gabriel talked to some guy, and the four of us went to the guy's car, and they drove us home. I sat in the front seat, while Dagmar and Gabriel murmured in the back. A leaf was stuck under the windshield wipers. Nothingness began to seep into me.

Gabriel helped me out of the car. "When is the funeral?"

"I-I d-don't know."

"It's okay. I'll check the newspaper. The funeral parlor will put in an announcement. You take care of yourself. I am so sorry."

Dagmar draped herself across Gabriel's shoulder. "I can't bear to take one more step on my own," she told him. I walked ahead of them and opened the front door.

Dad met me there, his face haggard, his eyes dull. "Thank the Lord you found her."

I nodded and stepped out of the way to let Gabriel and Dagmar come in together. "This is unacceptable behavior," Dad told Dagmar. "Where have you been?"

Gabriel cleared his throat. "Let me explain, Professor Friis."

I hurried away. I'd done one more item on the list. Bring home sister? Check. That hollow feeling continued to eat at me. I wandered downstairs.

Serakh was sitting on my bed.

I leaned against the doorway and shook my head. "I don't have any answers. I'm sorry. I can't. Today isn't a good day."

In three beats she was by my side. I buried my face in her neck. Sobs erupted from all that nothingness. Tears. Finally.

"Oh, my sweet Hope. Oh, my dear friend. Ephraim was a good soul, and he loved you with his whole heart." Serakh stroked my hair and let me cry and cry until my insides felt scraped out, empty, and raw.

When I was done, she took both my hands in hers. "You can do no more for him now," she said softly. "But there are others who need your help. There is a baby whose life depends on you."

I shuddered. "Yes, I know."

"Whenever you are ready, I will meet you in Ephraim's room. In an hour or a day. No longer than a day. I wish I could leave you to grieve in peace and to come again as you are healing. But I cannot."

I thought about telling Serakh that my grandfather had forbidden me from wearing my grandmother's prayer shawl. I thought about asking her what she did with my grandmother that so frightened him. Instead I said, "I understand."

She kissed my forehead, and I turned away from the flash.

CHAPTER TWENTY-EIGHT

D AD AND DAGMAR WERE still arguing, their muffled voices raining down through the stairwell. I wasn't surprised when the front door slammed and I peeked through the window to see Dagmar running down our walk. The car we came home in was gone, so Gabriel and his friend must have left.

With Serakh gone, Sylvester reappeared and butted his head against my hand. I gave him a half-hearted scratch behind his ears. Not even he could ease the icy ache inside. Finally I managed to change out of my school clothes and into my good white blouse and black slacks. That felt right. Then I remembered Grandma Miriam's album. I stretched out on my bed with a box of tissues.

The maroon leather binding was worn around the edges, but I could still see "Double-J Printers" embossed in silver in the lower right hand corner of the cover. A faintly sweet smell rose from the first page, a luncheon invitation for March 4, 1917, to celebrate the inauguration of Jeannette Rankin as the first woman elected to Congress. A couple of pages later, I found the 1920 program for a "Ratification Ragtime Ball," when the Nineteenth Amendment went into effect and women got the right to vote.

I turned page after page, pieces of other people's lives. My favorite, the one I wanted to show Gabriel and his friends at CORE, was an invitation to a barbecue in 1947 to honor Jackie Robinson for taking the field with the Brooklyn Dodgers and breaking the color barrier in Major League Baseball.

My family history was there, too. Birth announcements and

wedding announcements for my mom and her two brothers. Birth announcements for Josh and Dagmar, and my cousins. Nothing about me, since I didn't come into this world until after Grandma Miriam left it.

I ran my finger over a pale blue ribbon on the yellowed birth announcement for my Uncle Paul, Grandma's firstborn. She must have loved him so much—and Grandpa, too. They were a family. What would Grandma have done if she were in Dolcette's place? Or in mine? Suppose she knew about the link between ergot and LSD? And she had doses? How far would she go to keep a loving family together?

No! Don't even *think* that! I snapped the album shut and hugged it to my chest. The lilies on my Monet poster sparkled and danced. I blinked. The lilies went back to normal. Muted and still. *A trick of the light,* I told myself. *Or a warning about tricking someone into blowing their mind.*

Later, Dad and I shared the cheese omelet he'd made. "Josh is flying up from LA tonight after class," Dad said, his hand reaching for a legal-sized yellow notepad and a ballpoint pen he'd brought to the kitchen table. "He'll find his own way home. Your mom will be home tomorrow evening. Rabbi Cohen is available for funeral services Sunday morning at the temple." A weary sigh escaped. He folded his napkin in quarters. "I wish Jews weren't so set on burying their dead as quickly as possible."

What did Lutherans do? I didn't bother to ask.

"The rabbi called with his condolences," Dad continued. "He'd like us to go to Friday night services tonight. I told him maybe. Mrs. Nash is organizing food and whatever else needs doing."

Dad's whole face seemed to sag. "There's your grandfather's family from Portland. Five of them are coming so far, maybe more. And your mother's great-uncle Albert." He shook his head. "I don't know where we are going to put everyone. Maybe some of them will stay at your Uncle Paul's house in San Francisco."

Honesty bubbled up inside me. "I w-w-wish they wouldn't c-c-come."

"Me too," he admitted, taking off his glasses and pinching the bridge of his nose. "I'm sorry to put the burden on you, but would you mind cleaning up Grandpa's room in case someone stays there? After the company leaves, his room will be yours if you want it. Dagmar can keep the room downstairs. You've put up with your sister long enough."

My room? I rubbed my forehead. I'd never had a room to myself.

The damn phone rang again.

"Friis residence," Dad said. Then, "Yes, operator, I'll accept the call." He closed his eyes. "Rachel, honey, where are you?"

I left my parents to their private conversation.

Focus on the linens, I told myself, as I stripped Grandpa's bed. It's just a bed. I opened the window, letting in fresh air. How long would this room smell like my grandfather?

I managed to clear off the papers on his desk and put his slippers back in the closet. No way could I disturb the bits of his life he'd left on the top of his dresser: a saucer of coins, a pill bottle of digitalis for his heart, a nail clipper, last Sunday's crossword puzzle—nearly finished—and a small framed picture of my grandmother.

I opened the top drawer of his dresser and touched two of Grandpa's treasures—Grandma's faded yellow suffrage bow and the Vote for Justice postcard he'd helped Grandma print in Portland. I wondered what my outspoken grandmother would have thought of having me as her namesake. Inspoken me.

Making space for someone else's clothes in my grandfather's dresser was completely out of the question. It was too soon to admit I could shuffle his things without asking him first.

Leona's mother showed up at about 4:30 with a chicken-and-rice casserole, her twelve-cup coffeemaker, a pint of half-and-half, and three dozen butter cookies. Dad was in the den on the phone, so I had to answer the door. She held me and murmured all the right things about my grandfather. I nodded in appropriate places. "Leona has ballet class," she said. "Otherwise she'd be over here with me. She's so terribly sorry, you know that."

I nodded again.

Dad appeared. "Sheila," he said, extending his hand, "thank you for coming."

Mrs. Nash took Dad's hand in both of hers. "It's the least I can do, Henry. Harvey and I offer our deepest condolences. May Ephraim's memory be a blessing. Have you been in touch with Rachel?"

"She's coming home tomorrow. The funeral is Sunday at ten o'clock at the temple. Then we'll sit *shivah* on Sunday, Monday, and Tuesday, possibly the whole seven days. I'll see what Rachel wants."

Seven nights of people and prayers. Crap.

Mrs. Nash dipped her chin several times in sympathy. "You'll be at services tonight?"

I bit my lip and willed my father to make an excuse for us. If Mom were here, we'd go to support her, but under the circumstances, couldn't we be alone for one night?

"It's the right thing to do," he said. "Miriam Hope and I will be there."

I went downstairs and threw up.

The Sixth Day

PARIS
1 Tevet 4860
ANNO DOMINI 1099, FESTIVAL EVE AND
FEAST DAY FOR SAINT ADÉLAÏDE OF BURGUNDY
Sunset, Thursday, December 15–
Sunset, Friday, December 16

BERKELEY
30 Kislev 5725
Sunset, Friday, December 4, 1964–
Sunset, Saturday, December 5, 1964

CHAPTER TWENTY-NINE

EVERYONE BUT RABBI COHEN's son, Matthew, looked at Dad and me when the rabbi announced, "Ephraim Jacobowitz was called to his eternal rest today." Murmurs of sympathy filled the sanctuary.

I focused on eight-year-old Matthew. He sat on the side of the sanctuary in a world of his own, clutching some sort of solider doll and silently mouthing, "Bam! Bam!"

The rabbi droned on about the week's Torah portion—how Joseph told Pharaoh that Pharaoh's dream was about good and bad harvests, and how Joseph acted to save the people from famine. He connected that story to James Chaney, Andrew Goodman, and Michael Schwerner.

"Like Joseph and these young men, brutally killed in Mississippi last summer, we must act for a better society. It is not for us to finish the work, but neither can we turn away. The prophet Zechariah reminds us in his dream about a golden candelabra, 'Not by might, not by power, but by My spirit,' says the Lord of Hosts. As you look upon your Hanukkah lights, remember that when you seek justice you walk in the spirit of the Lord. And let us say..."

"Amen," I said.

Matthew mouthed, "Zap! Bang!"

After services, I left Dad to deal with the brunt of the condolences and I joined Matthew in the corner with a slice of challah and a glass of grape juice. He showed me his doll, which he called G.I. Joe. "My uncle had to order him from New York City," Matthew explained. "He's not a doll like Barbie. He's

America's first movable fighting man. See, he has a big scar on his face."

I nodded. G.I. Joe and I had something in common.

The light was on in the living room when Dad drove up to the house. Josh? Uncle Paul and his brood? I had an urge to sleep in the car. Not one more person. My mouth felt dry, and a lump of lead grew in my chest.

The lump melted when I saw Gabriel open the front door. He smiled at me, a soft, sympathetic smile, with no sparkle to his eyes, and he shook hands with Dad. We three stood together on the front porch.

"Dagmar is downstairs sleeping," Gabriel said. "She's had a hard day. I know you all have. I didn't want to leave her alone, in case…well, she's sleeping it off actually. But she should be fine in the morning."

Dad's shoulders slumped. "I see you make a habit of rescuing my daughters."

I bit my lip. No way was I one of a pair. I wasn't anything like Dagmar.

"Just trying to help out. Your son Josh called with his flight information. Under the circumstances, Dagmar volunteered me to go pick him up from Oakland later, if that makes sense to you."

Dad looked relieved. He thanked Gabriel, invited him to stay a while, announced he still had arrangements to make, and headed inside for the den.

Gabriel put his hand on my shoulder as we walked to the living room. "How were services?"

I shrugged.

He waited.

"Awful," I whispered.

Seven candles waited in the menorah. I'd forgotten to light them earlier.

"There's leftover fudge in the kitchen," Gabriel said. "Dagmar got a sudden craving for fudge, and I bought a pound. It was the only way I could get her to come home. How about we light the candles and eat some?"

"N-no. It's too l-late."

"Every good boy deserves fudge, Hope," he said, reminding me of the hours we'd spent together at Sproul.

I shrugged. His voice was gentle, comforting, the kind of voice that made me wish he'd never leave. "Hey, maybe it'll make you feel better. Give yourself a break. I'll sing the Hanukkah blessings with you, if you don't mind listening to me squawk."

"B-baritones d-don't squawk," I informed him.

"You haven't heard this one."

Gabriel was pretty much on target about his singing ability—and in awe of mine. We shared a cube of pistachio chocolate fudge and watched colored wax decorate the lion's back. I said even less than usual, but Gabriel didn't seem to mind. He didn't say much either.

When he got ready to go, I mangled a thank you. "It gets easier," he said, his face only inches from mine. "But not for a long time. Don't rush it. I lost my mother four years ago, and I still get a cramp in my gut whenever I meet a woman wearing Mom's Shalimar perfume."

I started to say something, but he touched his finger to my lips and shook his head. "Hey, let's not talk about it," he said, his voice husky. He took a breath. "Go easy on yourself, Miriam Hope Friis."

Still, as I watched Gabriel walk away, I counted my failures. I shouldn't have trusted Dagmar with money I needed for the music festival. I shouldn't have refused to sing Psalm 150 when Grandpa asked me. As much as I wanted Gabriel, I didn't have the guts to compete with Dagmar. And, worst of all, I couldn't keep Grandpa alive until Mom came home.

But when Dagmar's snores woke me about 4:15 Saturday morning, I felt strangely calm. I felt that I had work to do before Mom came home and the world of 1964 smothered me. I put on my slippers, took my prayer shawl to Grandpa's room, and locked the door.

"I LEARNED MORE ABOUT Mainz from a history professor," I told Serakh as I paced, energy seeping into the hollow places. "I understand everything better now."

Serakh sat in Grandpa's chair. "So you have found the answer."

"Wait. No, don't go that far. Have you heard of Saint Anthony's fire?"

Serakh winced. "A terrible affliction. It blackens the hand and foot, and causes terrible pain."

"Remember when I tried that dreidel experiment with Avram in the bakery, and I told you that he probably ate rye bread containing a fungus called ergot? Well, Saint Anthony's fire is really ergotism, the disease you get from eating this rotten rye. Mostly ergot causes gangrene, but sometimes it affects the nerves in your brain. You get visions. That strain of rye fungus is more common in Germany, north of the Rhine."

Serakh arched her eyebrows. "This is why Avram had his vision during his travels?"

"Exactly. Remember I told you that the ergot that caused Avram's hallucination is linked to the chemicals in LSD that blows people's minds these days."

"Blows the mind?"

"It makes people crazy, temporarily anyway." I touched the bandages by my right ear.

Sadness spread across her face. "This you know."

My face grew hot. "Oh, yes, this I definitely know. You can't undo LSD once you've taken it. I took LSD once by mistake and wound up with forty-seven stitches in my face. There's no cure, remember I said that? And the doctors told me there's no way to get it out of your system."

Serakh tapped her fingertips and seemed to stare into nothingness. Finally she said, "Perhaps you can cure by adding more."

"What?"

The finger tapping stopped. "At the time of the Second Temple in Jerusalem, there was a Greek by the name of Hippocrates. He sought to cure an affliction by giving a tiny dose of the poison that caused the affliction."

Homeopathy? I shook my head. "There is no way I'm giving Avram a dose of LSD. I thought of that already, and I'm totally against it. It's wrong. It might make matters worse. It couldn't undo the first hallucination, and who knows what kind of vision he would have the second time. Plus LSD is totally unpredictable. You can have flashbacks afterward—the visions return, or other ones do. We can't control what he'd see or how he'd think afterward."

Serakh cleared her throat. I waited.

Finally she said, "But surely you are intertwined with Dolcette because of your knowledge of this potion. Do others use it in this time and place?"

"Others beside me?"

She nodded.

"Yes, lots of people do. My sister for instance."

I stopped pacing and faced Serakh. "I wouldn't know what dose to use. Or how long this would take. Avram might have flashbacks later and…and…and I don't know what. Go crazy. Kill everyone in his family. Walk into the Seine and drown, thinking it's his bathtub. I could list a gazillion reasons why giving Avram a dose of LSD isn't a good idea."

"Have you another?"

"Another what?"

"Another good idea."

I crossed my arms over my chest. "You haven't heard a word I said. Using LSD on Avram to change his vision is way too risky."

Serakh's hazel eyes sparked with determination. I had to look away.

"What you mean is that you are frightened of this potion," she said. "You are more frightened of this potion than Dolcette is about losing her child. She is willing to give up her baby to save his life. What are you willing to do?"

I shook my head. "Dosing Avram is out of the question."

"Look to your garment of fringes," Serakh said. "*Tzedek tzedek tirdof.* Justice, justice you shall pursue. Dolcette's mother embroidered those words. She would tell you to take the risk.

Your grandmother Miriam wore this garment before you. She would tell you to take the risk. There is justice in showing a man a better way to walk in righteousness, do you not agree? And so you must do this."

"I can't," I whispered, managing to face her again.

Her voice softened. "The *brit milah* is in two days now. The One has led me to you for a reason. This must be the answer. What else can we do?"

"We'll go back to Paris and figure that out." I wrapped the prayer shawl around me. "Serakh, about your...um...intertwinings. Have they ever gone wrong? Have you ever failed?"

Silence. A line of tears ran down her cheek. And it was her turn to look away.

I reached for the blue thread.

CHAPTER THIRTY

A RED-FACED MON TRÉSOR WAS screaming in the kitchen. Celeste jiggled him as she paced, cooing and patting his back.

"Nothing helps," she told us as we stepped inside.

Serakh took the baby and sat on a stool. She laid him with his belly on her knees and she rocked her legs up and down. Three shrieks later, Mon Trésor let out a belch that would have impressed even Josh and immediately stopped fussing. Serakh cradled him in her arms and gave him her knuckle to suck on.

Celeste blinked. "I have never seen such a thing."

"It is nothing," Serakh said. "I have been with many babies. Rest from your labors, Celeste, and we will bring him to Dolcette upstairs."

Dolcette was not as easy to comfort. "Mama is not coming at all," she wailed. "Yom Tov contracted an ailment of the bowels while the wagon wheel was being repaired, and my parents are returning to Falaise."

Yom tov meant "good day" in Hebrew. Actually "day good," but either way it made no sense.

"Yom Tov," I whispered to Serakh as I sat on the edge of Dolcette's bed. "What kind of a name is that?"

"It is the name that the parents of daughters and more daughters might give to the first child who is a son."

I couldn't help rolling my eyes. "Can't your father return to Falaise with Yom Tov while your mother travels here? You need her."

"My mother leave my sniveling, little, overprotected, brother?

Ha! And he is already eight." She stared at me, desperation in her eyes. "Now who will help me after the *brit milah*? Who will take Mon Trésor from me and save him from Avram?"

Serakh paced with the baby. "We will not let your child come to harm. Tikvah will see to that, even if she has to raise him herself."

What?

Dolcette flung herself at me. "Oh, Tikvah, would you, please? I beg you!"

I suddenly imagined myself zapping back from medieval Paris with Mon Trésor in my arms. Mom would come home from Israel to a new addition to the family. Dad would add Buy Cradle to his to-do list for the funeral and *shivah*. Ridiculous.

Still, Dolcette needed reassurance, and I needed time to think of a better alternative. What could I say? "I'll do anything to save your child."

Dolcette kissed my hands and cried, and finally calmed down enough to nurse Mon Trésor.

Serakh turned to me, gratitude spreading across her face. I answered her with a skeptical look, one that I hoped she knew meant I was stalling.

Dolcette smiled at her nursing baby. "I know that you speak with Avram at the bakery, and Celeste has hidden a ball of wheat dough in her chambers, where Tante Rose does not go. Tante Rose does not trust you as I do. Celeste is unsure, but she's loyal to me."

Wheat? "But Avram eats rye bread, doesn't he?"

Dolcette nodded. "Oh, yes, it is his favorite when he goes to the Rhineland. But Tante Rose insists that rye is for the poor, and we can afford to eat wheat and barley. She says that she would be embarrassed to have my mother visit and see a loaf of peasant rye on the table. Silly woman."

Thank you, Tante Rose.

THIS TIME SHMUEL WAS nowhere to be seen. Serakh put our loaf on a pallet and angled it into the oven. Avram was hunched over his open ledger book again.

I mustered a bright smile in counterpoint to his haggard face. "I hope that you are enjoying the Hanukkah top," I said. Our small loaf wouldn't take long to bake, and there was so much I wanted to know.

He patted the pouch that hung from his belt. "Yes, that was a most gracious gift," he said, his voice a monotone.

"The rabbi's wife has invited my…um…sister-in-law and me to attend the *brit milah*. We are so happy that you have started a family after the…um…catastrophe in Mainz. Your wife says you've suffered terribly."

Avram scowled. "My wife knows better than to talk to me about Mainz. I expect that you will do the same." Dismissing me with a wave of his hand, he dipped his quill pen in a bottle of ink and scribbled something in the ledger.

So much for that. Serakh frowned in disappointment. Trying a different approach, I complimented Avram on the quality of his rye flour. "Is it from nearby?"

"From further north," he said.

"Oh, do you travel there often? Along the Rhine, perhaps?"

He stopped scribbling. "There is another oven that is open to Jews on the east end of the island," he said.

I stepped back and wiped imaginary flour from my hands. "I was just curious."

"Watch the loaf for us, dear sister-in-law," Serakh said. She let the silence build, and then asked Avram whether he had heard the news from Jerusalem. Hiding my confusion, I took a sudden interest in a stain on my gown. "Did you know the Christian knights took the Holy City last summer?" she asked.

I dared to peek at Avram. He was kneading his forehead, his lips tight against his teeth.

Serakh shook her head and sighed. "Such bloodshed. A travesty. They say that all of our kinsmen have been banished from our sacred places."

Avram slammed his fist on the table, sending a small crock of yeast skittering to the floor. "Are you here to bake your loaf or to punish me with cruel news I have already heard?"

Serakh sighed again, then asked in a quiet voice, "What have we done that The Holy One, blessed be He, has turned His countenance from us?"

Avram seemed to shrink into himself, "Not enough," he said. "We have not done enough." He stared at the ledger. Then he rose slowly and came toward me. Reaching into his pouch, he said, "Thank you for your reminder of the vision that has led to a vow I have made. The time to fulfill that vow is soon upon me. Your gift is no longer needed."

He dropped my dreidel near a bowl of salt and walked out of the bakery.

"Could I have made more of a mess, Serakh?" I marched back and forth under the oak trees, my stomach in knots. "Could I?"

She sat on a dry patch of ground. "Before you gave the token to Avram, he was firm in his vow. You have changed nothing."

"Why did you remind him of the Crusader victory in Jerusalem in 1099, which was, what? Last summer in this... um...time?"

"The great tragedy in Mainz happened three years ago. I wanted to see why Avram should have such a vision now."

I tripped over a rock. "So, if Avram feels guilty about not being in Mainz when the Crusaders attacked, then he feels doubly guilty now about what happened in Jerusalem? Yes, I suppose that makes sense. Avram believes that it's all his fault, even though he has no control over the situation. Does he really think that one more sacrifice will make things better?"

"Perhaps he believes this to be true. Perhaps it is the affliction." Serakh cradled the warm loaf. "Perhaps we must prepare to take Dolcette's child."

I put my hands on my hips. "That's impossible. I can't suddenly appear in Berkeley with a week-old baby."

"To save a life you would do this."

I sat next to her. "What about you, Serakh? Can't you take him?"

"I do not live in a single place and time. I travel often. The child could not survive in my care. Avram cannot cure himself. He has tried and failed. Dolcette has told of us the leeches and other trials he has put himself through. What is left but your giving him this potion, this SLD?"

"LSD," I corrected.

"Is it hard to find?"

"Ha! I wish it were. My sister's blotter of doses is under my bed."

Serakh grabbed my shoulders. "You *have* this LSD in your possession?"

I nodded.

Her eyes flashed. "And you *choose* not to *use* it?"

"How can I? I have no idea how to give Avram a vision that will make him break his vow. I could kill him."

She touched her forehead to mine. Two beats later she whispered, "You have more within you than you imagine. Do not live in fear."

CHAPTER THIRTY-ONE

AWN DRIFTED THROUGH THE slats in Grandpa's blinds. I sat on the chair by his bed, waiting for my body to adjust, the Paris snow to melt from my slippers, and my wobbly emotions to sort themselves into something that would hold me together. The last thing I needed when I left Grandpa's room and walked through the kitchen to go downstairs was Josh.

"H-hi," I said in the most civil tone I could muster.

He retied his bathrobe belt and closed a little spiral notepad on the kitchen counter. "I thought I heard you in your old bedroom up here. I'd paint the walls a warm yellow, if I were you. Ephraim would have liked you to get a fresh start in there. He was so generous and kind, an outstanding human being."

I gritted my teeth. Ephraim? Since when did Josh stop calling him Grandpa? My brother sounded like he was rehearsing the first lines of a speech.

"Man, you look beat. Rough day yesterday. I can imagine. Dad sprang for a puddle jumper from Lockheed Air Terminal to Oakland, and some guy named Gabriel answered the phone here and said you and Dad were at services. Dagmar was here with him. Can you believe it? She has no sense of decorum. You can imagine what the two of them were doing."

"S-stop it, J-Josh."

"Hey, I'm just sayin'." Josh got out the butter and a carton of eggs. "He picked me up in a station wagon that smelled like cigars. Not even his station wagon. It's probably owned by the commune."

I let it go. Why bother? "T-two f-for m-me," I managed,

pointing to the eggs. Food was food, and I was famished. How long had it been since I'd eaten? How long had I been in Paris?

"Scrambled." Not a question. That's how they were going to get done, period.

"Dagmar plans to stink up the house with some smoldering clump of dried sage. She says it clears the air. I told her to stay the hell out of my room."

He pointed the spatula to a yellow-lined pad on the kitchen table. "There's the list. Dad borrowed Mr. Nash's car. He's getting Mom later. I'm leaving after breakfast to get Dad's suit and my suit pressed. If you need anything, write it down. We've got everything under control."

He made the funeral sound like a stockholder's meeting. I poured a glass of orange juice and ran down the list of who was supposed to do what when. Dad had included everything from when the rabbi was going to visit us (tonight at 7:15) to notifying the school Monday morning that I'd be out until at least Wednesday. If death is about phone calls, then funerals are about lists. Grandpa would have been appalled to see the fuss we were making over him.

A plate of scrambled eggs appeared under my nose. Josh announced he was off to do…whatever he was off to do. He sounded official. I gave him my official nod.

The rest of the morning and half the afternoon was a blur. I wandered through the day on automatic pilot. Dagmar appeared at some point, and then disappeared. Dad came and left. Sylvester stayed next to me everywhere I went. The phone rang. I ignored it.

Mom looked smaller than I remembered her. She gathered me up in her arms and I clung to her. She smelled like the sandalwood soap she always brought back from Israel.

"I-I tuh-ried, I r-r-really tuh-ried. I-I d-did the b-best I could."

"Of course, you did," she whispered in my ear. "Of course, you did."

Tears flooded my face. "I-I w-w-anted s-s-o m-much to k-keep him alive until you c-came home."

She stroked my hair. "Shhh… It's okay, sweetie. I understand. I couldn't keep your grandmother alive another few weeks until you were born. And now you have her name, which is a beautiful reminder of her every day. Honey, we can't control life and death."

Dad enveloped the both of us, and we stood silently together for one precious moment. Then he said, "We have to let your mom rest, *Nudler*. She needs to get off her feet."

"Just for a little while," Mom said. She studied my bandages. "Is everything healing properly? No redness? No pus?"

"F-fine."

"Good," she whispered. She seemed to shrink before my eyes. Dad handed her his handkerchief and guided her down the hall toward their bedroom.

I sat on the back porch for who knows how long, the sun warming my face. Our little Meyer lemon tree had started to bear fruit. I thought of my grandmother's prayer shawl—the "garment of fringes" as Serakh had called it—that was passed down from Miriam to Miriam. Who would have worn it if my grandmother had lived until I was born, and my parents named me for another dead relative?

"There you are." Leona's voice pierced my thoughts. "I've been looking all over the house for you. My mom let us in, so we wouldn't disturb anyone. We brought over chicken noodle soup and corned beef sandwiches for dinner. And a roast beef sandwich for you. I told her you like roast beef better."

I stood long enough to hug her. Leona pulled up a chair and sat beside me. "How are you? You must be devastated."

"I f-feel like a l-lump of n-n-nothing."

"I am so sorry. It must be awful. I mean you two were so close. Just a couple days ago when we got Chinese takeout— remember? You were especially careful to get exactly what he wanted."

I touched her hand and shook my head slowly.

"You'd like me to shut up for a change? Sure. Do you want to be alone? I wouldn't feel bad about that. I can go into the kitchen."

I shook my head again. "Stuh-ay."

"Okay. But I'll be quiet."

And she was, which is hard for Leona. I sighed once. Leona sighed back. I stared at the lemon tree and thought about my prayer shawl. One thought led to another, and soon I was back to Avram and that damned LSD. "L-Leona?"

"Hmmmm?"

"S-Suh-pose y-you c-could d-do s-s-omething t-terrible to s-someone. S-someone s-s-sick. Thuh-ey w-wouldn't know. B-but it m-might c-cure them. W-would you do it?"

Leona frowned. "I'm not sure what you mean? Is this anybody we know?"

I shook my head, took a breath, and started again. "S-say y-you g-gave them a duh-rug that c-could m-make thuh-ings w-worse or or k-kill them. Or or c-cure them."

"Would I give them the drug?"

I nodded.

"What are the chances of curing them?"

I shrugged.

She studied her fingernails for a minute. "Sort of like chemotherapy and cancer. The poison could kill you, but it might save you. Only there you can ask the patient, right? And what you're saying is the patient doesn't know. You have to make the decision on your own."

I nodded again.

"That's a tough one." She brushed her bangs off her forehead. "I guess you'd have to figure out what that person would want you to do. I mean, if you think they would take the risk, you should, too. Does that make sense?"

What did I know about Avram? Practically nothing. I bit my lip. Still…

"Thanks," I said. "H-how was b-ballet cuh-lass?"

Leona smiled. She launched into paragraph upon paragraph. I barely listened to a word, but that let me sink into my own thoughts and I knew she'd understand.

What was Avram's vision? Something about an angel, but what? Why hadn't I asked Dolcette? Did she know? I couldn't just grieve the days away in my Berkeley world while the clock ticked in Paris back then. The day after Grandpa's funeral would be Mon Trésor's circumcision and naming. They'd call him Ysaak. Isaac. And the day after that?

I lived in two worlds. Both of them were falling apart.

The Seventh Day

PARIS
2 Tevet 4860
ANNO DOMINI 1099, FESTIVAL EVE AND
FEAST DAY FOR SAINT OLYMPIAS OF CONSTANTINOPLE
Sunset, Friday, December 16–
Sunset, Saturday, December 17

BERKELEY
1 Tevet 5725
Sunset, Saturday, December 5, 1964–
Sunset, Sunday, December 6, 1964

CHAPTER THIRTY-TWO

LEONA ANNOUNCED IT WAS time for the two of us to light the Hanukkah candles, and I didn't say no. We sang the blessings together, her strong, clear voice helping mine along.

"You're nearly back to normal," she said. "Once the bandages come off you'll sing even better."

"He wanted m-me to s-sing Psalm One-one F-fifty when w-we l-lit the c-candles on Thuh-ursday. I s-said I was t-too tired."

The flames blurred. She gave me a fresh tissue. "You didn't know it would be the last time, Hope. Cut yourself some slack."

I couldn't. The truth was that I had let my grandfather down, and I wasn't going to get a second chance.

Then the onslaught began. Rabbi Cohen arrived to pay his respects and help us get organized for the funeral. Mom's brothers, their families, and Grandpa's niece, Bella, invaded. Leona and Mrs. Nash offered everyone coffee, tea, and cookies, and were able to escape to the kitchen. I wished I could go with them, but it wouldn't have been polite. Dagmar wasn't even home, and I refused to think that she might be out with Gabriel.

Josh and Dad took charge, which was a relief. The less I had to say the better. Mom barely spoke.

I pretty much tuned out while they talked about my grandfather. Grandpa and I had spent a lot of time alone together in this house over the last six years. Never once had he asked me to sing that soprano part from Psalm 150. And the one time... the one time...

"You don't have to say anything. Josh can speak on your behalf." Mom had her hand on my knee.

Rabbi Cohen was focused on me with an expectant look in his eye. So was Dad.

"S-sorry," I said. What did I miss?

"Rabbi Cohen was telling us about tomorrow's service," Dad explained. "We're deciding who is going to take part."

"I'll sing." It just slipped out, when I wasn't thinking. I put my fingers to my lips.

Two beats of silence. Then Rabbi Cohen stuck his finger in the air, as if I'd just answered the $64,000 question. "What an excellent idea! Ephraim loved your singing, Miriam Hope. He always told me you sang like an angel. You know Psalm 23 from choir, I'm sure. That would be perfect."

I shook my head.

"No? It's traditional to sing at a funeral service. Song is prayer. Your voice would lift us up."

"It h-has to be Ps-psalm One F-fifty." I took a breath, hoping I didn't have to explain.

Rabbi Cohen cocked his head and tented his fingertips. "Well…then…yes, let it be Psalm 150. I've never heard it sung as a solo, but I'm sure you can do it." He turned to Mom. "Will you want to say something, Rachel?"

Mom shook her head. "My daughter will sing for the both of us. Thank you, sweetie."

I closed my eyes and rubbed my forehead. *Idiot!* I'd never sung such a difficult part solo. As soon as I could, I escaped to the kitchen.

Bad news travels fast. "My mother just told me you're singing Lewandowski's 150 tomorrow," Leona said. "Perfect!"

I shrugged.

"Oh, come on. You'll be great. Here, have a cookie."

The ginger snap tasted like cardboard.

Later, Leona sat on my bed while I warmed up my vocal cords and extracted Psalm 150 from my choir notebook. I went through the song once, just on the soprano lines. Without the rest of the voices, the soprano part sounded thin and screechy in places, but my singing wasn't a total disaster. Leona and I studied every measure and penciled in a few adjustments. She assured me no one would notice. I tried again. Better.

THE NEXT MORNING, THE tip of my nose was numb and the room felt like the inside of a refrigerator. The window was wide open.

I charged out of bed toward the mess on Dagmar's side of the room. There she was, snoring, still in her clothes, with her feet on her pillow and the gray skirt I'd put out for her to wear to the funeral crumpled under her head. She must have climbed through the window and forgotten to close it. At least she was home. I closed the window and took a deep breath. We'd get through the day okay.

When I came back from the bathroom, my semicomatose sister was still in bed, slumped against the wall. Mom stood by my desk, a Macy's shopping bag dangling from her hand. Her bathrobe pocket bulged with tissues. Her face sagged.

"I will not have my father's memory dishonored by your wearing army boots and the hippie regalia you call clothing. Do this for me, Dagmar. I'm not asking much."

Dagmar's eyes were puffy. She looked incapable of brushing her teeth, let alone getting dressed. Mom put the Macy's bag on my desk and turned toward me. "There's an ecru blouse for you that will go nicely with your navy suit. I made time to shop in New York between planes. Lord knows I needed a diversion. Can you manage?"

I nodded.

Dagmar grumbled, but later I caught her admiring herself in Mom's choice of clothes—a flowing, black-and-white, calf-length skirt, an old-fashioned high-collar lace blouse, and soft black Capezio flats. If my new blouse hadn't been beautifully tailored with little pearl buttons, I might have been jealous. I take that back. I was jealous as hell.

THOSE PEARL BUTTONS SAW me through the funeral service. I rested my right hand on the second button down from my neck. The pearl was round and smooth, cool to the touch at first, then warm as a kiss. I focused my eyes on the floor when it was time to stand, and on the weave of my navy skirt when it was time to sit. I closed off into a tiny world inhabited only by Grandpa and me—and our pearls.

Pearl Harbor. I imagined the story Grandpa would have told me tomorrow, the same story he told me on December seventh ever since I could remember. I imagined how he and Grandma were eating Chinese food in a restaurant in Oakland when they found out about the Japanese attack on Pearl Harbor. And how the next day he heard President Roosevelt over the radio. "December 7, 1941," he'd quote, "a date which will live in infamy." I wondered if I would remember President Kennedy's assassination last year the way my grandfather remembered Pearl Harbor.

And then I could see Grandpa sitting in his chair and telling me for the gazillionth time how Pearl Bailey was the best actress and singer to come out of vaudeville. How brilliant she was when she played her part in the *Porgy and Bess* movie he took me to when I was in sixth grade. And then we'd sing *Porgy and Bess* songs about summertime when the living is easy.

And there was the pearl necklace that Grandpa and Mom gave to me for my sweet sixteen birthday last May. "The Marie Antoinette necklace," Grandpa called it. He told me how my great-grandmother Lillian gave it to Grandma to wear with a Marie Antoinette costume on the night that Grandpa printed those Vote For Justice cards for Grandma and drove her to a Halloween ball. Lillian later gave those pearls to Grandma when she left Portland, and then Grandma gave them to Mom when Mom turned sixteen. But Mom never dared to wear something so precious to a Halloween party.

I caressed the pearl button and wished with all my heart that I'd stayed home with Grandpa this past Halloween.

Josh nudged me. He was burying three-by-five cards in his suit jacket. "It's your turn," he whispered. I stood and stepped up to take his place.

Focusing on the windows in the back of the sanctuary, I clutched the pearl button and hummed a D. *For you, Grandpa.* Inhale. Slow release.

I hit the first note almost perfectly. But almost perfect was good enough. Grandpa wasn't about perfection. He loved me just as I was.

I closed my eyes and let the music fill the hollow places inside me and reach out to my grandfather. At some point in the psalm, the rabbi's voice joined mine at an octave lower, then another voice came in, an alto. I heard a quavering voice in the mezzo-soprano range. By the last measures, it sounded as if the whole sanctuary had joined in the final hallelujahs.

For a moment the air in the sanctuary seemed to vibrate with something beyond silence. I opened my eyes and took my seat. Mom whispered, "Thank you."

Later Rabbi Cohen announced, "*Shivah* will be held at the Friis residence. Everyone is welcome to come tonight, and Monday and Tuesday evenings, starting at seven o'clock, to participate in a short prayer service. Instead of flowers, a contribution to the charity of your choice would be appreciated."

Mom touched my arm. I stood with the family and walked down the aisle behind Grandpa's plain pine casket. That's when I saw Gabriel, sitting toward the back, his eyes on me, his face a mixture of sadness and comfort. *You would have liked him, Grandpa.*

At the cemetery, a large rectangular hole pierced the ground next to my grandmother's burial plot. I stared at her gravestone:

Miriam Josefsohn Jacobwitz
Beloved Wife, Mother, Grandmother
July 11, 1896–April 2, 1948

Grandma Miriam. Always a phantom to me. A story, a picture, someone else's memories. I had her pearls now. And her prayer shawl. Did I have her courage?

The few people who came with us to the cemetery perched on folding chairs next to a mound of newly turned earth.

Gabriel wasn't among them. The morning's warm breeze had turned cooler, and clouds threatened afternoon rain.

I planted myself at the back of the line so that I could be the last of the mourners to put a shovelful of earth on my grandfather's grave. I wanted to tuck him in, to spread out his pajamas and get him a glass of water. I wished that Sylvester could be with us. When my turn came, I stared down at the hole. Is there a special spot on the olam set aside for grief?

The Eighth Day

PARIS
3 Tevet 4860
ANNO DOMINI 1099, FESTIVAL EVE AND
FEAST DAY FOR SAINT GATIEN OF TOURS
Sunset, Saturday, December 17–
Sunset, Sunday, December 18

BERKELEY
2 Tevet 5725
Sunset, Sunday, December 6, 1964–
Sunset, Monday, December 7, 1964

CHAPTER THIRTY-THREE

THE HOUSE WAS BLISSFULLY quiet for the moment. Mom and I stood alone in front of the lion-cruet menorah, which was fully bedecked with Hanukkah candles.

She handed the box of matches to me and extracted a tissue from her skirt pocket. "We can't leave them like this," she whispered. "We can't leave Hanukkah undone."

I lit the candles and sang the blessings. We watched the wax drip, covering the entire lion.

Mom grabbed my hand as if it were a lifeline. "Your singing was the best part of the service."

"Thuh-anks." Six beats of silence. "H-how was Is-Israel?"

"I don't remember. Let's talk about it another time."

I started to leave, but she didn't let go of my hand. "We used to get salt water taffy for Hanukkah. Mama and Daddy had a customer who sent them taffy from Atlantic City every year. It was a real treat back then, when we didn't have much. My brothers gobbled theirs on the spot, but I made my share last for weeks."

I nodded, knowing how memory can dull the pain of here and now. Then she turned into my mother again. "It's been a terrible month for you. Halloween, and now…this…" She frowned. "The doctors said you should take off your bandages by Thanksgiving," she reminded me, sounding the most like herself since she'd come home. "At this stage, air will help with the healing process."

Plastic surgery will help with the healing process. "I'm f-fine," I lied, sounding like my grandfather.

LATER, I SAT NEXT to Leona, and tried to be the polite, attentive, dutiful version of myself. I tried to graciously accept people's condolences, to be the good daughter, in contrast to Dagmar, who left right after the *shivah* prayers. I owed that to my parents and to Grandpa.

"So tomorrow I'll tell Mr. Z. that you won't be in until Wednesday," Leona said. "I'm sure he'll understand. Your singing was amazing today. I wish he had been there. Not that I expected him to come, although you never know. There was a bunch of people I didn't recognize. Who was the cute guy with the scar on his lip? He was positively transfixed by your Psalm 150. You're holding out on me."

I reached for the bowl of mixed nuts. "G-Gabriel Altman. D-Dagmar's l-latest c-catch."

"Not from where I was sitting. I'm telling you, Hope, he hardly noticed her."

I shrugged. If Gabriel wasn't interested in her at the funeral, Dagmar would make sure he'd be interested in her later.

And I was right. Dagmar made her grand entrance after every guest but Mrs. Nash had left, my parents had trudged to their bedroom, and Josh had taken the car to who knows where. I was helping Mrs. Nash clean up in the kitchen.

Dagmar arrived wearing a bright orange shawl I hadn't seen before over her black and white funeral outfit, and she'd stuck a wilting rose in her hair. By some miracle, she seemed to be completely sober.

"Gabriel and I found the perfect spots in Tilden Park to commune with Grandpa," she announced, unwrapping the cheese platter and popping a cube of Gruyère in her mouth. "Lake Anza was gorgeous, positively gorgeous, right Gabey-Baby?"

Gabriel stood next to her. He'd exchanged his funeral suit for a blue oxford shirt, brown sweater, and chinos. He smiled at me, his face strong and gentle, his eyes filled with concern.

"How are you doing, Hope?"

I felt my cheeks flush. "B-better"—which was true. He clearly hadn't shaved since Grandpa's funeral, and for one crazy moment I imagined how it would feel to touch the stubble on his chin. Gabriel wasn't drop-dead gorgeous, like Avram, but gorgeous can be overrated.

Dagmar's right index finger caressed Gabriel's face, and I squelched a sudden urge to drop an open container of sour cream on her lovely new shoes.

"I'll just tidy up the guest bathroom," Mrs. Nash said, in full retreat.

Then it was just the three of us. Dagmar looked like she wanted me to leave, but I decided to dry the serving trays. She announced she was going to soak her weary body in the tub downstairs. She made it sound like she wanted Gabriel to join her.

"I've got a bunch of work to do, so I'll see you tomorrow morning," Gabriel said.

Dagmar kissed him good night, a full, sloppy kiss on the lips. He jerked his head back slightly, and I wanted to imagine that he wasn't entirely enjoying the experience.

She pouted. "Be that way. It's your loss." Then she swooshed downstairs.

So now it was just the two of us, with Mrs. Nash coming back any minute.

I cleared my throat and picked up a dishtowel.

Gabriel handed me a serving tray from the drying rack. "Look, Hope, I'm sorry to bother you with this, but I have a couple of favors to ask."

Crap. I bit my lip and waited, figuring the favors would involve my sister.

They did.

"So the first favor is. There's the arraignment tomorrow for everyone who got arrested at Sproul Hall. I'll pick Dagmar up at 8:30. Could you see that she's ready, and...um...maybe wearing the same outfit she wore today? Minus the orange shawl. She should look presentable."

"Sure." I scratched the edge of the bandage along my jaw where it itched the most.

"The stitches must be out by now. How is it healing?"

I shrugged.

"No. I mean it. How bad is the scarring?" He touched the place on his face where I imagined he'd never grow the perfect mustache.

"I d-don't want to t-talk about it."

He raised his left eyebrow and then his right eyebrow. They danced on his forehead independently, forcing me to smile.

"Okay, another time. Anyway, the second favor is that I'm not going to tomorrow's arraignment. My lawyer will represent me. It's risky, but sometimes you have to take a risk. President Kerr has scheduled a campus gathering at the Greek Theatre tomorrow at eleven o'clock. That's conveniently close to the time of the arraignment, don't you think?"

I nodded.

"So if the judge doesn't cooperate with us tomorrow, hundreds of Kerr's most vocal critics, namely those people who occupied Sproul, will miss the campus gathering. That's why I'm going to the Greek Theatre instead. I'd like you to come along. You were with us at Sproul and you might be a student at Berkeley in a couple of years. It's fine if you'd rather not. But if it's okay with you, I could come by here around 10:30. Is it a date?"

Is it a date? I wish! If the arraignment had been at a different time, Gabriel wouldn't have asked me. This wasn't a date for real. Not the kind I wanted. "I d-don't know."

He handed me another serving tray. "Yeah, I know, Hope. Bad timing. But I figured you weren't going to school tomorrow because of your grandfather's passing, and the *shivah* service isn't until the evening. How about I stop by, and you can tell me then? It's not out of my way." He put his hand on my shoulder. "I'd like to see you anyway. If you don't mind."

I leaned toward his hand and took a breath. Did he mean that? Not that it mattered much. Dagmar had already claimed him.

Still…

I licked my lips. "I-I'd l-like that," I said.

He squeezed my shoulder. "Great!"

Mrs. Nash made an untimely appearance. Gabriel shoved his hands in his pockets. I dropped a tray.

CHAPTER THIRTY-FOUR

Monday morning, I woke up three minutes before the 6:30 alarm—the only normal thing I'd done in the past few days. Dagmar had taped a note to the clock. "Wake me at 6:45."

Resting against my pillow, I fixed my eyes on the ceiling and struggled to unravel tangled dreams: Avram with rye bread where his eyes should be; Grandpa at Pearl Harbor with two fingers missing; Gabriel zipping and unzipping his mouth; Dagmar's feet shrouded in sour cream; Serakh bathed in blue.

At 6:40, I jostled the lump on Dagmar's bed.

The lump mumbled, "What time is it?"

"T-t-time to g-g-get up," I said.

"Wake me again in ten minutes."

"I'll be in the sh-shower."

Mumble. Mumble. Mumble.

Twenty minutes later I collected the clothes Dagmar had worn to the funeral and draped them over the chair. Then I dribbled cold water on my sister's forehead.

Her eyes jerked open. "Whoa! That wasn't very nice!"

"B-but euh-fective." *Why didn't I think of this sooner?*

She bolted into a sitting position. "You haven't told the parents about the arraignment today, have you?"

I shook my head.

"Good. Gabriel says that the defense lawyers are going to ask the judge for a postponement anyway. We met last night at Garfield Junior High. You would have been so scared, because I know how you hate crowds. It's a wonder I managed to keep you safe at Sproul Hall. Hundreds of kids, I'm telling you, there must have been a thousand people."

"I thuh-ought you w-went to T-Tilden Park?"

She arched her back and stretched. "We did that too. But no way was I going to talk about the meeting last night while Mrs. Nosy Nash was around. Remember when I asked you where the Municipal Court Building was?"

I shrugged. No, actually I didn't remember.

"Well, forget that. There are so many of us that the arraignment is going to be at the Berkeley Community Theater. Isn't that ironic? Community theater. Gabriel calls this whole thing 'theatre of the absurd.' I have to borrow five dollars from the dreidel fund. I'm tapped out. You'll get back every penny, I swear."

I closed my eyes and shook my head. How was I ever going to get enough money for the music festival trip? I heard the bathroom door close. Too tired to argue, I went back to bed.

By 8:30, DAGMAR PRONOUNCED herself presentable for municipal judgment. She had surrendered her breasts to the bra Mom had made her wear to the funeral, and she wore the same blouse and skirt. Army boots instead of those beautiful Capezios.

"W-what about the n-n-new shoes?"

"They are so totally not my style, Hopeless. Combat boots work better when you have to face the enemy, don't you think? Wish me luck." She smothered me in a hug on her way out. "Tell the parents I had an early class."

"Dagmar is up to something again," Dad said, when hunger drove me upstairs for breakfast. "President Kerr called an assembly of the faculty and students at the Greek Theatre for eleven o'clock. Morning classes are cancelled."

Heading for an apricot Danish someone must have brought us, I debated whether to tell my father about Gabriel asking me to go to the Greek Theatre with him. I still wasn't sure whether to accept Gabriel's non-date date. As a Berkeley High student, I had no business getting involved in campus politics. If Mr.

Zegarelli found out, he could ban me from the music festival. But it would feel marvelous to be with Gabriel again, even if only for a little while.

Dad sipped his coffee. "I'm staying home, of course. Your mother needs me."

We sat quietly together, until I stopped in mid-chew, my stomach suddenly unwilling to accept another bite of pastry. Two beats later, my brain registered what my gut already knew. As much as I wanted Gabriel, someone else needed me. I had to get back to Paris. Now.

I dumped my half-eaten Danish in the garbage.

"Miriam Hope, have some protein at least. A slice of lox."

"S-sorry," I said. "I-I j-just…I-I…I-I'll be b-back s-s-oon."

As I raced downstairs, I heard him ask me where I was going. I pretended not to hear. *It's complicated.*

"MON TRÉSOR's CIRCUMCISION IS today, isn't it?"

Serakh sat on the floor near my bed. "This very morning. Last night the rabbi and Madame Léa gave a feast in their home, where the *brit milah* will be. The women have prepared a beautiful garment for the baby. Today Avram sees his son for the first time."

"Maybe Avram will break his vow when he sees Mon Trésor."

"Perhaps."

Wishful thinking. Inhale. Slow release.

"There is weariness in your face, but determination in your eyes," she said. "Have you found all the answers you seek?"

"Ha! Not a chance. Not even close."

She didn't say anything, but we both knew. I stood up and squared my shoulders. "I have to do something anyway today, don't I? We're running out of time."

CHAPTER THIRTY-FIVE

CELESTE USHERED US INTO the kitchen. The large wooden table had been scrubbed clean, and judging from the stains on Celeste's gown, it was easy to see who had done the scrubbing.

"Thank the Holy One, blessed be He, that you are here. My mistress has been asking for you since dawn. Tante Rose took Mon Trésor to Madame Léa's to prepare him for the *brit milah*. Tante Rose told my mistress to rest here until the baby returns, but my mistress will not."

Celeste looked toward the stairs. "If you please, sit by the table." She was gone before my bottom hit the stool.

My heart pounded in my throat. "Dolcette must be frantic."

Serakh smoothed my headscarf. "We will tell her that perhaps we have a plan."

"Giving Avram a dose of my sister's LSD is not a plan. It's a recipe for disaster."

She arched her eyebrows and pursed her lips. I shook my head and was about to explain the dangers again, when I heard Dolcette and Celeste on the stairs. Dolcette grasped Celeste's arm for support as Celeste guided her to a stool.

"You look beautiful," I told Dolcette, despite her ashen face and bloodshot eyes. She wore a pale blue dress with long flowing sleeves and embroidery around the bodice.

"My wedding dress." Her hands slid over and under themselves on her lap, as if comforting each other. "I must go to the *brit milah* and see Avram. Surely the feel of our baby in his arms will tell him that his vow comes from a place of evil, not the will of the Holy One, blessed be He. I will take Avram and our son to a quiet spot, and I will plead once more. If my beloved will not renounce his vow, I will give Mon Trésor to you."

I glanced at Celeste.

"She knows," Dolcette said. "Celeste is more than my servant. She is my trusted friend. She and Shmuel have done all they can."

"Shmuel? From the bakery?"

Dolcette closed her eyes and shuddered. "Celeste, you tell them. I can't bear to."

Celeste cleared her throat. "You have heard of Madame Juliane, the wife of the herbalist?"

"The woman with the willow bark tea," I said.

Celeste nodded. "Madame Juliane was sure that an infusion of horehound would lower the black bile of our dear Avram and drive away the evil that bedevils him. The monks at Saint Étienne gave Madame Juliane's husband the leaves. She made the infusion on the feast day of Saint Adélaïde, exactly one hundred years after the day of Saint Adélaïde's death. Madame Juliane said this was propitious, because Saint Adélaïde had been the empress of the Holy Roman Empire and her daughter the queen of France, and the royal families have been good to us Jews."

Saint Étienne. Those must be the church bells I heard. I remembered now that Notre Dame Cathedral wasn't finished until the fourteenth century. I was in Paris at least two hundred years too early.

Celeste put her hands to her lips. I smiled encouragement and waited, because you have to give people time to tell a story their way.

"Avram has stayed with Shmuel since the birth of Mon Trésor," Celeste continued. "I gave the infusion to Shmuel, and I told him that this would cure Avram's melancholy. I said nothing of the vow. That would be too great a burden for him."

Meaning he'd tell everybody and who knows what would happen.

Celeste sighed and shook her head. "It was yesterday, during their Shabbat meal together. Shmuel put the infusion in Avram's wine. After a moment, Avram spit out the wine and threw the goblet across the room. He cursed Shmuel. Horrible curses I will not repeat. He accused Shmuel of trying to poison him. And then he cried and said that he wished Shmuel had given him poison because his burdens were so heavy. Shmuel says that Avram's melancholy has gotten worse."

Dolcette grabbed Serakh's robe. "Have I sinned? Is horehound a cure for Christians and a plague for Jews?"

Serakh brushed a strand of hair from Dolcette's face. "This plant does not know the faith of the person who partakes of it. Be calm now. You have not sinned."

Horehound. Was LSD a better solution? I stood there, my fingers rubbing a knot of wood on the table.

"If Avram refuses to renounce his vow, then tomorrow I will surely sin," Dolcette said. "Tomorrow, after Mon Trésor is safe with you, we will take a bundle to the river. Later Celeste will testify that the baby and I slipped in the mud and fell in. She will say that I recovered, but that the Seine took Mon Trésor away, out toward the sea. Only she and I—and you—will know that my child will be like the baby Moses. He will survive. Maybe one day he will return to Paris, and I will see him again."

I bit my lip. Serakh touched my shoulders. "Tikvah has another plan. It is filled with great risk, but it offers hope that you will keep both Avram and your son."

I shook my head. Serakh shouldn't have spoken for me. I wasn't ready.

Dolcette's hands fluttered to her face. Her eyes grew wide. "Oh, Celeste, what did I tell you? Our prayers have been answered!"

Celeste rushed first to Dolcette, then to Serakh and me, crushing us in a tear-filled embrace. How could I disappoint them now?

I touched the right side of my face, where the bandages itched. "Dolcette, my plan will work best if I know what Avram saw that caused him to make this vow."

Dolcette shivered.

Serakh squatted by Dolcette. "Tell us, child. What was his vision?"

Tears streaked down Dolcette's cheeks. "I begged Avram to reveal the vision to me," she whispered. "At first he refused, but I gave him no rest." She took a shuddering breath.

"Avram told me he was in a farmer's field under an apple tree. He heard heavenly music but he could see no instruments. He looked up into the tree. The apples dripped with blood. And then a winged messenger from the Holy One, blessed be He, hovered over Avram with a bloody apple in each of her hands. She called out to him 'Avram, Avram' and he answered 'here I am.'"

"*Hineni*," Serakh said, translating "here I am" into the Hebrew word in the Torah from the story of Abraham and Isaac.

Suddenly it all fit. Avram had conjured up a cruel distortion of the Abraham and Isaac story, the binding story, the Akedah passage from Genesis. I'd read that story every year on the High Holidays. But hadn't the story ended with Isaac safe? I felt my shoulders relax. For a moment I imagined that Avram expected an angel would stop him at the last minute, the way it happened in Genesis. It might be easier than I thought to convince him to spare Mon Trésor.

Wishful thinking. If this were the case, Avram would have told Dolcette. More likely Avram believed that sacrificing his son would somehow restore the exiled Jews to Jerusalem, or sanctify God's name, or whatever. A preposterous, revolting idea, but then I didn't live in the Middle Ages, and I hadn't witnessed the horrors that Avram must have seen in Mainz.

"Tikvah? Please. What are you thinking? Tell me. Is Avram possessed?"

I couldn't add to Dolcette's agony, so I managed to give her a comforting smile. "I am thinking of possibilities. Let's go to the *brit milah*. We will find out more there."

The overcrowded main room in the rabbi's house smelled of garlic. I gagged on the collective body odor and longed to be outside. Dolcette introduced us as her mother's friends from Falaise. We gave vague answers to a few polite questions and soon the people there ignored us, which was fine with me. Serakh and I stayed together toward the back of the group of a dozen or so people, while Dolcette and Celeste left through a small door to another room.

Later, Avram entered through that same small door. He cradled his sleeping son in his arms and nodded to his neighbors. Avram's face could have been cast in stone. There was no life behind the thin smile and dull eyes. He looked like a zombie. Dolcette walked beside him, just as pale and deathlike as he.

I squeezed my way closer to the front of the room. Leatherbound books were stacked on a low wooden shelf next to two silver candlesticks, a small silver goblet, and a silver filigreed box with a lid. Avram handed a beautifully dressed Mon Trésor to the rabbi's wife, who placed him on an exquisitely embroidered pillow resting on the lap of an older man with a leathery face and flowing white beard. Avram chanted Hebrew blessings. Another man stepped toward them, his back to me. A moment later the baby wailed.

I winced. Everyone around me smiled and murmured their approval at the loss of a baby's tiny foreskin—his official entrance into the covenant of Abraham. Mon Trésor was now Isaac, a member of the Jewish community.

I turned toward the back of the room. And that's when I saw my grandfather.

CHAPTER THIRTY-SIX

I BLINKED AND LOOKED AGAIN. No. I was wrong. This man's ears were larger than Grandpa's and his eyes a deeper brown. His face didn't melt or his chin sprout dandelions. Nothing crazy. Not a flashback. Simply the sad duet of memory and grief.

The old man was holding a goblet of what I assumed was wine, perhaps the same Manischewitz type of wine that my grandfather loved. That I'd served to Grandpa, what? Two days ago? Three?

No matter which kosher wines Mom brought back from Israel, Grandpa always insisted on the Manischewitz wine you could buy at Andronico's supermarket. I wondered if Grandpa's father served this type of sweet red wine when Grandpa suffered through his circumcision in Bialystok.

Tears blurred my vision.

Serakh wrapped her woolen cloak around me and led me outside. "Surely you have been to a *brit milah* before. The baby will soon recover."

A damp wind blew in from the Seine. "It's not that. I was just thinking about my grandfather. He was such a brave man."

Serakh huddled against the cold. "Ephraim had a family. He did his best to protect them."

I told her about the Bialystok pogrom, when Grandpa cut off the fingers of his dead brother-in-law and risked so much to bring his sister and her children to America. "I could never be that brave."

"How can you say that? To overcome your fears, is that not bravery?"

Before I could answer, Serakh cocked her head and then put her finger to her lips. She led me around the corner of the rabbi's house. "Look there," she whispered. "We must hide."

We ducked into a doorway, and she wrapped the cloak around us both. It hardly mattered. Dolcette and Avram looked so involved with each other and their baby that they would have ignored a parade. Dolcette held their baby against her breast, and Avram had wrapped his arms around them both. She buried her face in his chest. He kept kissing Dolcette on the top of her head, his face twisted in anguish.

I touched my lips and remembered Dad enveloping Mom and me when Mom got home. Love, pure and simple; a bond so deep and so fragile. I struggled to listen to the voices inside screaming at me to take the safer way out and rip this baby from his parents. But how could I? As I watched these two lovers clinging to each other in the muddy snow, with their child nestled between them, I thought about my grandfather, about Chayim's wedding ring, and what it means to risk everything. I knew that I had to give Dolcette, Avram, and baby Isaac one more chance to be a family.

I SAT WITH SERAKH on a fallen limb in the grove of trees by the river. Sunlight warmed my back. "Avram's hallucination about the angel and the bloody apples is based on the *Akedah* story," I told her, although I realized she understood this already. "The binding of Isaac. This vision of his is a gross distortion, but there's a link."

I collected a handful of twigs and started to break them, one by one.

Serakh nodded. "The *Akedah* is a powerful image for a pious man."

My head pounded. "Exactly. So Avram needs an equally powerful image to make him change his mind."

"An angel," Serakh said. "He must see an angel who will make him vow not to harm his son."

I rolled my head from side to side, trying to ease the tension in my shoulders.

"You would make a perfect angel, Serakh," I said. "You could appear in a blue flash the way you do. Avram will be so astonished he'll do anything you ask. He'll make a new vow never to harm his son. Then you could disappear in another flash of blue. It's as simple as that."

Two beats of silence. Then Serakh put her hand on my knee. "You are right, my dear friend. That is simple. But surely you see now that Avram needs you. You shall be our angel."

No. My stomach cramped. "That's not going to work." I frowned, digging for arguments to bolster my gut reaction. "Avram knows me too well from the bakery. I'm not magical like you. I wouldn't know what to say. I wouldn't be convincing."

Serakh's voice was smooth and even, barely above a whisper. "I have heard you sing to the baby. Your tone echoes with the divine. But you are afraid."

I bent and twisted a greenish twig that refused to snap. "Of course I'm afraid. That's not the point."

Serakh took my hands in hers. "Avram has seen me as well. My blue flash will frighten him. He will think I am a witch or a conjurer. He will think I am the devil luring him away from what he believes must be done."

I shook my head.

"If you are Avram's angel, then I can watch from nearby," Serakh said. "I can rescue Avram in an instant if he falls into danger. I have been guided to you. You must give Avram your potion so that he does not see you as yourself. You must present to him in your beautiful voice the vision that speaks to his soul and guides him in the path that will save him. In your heart you know this to be true."

"I don't know how much of a dose to give him."

"This is so."

"I don't know what words to use."

"This is so."

"The dreidel I gave Avram only made him more determined to kill Mon Trésor. My angel idea might be another terrible mistake."

"This is so."

Serakh leaned over and kissed my forehead. "But still you will be Avram's angel. You will use your potion and your powers. Now you must go back to your spot on the *olam* to rest and gather what you will need. Avram would not harm his child on the day of the *brit milah*, nor will he make a sacrifice after sunset. Shall I meet you in Ephraim's room just before dawn?"

I nodded. What more was there to say except the obvious? So many things could go horribly wrong. When you fight fire with fire, your whole world could go up in flames.

CHAPTER THIRTY-SEVEN

AFTER SERAKH LEFT, SYLVESTER refused to come out from a pile of Dagmar's clothes. Midmorning light streamed through the window. This wasn't right. Hadn't I just spent half a day in Paris? My head throbbed.

I stared at my alarm clock—10:05, Berkeley time and place, Monday. I'd already gotten Dagmar ready for the arraignment. Gabriel picked her up at 8:30. He was coming back for me at 10:30. For me. Yes. Time flexed in my crazy world, and I could make time, still, to be with him.

Do this. I stumbled to the bathroom and managed what Dagmar calls her "PTA dance" in front of the sink. "Wash your essentials," she'd instructed a twelve-year-old me. "Pits, tits, and ass."

I threw on my black slacks, white turtleneck, and gray sweater—an acceptable outfit for a granddaughter in mourning. No time to change the bandages. I had barely finished inhaling a hard-boiled egg and finding Dad in the den when the doorbell rang.

"I-I'll get it," I told him.

Gabriel presented me with a box of peanut brittle. "For the *shivah* house," he said. "I refuse to bring you one more fruit basket or box of butter cookies. So, here you go. Certified kosher-dairy. Peanut brittle lasts forever. Invite me over for New Year's Eve, and it will still be good."

My exhaustion vanished. I waved him into the living room.

"I hope you like peanut brittle. I'm a huge fan. I could live on peanut brittle and Cheerios. Well, not exactly. You look good in gray. So, Miss Friis, would you like to join me this morning?" He voice was clipped and breathy, with a Chatty Cathy quality like Leona. He almost sounded nervous, which didn't make sense for a guy who was twenty and one of my sister's "close friends." Or was he?

"I-I just g-got up and…um…"

"Peanut brittle is one of my favorites," Dad said, advancing on Gabriel with his hand extended. "Good morning, Gabriel. It's good to see you."

"Professor Friis." Gabriel shook Dad's hand. "I was wondering if Hope could come with me for an hour or so."

"D-Dagmar is g-gone again," I said, which was true.

Dad ran his fingers through his hair. What if he asked how Gabriel knew she was missing?

He didn't. Instead he looked at his watch. "If you can't find Dagmar, let me know. I'll leave Josh here to help Mrs. Friis, and I'll go help you look as well."

Done.

"That was clever," Gabriel said, escorting me to his uncle's station wagon.

I smiled for the first time in eons. "I know."

This is not a date. This is not a date. I sat two feet away from Gabriel in the front seat and looked out the car window at the stores along Shattuck. Still, I felt physically closer to him than when we sat nearly thigh-to-thigh at Sproul Hall. Just the two of us in this enclosed space, his aftershave insinuating itself up my nose. A tightness thrummed deep inside.

Gabriel tapped a three-four rhythm on the steering wheel.

"I-I h-have to be b-back by one th-thirty," I said, picking a time that seemed to make sense in the nonsensical collision of Paris-Then and Berkeley-Now.

Gabriel turned on Hearst into campus. "I'll have you home by then. Holler if you see a parking space."

Holler is hardly my style. I glanced at the scar between Gabriel's lip and nose. My LSD brain had conjured up Mr. Zipper Mouth. I must have been looking at his scar in the hospital, and at the party, too, whenever he found me. Did I ever call him that to his face? I bit my lip and felt embarrassment creep into my cheeks.

"Well, I'll be damned. Would you look at that?" Gabriel pointed to a group of people marching up the street, row upon row of them, four across. "The judge must have dismissed them early so they could make it to the assembly. I can't believe it."

I folded my arms across my chest and looked away.

"We'll catch up with them later," he said. He didn't mention Dagmar.

The Greek Theatre was mobbed. If it were indoors, we would have been turned away, but this was one of those open-air amphitheaters. Gabriel took my hand and led us to a grassy spot by the top tier. We sat further apart than we did at Sproul, but closer than we were in the car. His hand stayed on top of mine. The birthmark on his left earlobe looked like a tiny onyx earring.

The back of my neck tingled. I dragged my focus away from Gabriel to the reason why we were here.

The stage far below us looked like the square in front of an ancient Greek temple, but we were definitely in the middle of the twentieth century. President Kerr stood in front of a podium with a microphone. Dozens of people, men mostly, were on the stage with him, along with a few policemen.

"There's Mario Savio," Gabriel told me, pointing to a curly-headed guy a couple of yards from the stage. "He looks like a munchkin from here, but don't underestimate Mario. If you want to organize an act of civil disobedience, he's your man."

"W-was it w-worth it?"

Gabriel cocked his head. "To disrupt the university and occupy Sproul?"

I nodded.

"Absolutely. We aren't out to overthrow the administration, Hope. That's pure bull. We simply want to set up tables and distribute pamphlets on campus. It's a basic right in a free society. So what if some of us lean toward the far left politically. You should see how many libertarians and conservatives have joined the Free Speech Movement. And it's not just the students and some of the faculty. Ed Landberg, the guy who owns

Cinema-Guild? Well, he's giving the money from tonight's showing of *Chushingura* to us. And he lent us the movie projectors and films for the sit-in at Sproul."

I nodded again, and licked my lips.

"Hey, I'm sorry. I must sound like I'm on a soapbox here. It's just that this matters to me."

"M-me, too," I said automatically. *Really?* I thought about the protests on campus and the occupation at Sproul Hall. That's what my grandmother's prayer shawl was all about. Pursuing justice. Sometimes you have to act. Sometimes you have to open your mouth.

I looked back at the stage. President Kerr was talking about "the full and free pursuit of educational activities on this campus," whatever that meant. He promised to "abide by the new and liberalized political action rules and await the report of the Senate Committee on Academic Freedom."

What new rules?

"The departmental chairmen believe that the acts of civil disobedience on December second and third were unwarranted," Kerr said, "And that they obstruct rational and fair consideration of the grievances brought forward by the students."

Gabriel shook his head and muttered something I didn't catch.

Kerr continued. "The cases of all students arrested in connection with the sit-in at Sproul Hall on December second and third are now before the Courts. The university will accept the Court's judgment in these cases as the full discipline for those offenses."

I wondered what happened to Dagmar at the Berkeley Community Theater and whether she was going to go to jail again.

"The university will not prosecute charges against any students for actions prior to December second and third; but the university will invoke disciplinary actions for any violations henceforth."

Mario kept shaking his head, too. I saw his mouth moving, but we were too far away to hear what he was saying. As soon as President Kerr stepped back from the microphone, Mario walked toward the podium. Gabriel leaned forward, his body tensing, his eyes on Mario. I shaded my eyes and craned my neck, straining to see what was happening.

A rumble of protests echoed from the crowd nearest the stage. Then I saw two policemen grab Mario. My stomach lurched. He hadn't done anything wrong. What about these new, improved rules for political activity on campus that we just heard about?

One of the policemen wrapped his arm around Mario's throat and forced his head back. The other one seemed to twist Mario's arm. As Mario went limp, they dragged him off the stage.

So much for free speech on campus.

Suddenly I was on my feet.

"Unfair," I shouted, making a megaphone of my hands.

Why are people so afraid of other people's ideas, or values, or religions? What had we, supposedly civilized human beings, learned in nearly a thousand years since…well, for me, since this morning?

Anger blasted through me. "Unfair! Unfair! "

And then my words were swallowed up with others, all over the Greek Theatre. Some men had scrambled on stage to help Mario, but the police and faculty members were holding them back.

I felt Gabriel's arm around my shoulder. "You tell 'em, lady. Now let's go before the rush."

I frowned. "It's n-not over."

"I have to talk to you someplace quiet, and we only have until one thirty."

Curious, I didn't say no.

We found a parking space on Telegraph Avenue—which Gabriel dubbed a minor miracle—and walked past Caffé Med. "There will be a mob here tonight," he said. "Maybe even for lunch. Let's try that new café on the corner."

Tidbits on Telegraph had red-checkered tablecloths and plastic daisies in tiny wicker baskets. "A throwback to the fifties," Gabriel said, after the waitress seated us. The place was nearly empty.

The tuna sandwich looked good, but who wants fish breath when you're out with a guy? I chose egg salad on whole wheat—rye was out of the question—and a cherry coke. Gabriel ordered a Reuben and coffee, plus fries for us to share.

Then silence. We sat across from each other. I cleared my throat. One of the plastic daisies had a fake ladybug on its petals.

Gabriel coughed. "Dagmar is a force of nature. I don't want to see you get hurt."

My mouth turned sour. I folded my napkin in thirds.

CHAPTER THIRTY-EIGHT

I DIDN'T DARE LOOK AT Gabriel. *It's always about Dagmar. I shouldn't have come.*

"Hope, I'm just going to spit it out, so please let me finish before you say anything, okay?"

A chuckle bubbled up. I am the Empress of Non-interruption. "Okay," I said.

He reached across the table and touched my hand. "I know we got off to a bad start at the Halloween party and the hospital. The doctors at Alta Bates told me you would remember very little about what happened, but what do they know?"

I nodded and counted three beats. He started again before beat four. "But I'd really like to get to know you better. We had a good time together at Sproul, right? I mean even if it was a sit-in."

I nodded again. Yellow flecks highlighted his brown eyes. I wanted to ask him to make his eyebrows dance again, just for fun, but he was suddenly acting very serious.

"You're way more my type than Dagmar is, even though you're four years younger than I am."

He inhaled. I forgot to breathe.

"Dagmar has a way of getting what she wants, I don't have to tell you that. She and I know each other because she hangs out with friends of mine who are a lot more into the Merry Pranksters and Haight-Ashbury scene than I am. What I mean is, she's not my style."

The waitress stood over us with our food. Gabriel let go of my hand. He didn't take it again when she left. I dipped a

French fry in ketchup and munched, nurturing the tiniest hope that this monologue was going where I wanted it to.

Gabriel sipped his coffee. "So. I am wondering if you are interested in...you know...in —what do they call it?" He made little air quotes. "Exploring a relationship?"

He took another sip. "If you are, then I'll make it clear to Dagmar that she and I are just friends of friends."

Sip three. "But if you don't want to get into trouble with your sister, I totally understand."

Sip four. "Okay, now it's your turn."

I focused on my sandwich, the heat rising in my face. I wanted to reprise Gabriel's wonderful words, the parts where he said he liked me and wanted to be with me. Me. Still, I had to know. It mattered.

"H-how...um...c-close are are y-you and D-Dagmar?"

"You mean are we sleeping together?"

I put hands on my lips and shut my eyes, and I managed to nod. *Please, please, please tell me the truth.*

One full measure of silence. "We're not. But I've gotta tell you...Geez, Hope, I'm a regular red-blooded twenty-year-old male. I have... I've had... some experience. But casual sex doesn't do it for me. If you don't mind my saying so, that's what your sister is all about."

I dared to open my eyes. Gabriel's gentle, honest face seemed to match his words. Relief flooded through me. He bit into his Reuben. Sauerkraut landed on his sweater. "I'm such a slob," he said, picking it off. He had the kind of thick curly eyelashes Leona told me she always wanted.

Then I had to be honest, too. "If-If I c-called you M-Mister Z-Zipper Mouth, I-I'm sorry."

"What?"

"At the h-hospital."

He touched his scar. "You cussed like a pro in the kitchen, and in the ambulance, and in the emergency room, but you didn't say that. When I first found you, you came at me with a screwdriver and nearly drove it into my chest. The screwdriver, remember? You know, the one you were using to unscrew your jaw."

My face felt like lead. I did what? The table swayed. The room swiveled from side to side.

"Hope, you don't remember that?"

I couldn't even shake my head.

"You told me that the stork had put your jaw in crooked and that you were making adjustments. You were not happy when I took the screwdriver away and tried to stop the bleeding."

I almost killed myself over my damned stuttering? My mouth went dry. My sandwich blurred. And then Gabriel was sitting next to me in the booth, his leg touching mine. An un-pressed but perfectly clean handkerchief appeared in my hand.

"Mr. Zipper Mouth," he whispered. He touched my bandages. "I've been called a whole bunch of names, especially when I was little, but I don't remember that one. See, Hope? I knew you were someone special."

He pressed his lips to the ugly side of my face. "I bet you've been called a ton of names, too. And you know that saying about sticks and stones will break your bones but words will never harm you?"

My chin managed to dip toward the table and then come up again.

"Well, that's a crock, right? Words can gouge out your insides, right?"

I took a shuddering breath and wiped my nose.

"Here's the thing. We can't control what people call us or how they describe us. But we don't have to let them define us. You know what I mean?"

The best I could do was shrug.

Gabriel kissed my cheek. And then my lips. Once. Twice. Soft, gentle kisses that sheltered me from my thoughts about that horrible night until I started to feel fine. So fine. Oh, so fine.

Gabriel stayed on my side of the booth. I devoured my sandwich and we decided to share a hot fudge sundae for dessert. He told me about his cello, and about wanting to fight the disease that killed his mother. I told him that my grandmother died of cancer, too, and that, besides singing, which was my life's passion, I liked to hike, and I once had a pet snake. I told him that I adored licorice, just like my grandmother, but I had understandably lost my appetite for it since Halloween.

Then it was suddenly 1:20 and we had to leave. A guy with an FSM armband stopped us as we were walking hand-in-hand past Caffé Med. Gabriel introduced me as Dagmar's sister.

"Dagmar's back at her place," the guy said. He rolled his eyes. "She missed you something awful this morning, Altman."

Inhale. Slow release.

We didn't say much on the way home. After Gabriel parked in front of my house, he touched my cheek. "Are you ready for this?"

I nodded.

"Good luck," he said.

"G-good l-l-luck b-b-ack at you."

We walked inside together. Dagmar was still wearing her funeral clothes, which had begun to smell ripe. She flung herself at Gabriel. He held his arms out while she nuzzled his neck. I clenched my jaw—and my fists.

She frowned at me. "You didn't tell The Great Dane about the court case, did you? Because everything is going to be fine. Judge Crotchety was a trip."

"Judge Crittenden," Gabriel said.

"Well, he was crotchety to me, Gabey-Baby. You would know if you had been there. That was *such* a disappointment. Anyway, His Honor granted a postponement until December fourteenth. We have a whole week to figure this out. Plus, I saw the charade at the Greek Theatre, when they took Mario away, and then they brought him out again, and he told everybody to clear this disastrous scene and get down to discussing the issues. Cal is jumping! I can't wait to see what the Academic Senate is going to say tomorrow."

She tickled Gabriel under his chin. "How about staying for dinner tonight? We have to do the *shivah* thing. Poor Grandpa. I'm sure my parents won't mind."

Gabriel gently brushed her hand away. "Another time maybe. I have a strategy meeting tonight. I can't stay. Hope, thanks for coming to the Greek Theatre with me and…ah…everything. Are you sitting *shivah* tomorrow night, too?"

I nodded. Dagmar crinkled her forehead. "That's right. It's only Monday. So much has happened since Grandpa's funeral."

And it's not over yet.

THERE SEEMED TO BE a closed-door policy for each of the bedrooms at the Friis house for the rest of the afternoon. Which was just as well. Maybe everybody needed to be alone as much as I did. In Grandpa's room, I studied the white satin bible that the temple's sisterhood had given to me for my confirmation last spring. It had the holy scriptures and miriam hope friis embossed in gold letters, and I was supposed to carry it with me at my wedding. Squinting at the miniscule print, I read and reread the Abraham and Isaac story in Genesis, chapter 22. God tells Abraham to bind Isaac, and then to put him on an altar and slay him with a knife. When Abraham gets out his knife, an angel stops him. I memorized every word the angel said. That would be my speech. But would it be enough? And what strength of LSD should I give Avram? Was the current dose in 1964 more than what he would have eaten in ergot-infested rye bread in 1099? Less? By how much?

This whole plan was ridiculously risky, but I wasn't in agony about the decision anymore. I felt sure that if Avram knew how mistaken he was, he would want me to try.

Sylvester purred on Grandpa's bed. I watched the trees through Grandpa's window and waited for answers. When none came, I put the teakettle up to boil, consigned two innocent slices of cinnamon raisin bread to the hot electric coils of the toaster, and got the menorah from the living room. Time to give the lion a good de-waxing.

You can't scrape wax off enameled copper; it ruins the finish. You can freeze the wax, or you can heat it. I chose heat. I poured boiling water over the menorah and coaxed slivers of wax from the lion's back and mane. I picked wax and bits of parched string from the nine candleholders. Next Hanukkah the Friis family would light a beautiful menorah, even if I had to buy it with my now nonexistent money.

Wiping the menorah dry, I imagined Isaac playing with his parents during his next Hanukkah and the Hanukkah after that. I had to be the angel who made Avram change his vow, as well as the demon who would dose him with LSD.

The **Ninth** Day

PARIS
4 Tevet 4860
ANNO DOMINI 1099, FESTIVAL EVE AND
FEAST DAY FOR SAINT NEMESION OF ALEXANDRIA
Sunset, Sunday, December 18–
Sunset, Monday, December 19

BERKELEY
3 Tevet 5725
Sunset, Monday, December 7, 1964–
Sunset, Tuesday, December 8, 1964

CHAPTER THIRTY-NINE

D AD PUT A TRAY of sandwiches on the kitchen counter and
announced that dinner was self-serve. Dagmar and Josh were
doing who knows what. Mom would be resting until Rabbi Cohen
came—which would be about 6:45. All the relatives and guests
would be gone by about 8:30. Mrs. Nash would stay an extra half
hour to clean up and get everything ready for the next day. Tuesday
night the same thing would happen, and then we'd be done.

Wrong. Tuesday night is only the beginning. My back twitched.
Grandpa would be gone now for the rest of my life. I'd never be
done with missing him.

I leaned against the counter.

"Grief takes a toll," Dad said, kneading the knots in my
shoulders.

Grief and fear.

"Remember Dagmar's shiver story, *Nudler*?"

"Mmmm," I said, feeling my shoulders relax. Dad had made
all the arrangements when Grandma Miriam died and Mom
was pregnant with me. Dagmar had no idea that sitting *shivah*
meant staying at home and letting people pay condolence calls
and join in a mourner's service. "I thought you were supposed
to shiver," she had told me. "What did I know? I was only three.
Aunt Caroline kept putting an ugly brown sweater on me, and
I kept yanking it off, so I could shiver."

He rested his hand on my back. "It takes time." Then he
made up a dinner tray for Mom and left. I headed downstairs.
Maybe Dagmar could tell me something useful about ergot
versus LSD. Probably not, but still.

Dagmar's funeral clothes crowned the top of the clothes pile, but she was gone—again.

She came back just as we started the *shivah* prayers. Dagmar had clothed herself in an all-black Gothic ensemble complete with a lace shawl. Mourner's black, I suppose.

"Dagmar looks like a curly-haired version of Morticia in the 'Addams Family,'" Leona whispered after the service. She sat next to me, eating a mini-éclair. "She should be on TV. Want me to get you an éclair? They're super scrumptious."

I shrugged. Leona took that to mean yes.

I bit into the éclair, filling my mouth with thick cream custard. Leona leaned closer. "Mr. Z. can't wait to have you back in class. You should have seen his face this morning when I gave him your permission slip and the money."

"W-what?"

"Hey, watch out. You've still got éclair in your mouth."

While I closed my lips, and chewed, and swallowed, she said, "Didn't they tell you? Uh-oh, I guess I spoiled their surprise."

I looked around the room in confusion. Mom must have gone into the kitchen or bathroom. Dad was standing in the corner, talking to Mr. Nash.

"Your dad gave my mom the money and permission slip yesterday," Leona said. She told me that he and your mom decided your grandfather would have wanted you to go to Portland. I mean, after your singing at his funeral, there wasn't a dry eye in the house. Isn't that sweet?"

"B-but...but...the duh-reidel m-m-money..."

"Yeah, you must have made a mint. Hey, where are you going?"

I planted myself in front of my father and Mr. Nash.

"The Academic Senate is going to meet tomorrow at three," Mr. Nash was saying. "I know you're in a house of mourning, Henry, but this is a pivotal moment for the university. If the faculty breaks with administration policy, we'll have chaos on campus. There's a good chance the Senate will vote down Kerr's proposal and come up with something that caters to these student agitators. We mustn't let that happen."

I gave the tiniest cough. Dad touched my shoulder, but kept talking. "I'll see how things are with Rachel," he said. "In any case, the Regents have the final say in a couple of weeks. They could overturn a faculty vote. They've done it before."

Mr. Nash sipped his ginger ale. "True. But if the faculty comes out strongly in favor of the students, I'm afraid the Regents will decide to support them."

Dad gave a noncommittal nod and looked my way.

"L-Leona just told m-me about the f-festival. Thuh-ank you!"

Dad smiled and patted my shoulder. "We'll talk about the details later."

"Well, won't that be an exciting trip!" Mr. Nash crunched on a sliver of ice. "As I was saying, Henry…"

I escaped, thankful that Mr. Nash hadn't mentioned the coat and purse I'd left in his office during the occupation. Or maybe he'd told Dad and Dad hadn't mentioned it to me, yet—too many maybes. But one thing was for sure, it was up to me now. A place in the music festival and a chance for a prize-winning solo was mine to win or lose.

I headed outside to the back porch, because pirouettes of delight don't belong in a house of mourning.

Ten minutes later, sober-faced, I sat next to Leona again and listened to her talk about what we'd wear on the trip.

The doorbell heralded a visit from one of Dagmar's friends— Jerry Somebody, who knew Marsha and had a connection with Dagmar. Dagmar waved to Jerry, hugged Dad, stuffed her feet in her army boots, and was out the door in under a minute.

Crap! I rushed outside and grabbed her elbow.

"This is not a party you'd like," she told me.

I tightened my grip. "Yes, b-but…um…is-is r-rotten r-rye as stuh-rong as a d-dose of LSD?"

She sniffed. "How should I know?"

"At H-Halloween, h-how m-m-many d-doses did I take?"

"Let's talk about this another time. Jerry's waiting."

"N-now."

She rolled her eyes. "Well, don't ask me, Hopey-Dope. I

brought my own, of course. I wouldn't touch somebody else's. You must have stuffed your face on those little licorice sandwich candies. The kind with the white in the middle was just candy. The kind with the pink middles was laced. Didn't I tell you? How many did you eat? See what I mean? You don't know, I don't know. I told you to stay away from the licorice. I'm sure I did."

She brought her own doses? When did she take them? How out of it was she? Suppose Gabriel hadn't found me? I stood there, stupefied, while Dagmar pried my fingers from her elbow.

Afterward, I sat on the front steps. Pushing the Halloween party and the hospital out of my mind, I concentrated on the disaster at hand. Should I give Avram one square of the perforated blotter hidden under my bed? Two squares? Six? Too little and he wouldn't believe the whole angel performance. Too much and…

"Lovely evening." Rabbi Cohen stood over me.

Is there a prayer for trying to do the right thing, and risking someone else's life in the process? We shook hands good-night, and I took an extra two beats before I let go.

CHAPTER FORTY

FIFTEEN MINUTES AFTER THE last guest left, I fled down-stairs with Sylvester. I set the alarm for 3:10 a.m., an hour before Serakh was to meet me in Grandpa's room. It wouldn't be hard to sneak upstairs then.

We had decided that Avram would be the most suggestible at dawn, when dreams feel more real and the light plays tricks on you. He was still sleeping at Shmuel's house. Serakh would find a way to give him a dose and lure him outside. When I thought he was into the deepest part of his trip, I would use the words from the angel in the *Akedah* story and command him to renounce his vow.

Anyway, that was the plan.

I was supposed to get a calm and restful sleep before re-turning to Paris. No way was that happening. My mind refused to shut down. It paraded before me every possible scenario of everything that could go wrong. I sweated in my pajamas. And then, when I opened the window wider, I shivered with cold.

By 2:30, I gave up trying to rest. I extracted the paisley blotter from under my bed and tore off three squares. If one square didn't work, then maybe, just maybe, we'd have another chance, and I'd try two. Could I do the unthinkable—twice?

I stared at the rest of the blotter and clenched my jaw. Dagmar had promised that she wouldn't keep LSD in our bed-room after what happened on Halloween. This time, I was de-termined to see that she kept her promise. I stuffed the blotter in my bathrobe pocket, grabbed a hand shovel and gardening gloves from a shelf in the garage, tiptoed upstairs, and picked my way in the moonlight to the lemon tree in the backyard. I shredded the blotter and buried it. No eulogy other than "good riddance." No more dots or tabs. No more doses. Never.

Then I soaked in the bathtub, to ease the tension from my body. No good. Everything seemed coiled inside. I paced the room.

What do angels wear?

I couldn't remember if Serakh was going to bring me something appropriate or whether I was supposed come up with something. I rubbed my forehead. *This is not like the senior prom. He'll be so high, who knows what he'll see.*

Surveying Dagmar's pile, I decided on her purple caftan and a shawl with a yellow and gold floral pattern. Definitely the new Capezios. I'd be gone an instant in Berkeley time. She wouldn't miss them. I took my large white chiffon scarf to wrap my hair and most of my face. No jewelry, but I daubed White Shoulders on the scarf. Angels smell nice. I bundled everything in my bathrobe and tiptoed up to Grandpa's room. When I was ready—if terrified, but fully costumed, counts as ready—I held the blue thread close to my heart and shut my eyes.

"You look beautiful," Serakh said. She carried a thick woolen cloak, with a hood trimmed in fur. "It is snowing again in Paris, and we might be outside for a long time. You will need this." The cloak smelled like gym socks and musk, only worse.

"Weasel," she said. "It will keep you warm."

I shuddered.

"It will keep you warm," she repeated.

I cocked my head. "I have to ask this. Are there really such things as angels? Are you one?"

She sat in Grandpa's chair and stroked that long white braid of hers. "I have an abundance of years, although already I am feeling the weight of so much time. I am not an angel. I have never met a person with wings, as is depicted in the books and paintings I have seen. I believe that all beings have special qualities breathed into them from The One. Some have qualities we mistrust or we look upon with awe."

"I am practically petrified," I told her.

"This is natural. You hold lives in your hand. You have a thin possibility of success. That is a fearsome responsibility. Still you are here. You have called me to your side."

Even though Hanukkah was over, I slipped another dreidel into the pocket of Dagmar's caftan. My locally handcrafted, miracle-of-freedom, liberty top. My good luck charm.

"I'll say the same thing from the binding of Isaac story in Genesis," I said. "I practiced this afternoon."

"Excellent. Do you have the potion?"

I showed Serakh the three perforated paisley squares and explained that each one was a dose. "I still don't know how many to use. I'll start out with one and have the other two for a back-up."

Serakh put the squares in her pouch. "I have faith in you."

That made one of us.

CHAPTER FORTY-ONE

AFTERWARD, I SAT PROPPED against a log under the oaks by the river. The night air was clear and cold. Patches of snow glinted in the moonlight.

"Turn away from me," Serakh said. "Rest here until I return."

I did what she told me to do, and closed my eyes against the flash. I rehearsed my angel lines in my head, pretending that I was in control of the situation. If I gave a perfect dramatic performance, then we would have the perfect result.

And they lived happily ever after.

Then I sensed Serakh's return flash.

"Do not be alarmed," she said. "The baby is safe with Tante Rose. Celeste is with Dolcette and will see that Dolcette does not come to harm. I will find him."

I rubbed my forehead, struggling to make sense of her words.

"Dolcette searches for Avram," she said. "He is gone."

CHAPTER FORTY-TWO

A S SOON AS I could walk, Serakh guided me toward Dolcette's house. "Revelers were in the street," she explained. "Their noise woke Shmuel, and he discovered that Avram had left the house. Shmuel is fearful because of Avram's melancholy. He searched the streets within the Jewish quarter, but he could not find Avram. He awakened Tante Rose, and she told him that Avram had not returned home."

"Dolcette is out looking for Avram?"

"Yes. Poor child, she is sick with grief. Celeste is with her. I trust she will not be out long, for the sake of the baby. Come, we will tell Tante Rose that you will stay to help with the baby, while I look for his father to shorten the search. I will find him."

Alert now, and anxious, I hated to sit at Dolcette's and wait. "I know my way around this neighborhood by now. When I spot Avram, I'll touch the blue thread and you'll find me."

Serakh shook her head. "If you come to harm, all is lost. The intertwining will fail."

Tante Rose wanted nothing to do with me either. She pursed her lips. "Against my judgment Dolcette left with Celeste, and I am alone with the baby. I cannot share my company with you at the moment."

"Tante Rose, Dolcette might need you when she returns, and you will need someone to attend to the child," Serakh argued. "Surely there must be a place for my sister-in-law to rest here without troubling you. Surely Dolcette would want you to offer us hospitality during this grave time."

Tante Rose arched her eyebrows. I kept my woolen cloak

wrapped tightly around me, so she wouldn't see the angel costume. Finally she said, "There is an extra pallet in Celeste's bed chamber." She led us to a cramped room maybe twice the size of my bathroom and covered a pile of straw with a rough linen cloth. The first few measures of "Away in a Manger" rolled through my head, since it must be close to Christmas. My skin crawled just looking at the straw, but Celeste's bed wasn't much better—a more compact straw mattress resting on a slab of wood a few inches up from the dirt floor.

"You are most kind," I lied.

Tante Rose announced she would be in the kitchen or upstairs with the baby if I needed anything. The sour expression on her face told me not to bother her. Then she left, closing the door behind her.

I settled into the straw and wondered how Celeste managed. The room reeked of mold or mildew. A thin strip of animal skin—cowhide, maybe—covered most of the narrow hole in the wall that served as a window. But Serakh was right. I imagined her appearing and disappearing in a flash. I couldn't keep up.

There was nothing more I could do to help. The baby was still safe. My double days in Berkeley and Paris filled me with fatigue. A short nap wouldn't hurt.

I had just drifted off, my heart beating a slow legato, when I heard faint cracklings in the straw. Something slithered across my ankle and started up my leg.

I boosted myself on my elbows and lifted Dagmar's caftan. By now the feeling had reached my knee. I grabbed another handful of cloth and pulled up.

A yellow-collared, greenish brown snake was twisting himself around my kneecap, his head pointing toward the warmth between my legs. Before I could stop myself, I shrieked, then lost my balance, falling off the straw pallet and sprawling on my back.

Flashback or for real? My fingers reached out. Snake.

I exhaled my relief. He seemed to be some sort of harmless grass snake or garter snake, like Clarence, the red-and-yellow striped snake I had once, until he frightened Grandpa. We kept

Grandpa. This poor guy had probably come inside for warmth and mice, and was just as surprised as I was.

Figuring Celeste was as fond of snakes as Grandpa had been, I collected the French version of Clarence and was about to deposit him outside through the hole in Celeste's wall when I heard the door open.

Tante Rose looked way more venomous than the snake. She said something about *malade*—sick—but most of her French didn't sound anything like the language tapes in school. Her eyes grew wide, and she pointed to the snake whose head I was holding gently, and whose body was slowly wrapping around my arm.

"Blah, blah, blah, Lilith, blah!" She pointed to the snake. "Blah, blah, blah, *serpent*, blah, blah!" Without Serakh nearby, I was lost.

I took a step toward her. "D-don't w-worry," I said. "He's h-h-harmless."

Tante Rose flattened herself against the wall next to the door. She shook her head. "Blah, blah, *très mal*, blah, blah, blah."

Très mal. Very bad, or very evil. The snake was neither, if that's what she was talking about.

"T-Tante Ruh-ose," I stuttered. "See. I am f-f-fine." I brought the snake closer to my face to show her how harmless it was. "I j-just want t-to t-take it outside." I walked toward the door smiling, the snake coiling comfortably. It was cold out there, but not below freezing. I figured he—or she—would find a safe place.

Tante Rose rushed out of my room and shut the door in my face. I heard something scrape against the wood. The door wouldn't budge. She'd locked me in.

I knocked on the door. "Tante R-Rose!"

Nothing.

I pounded my fist against the wood. A moment later I heard Tante Rose's voice just outside my door—a hodgepodge of words in a singsong chant, high-pitched and urgent.

My heart set a faster pace. I pounded again. "L-let me out!"

Tante Rose shouted something. Then there was an odd

burning smell. Something oozed under the bottom of the door. Hot wax? Was she trying to seal me in? Or set the straw on fire?

My breath came short and fast.

Don't panic. Don't panic. Think!

I eased the wriggling snake through the hole in the wall. Then I got on my hands and knees and made a dirt barrier between the wax and any stray bits of straw. Fire lines work for California brush fires; they'd work here, too.

The room seemed to close in on me. I grabbed my prayer shawl, wrapped the blue thread around my finger and called for Serakh.

No glow. No blue flash. No Serakh. My temples pounded with the pulse of my racing heart.

I leaned against the far wall and stared at the crack under the door. What would that crazy woman try next? Boiling oil?

Stay calm. The doctors said flashbacks often happened when someone was under stress. Inhale. Slow release.

That tune from *The King and I* popped into my head, the one that Deborah Kerr sings to her son when they get to Siam. "Whistle a Happy Tune." I sang the part about holding my head erect and whistling a happy tune. A silly song, but still…I hummed, and sang. Then I switched to "Put on a Happy Face" from *Bye Bye Birdie*, and "I've Gotta Crow" from *Peter Pan*. No sad songs allowed.

"You did what?" Serakh's voice filtered through the door. Oh, thank God!

"She is possessed!" I heard Tante Rose shout. Serakh must be close enough for the communication to work. "I saw with my own eyes. She spoke in tongues. Her mouth quivered with the sounds Lilith made her utter. Even now she sings strange incantations to the devil. She came at me with a snake!"

I heard scraping. A thin shaft of light leeched under the door. "Serakh, I'm fine," I shouted.

The door creaked open. Serakh whisked into the room. "I have found Avram. I'm sorry I left you alone."

Tante Rose stood in the doorway, sniffed, and glared at us. She hefted a large ladle and a long iron roasting spit. "This vile creature cannot stay here," Tante Rose told Serakh. "I protect this house for Dolcette and I will guard her son with my life."

"Dolcette would be displeased," Serakh countered.

Tante Rose raised the ladle over her head in warning.

I'm not a monster! Half of me wanted Serakh to disappear in a blue flash. If Tante Rose was arming herself against terror, I wasn't the one she should have been afraid of. The other half of me would have been nearly as terrified as Tante Rose if Serakh disappeared then, leaving me stuck in medieval Paris.

Tante Rose backed away as we walked across the kitchen to the door. She tracked our every step, her eyes wide with fear, her fingers clutching the ladle and roasting spit.

Safe with Serakh now, I felt a surge of power. "Find a better bedroom for Celeste," I told Tante Rose. I remembered that red mark I'd seen on Celeste's cheek. "And if you *ever* hit her with that ladle or anything else, I will come back to *haunt* you!"

I heard a sharp intake of breath as I stormed out of the house. Yes!

An icy wind attacked us as we walked toward the familiar grove of trees. Pulling the fur-trimmed hood over my head, despite the putrid smell, I leaned close to Serakh. "Where's Avram?"

"On the other side of the river," she said. "When we are through with what must be done, I will guide him back to Dolcette. Celeste will care for her until then." She looked at the starry sky. "We still have about an hour before dawn."

"That's it? Only an hour? We have to give him the LSD *now*. It takes about an hour or so to really work. At least I think so." My stomach knotted.

"Then I must travel alone again. You will be safe in the short time I am gone."

Serakh took the paisley squares from her pouch. I showed her how to tear off a single dose. "Let this melt in his mouth if you can. At least I think that's right. No. I changed my mind. Use two. Two squares."

The instant I turned away, I felt I was wrong. Two squares would be too much. "Wait! Use one!"

But she was already gone.

CHAPTER FORTY-THREE

I SLUMPED TO THE GROUND. Stupid. Stupid. Why hadn't I stuck with my original plan? Frost gnawed at my ankles.

And then she was back.

"I have inserted two squares with the potion into his mouth," she said. "I have torn them into bits, and he has swallowed them without waking. Are you ready?"

"I made a mistake. I'm sure of it. We should have given him only one."

Serakh nodded. "Can we undo this?"

"No. Unless we make him throw up, but maybe not even then. It's probably already in his system."

"Then there is nothing to be done. So, now, we go forward." She helped me up and guided me toward the wooden bridge. "Tell me what happened with Tante Rose."

On our way, I explained about the snake. "Plus I stuttered," I said. "That's how I usually speak when I'm not with you."

"This should not have frightened Tante Rose. It is common knowledge that the great Moshe himself suffered from this malady. I think she feared the foreign words and the snake."

"Who is Lilith?"

"They believe in this place and time that Lilith is a she-monster, a demon who makes women do evil and who kills or deforms babies in childbirth. This is nonsense, but their belief is strong. Remember, I gave you one of their amulets against Lilith as a token when we first met? Lilith would have been pleased."

"You know her?"

"We have met. She is an independent woman with a sharp tongue. But Lilith is no more a she-monster than I am."

Peeking from my hood at the dark waters of the Seine twirling under the bridge, I wondered whether my assessment of Serakh or Sylvester's assessment of Serakh was the more accurate. Not that it mattered now. I couldn't go back to my Berkeley world without her.

I could barely feel my toes by the time we reached a forest. "He sleeps beneath the shelter of a large fir not far from here."

My voice shook. "I think I'd better be in a tree, someplace high where he has to look up at me and imagine I might have flown there."

Soon I was straddling the thick limb of an elm tree, my back against its trunk, my hands finding support in nearby branches. Serakh found a place in the thick branches of a fir tree a few feet away, hidden from Avram. We didn't have long to wait.

PINK IS A FEEBLE word. To call what I saw a rosy dawn hardly describes the power of the shift in the night sky that forces you to believe that yesterday's muck is gone, and that today everything can be made new and whole.

Down below us, Avram rolled on his side and crawled out from under the cloak that served as his blanket. He stripped off his thick woolen vest and tunic and sat there, shivering, staring up at the sky. Then he stood, wearing only his leggings and some sort of breeches, and wandered into the trees out of my sight.

Serakh motioned to me to close my eyes and look away. A moment later I heard her whisper, "He is bathing in a small stream that empties into the river. I believe that he is getting ready for his morning prayers. I will watch over him to see that he returns here safely."

For a moment, I was still nobody's angel—just virginal me who had admired Avram's body and now thought about Gabriel. I forgot to be terrified.

Then I saw Serakh back in the branches of the fir tree, and Avram, his shoulders still wet, stumbling back toward his clothes and a leather pouch. My shoulders twitched with tension again. It was too late to stop this craziness; he'd already been dosed. The rest was up to me.

Avram managed to put on his vest, but not the tunic that went underneath the vest. He seemed to be mumbling to himself as he reached into a pouch and took out his knife and a small wooden box. When he stood and faced toward the dawn, I guessed what was inside the box—*tefillin*. The black leather straps were similar to the ones Grandpa had brought to America. I remembered a snippet of prayer from temple: "Bind them for a sign upon your hand, and let them be for frontlets between your eyes."

Even from what little I knew about putting on *tefillin* I could see something was wrong. After Avram had laid a long leather strap across his bare arm and started to chant, he just stood there, letting the rest of the leather strap dangle. Then he stopped, the chanting unresolved. He took the strap off and squatted on the ground, sniffing the leather. He sat back on his heels and lifted the strap toward the sky. Then he made a loop and knot in the strap. A noose? *Oh, my God.*

"His sickness is upon him." Serakh said calmly.

"No! You have to stop him. He's going to kill himself."

"Avram is safe enough," she said, pointing toward him.

I followed her finger. Avram was lying on the ground, humming a strange tune in a minor key and whirling the *tefillin* over his head as if it were a lasso. I rubbed the back of my neck.

"Now, I put my trust in you," Serakh said.

Inhale. Slow release. And so I began.

"Avram! Avram!" I said, my voice full and clear, hoping I echoed the "Abraham Abraham" call of the angel in the Genesis story.

Silence.

He stood up and stared into the trees. Panicked, I waited for him to recognize me in the branches, to call out my name. But then he bowed his head.

"Avram! Avram!"

He gasped and fell to his knees.

"Avram! Avram!"

This time I heard the answer I wanted: "*Hineni*. Here I am."

Please, let me get this exactly right. I said the next words as I'd memorized them from my English translation in the confirmation Bible. Whether Serakh let Avram hear them in French or German, or in the Hebrew from the biblical passage he would have studied as a boy, I do not know. "Do not lay your hands on your boy as a sacrifice. For now I know that you fear God, and would not withhold your son."

He gasped again. His shoulders shook.

I wanted more. I needed desperately to make sure he understood. "Avram! Avram!"

He looked up again, startled, his voice shaky. "*Hineni*."

"Your son will be part of the generations that will return to Jerusalem. Avram, make a new vow!"

He frowned. Then he stared up at the tree. He grabbed his head.

"No," he shouted. "I am a pious man. I will not fall for your trickery."

CHAPTER FORTY-FOUR

AVRAM SCRAMBLED TO HIS feet and hurled a rock at my tree, barely missing the branch under my feet. He seemed all too lucid, frighteningly so. Was he seeing me or imagining something else? Could the LSD be wearing off already? Or was he seeing a monster instead of an angel?

I looked at Serakh. Her anguished face must have matched my own.

I shook my head and closed my eyes, half-expecting a flashback of a bloodstained screwdriver. How could I have done this to another human being?

Avram grabbed his knife and stabbed my tree, over and over. I wanted to scream at him, "You ate the wrong thing, just like me. It's your own stupid rye bread, not God!" I wanted to explain. I wanted to apologize. I wanted this whole horrible scene to end.

I wanted Serakh to step in and save me.

She didn't.

Instead she held out her hands and nodded. She trusted me, even now.

Then the bells rang. Peal after peal. Church bells. I remembered Celeste telling me about the monks of St. Étienne, the ones who collected the horehound leaves. I imagined the monks assembling for their morning prayer, standing to face each other in an echoing stone chapel and offering Gregorian chants in praise of the divine.

I looked at Avram's *tefillin*, his way to praise God, and I knew I had to give him pitch-perfect words, prayerful words,

words he could have faith in. They needed to express their meaning in a way that was clearly and utterly beautiful.

TODAY I AM AVRAM's angel. Today I will sing praise, not to commemorate a life, but to save one. I turned my face to a sky now suffused with visual variations on harmony and melody. Clinging to my elm tree, I shifted my weight and moved upright, until my feet felt more solid in the notch where the branch met the trunk.

I hummed a D, inhaled the dawn, and began to sing.

Ha-la-lu-yah, ha-la-lu-yah
Ha-la-lu Eil b'-ko-d'-sho
Hal-la-lu-hu bir-ki-a u-zo...

I sang the version of Lewandowski's Psalm 150 that I'd sung at Grandpa's funeral. The words came from a psalm that Avram must have recited a thousand times. The melody was one Lewandowski had composed in Germany about a hundred years before my time and eight hundred years after Avram's. Maybe, just maybe, Avram would believe that he was hearing an angel.

Again, and again, I inhaled the early morning air and I exhaled praise. Hallelujahs burst out of me, one after the other, each line without a ragged breath or a false note. I was praising and blessing God with all the instruments mentioned in the psalm: timbrels, lutes, harps, shofars, cymbals, and drums.

Toward the end I sang: *Kol ha-n'sha-mah t'-ha-leil ya.* Let everything with breath praise the Lord. And I had breath. I was praising. And now I was praying—praying to all that was pure and right and holy, praying to the divine essence that guided my Jewish mother and my Lutheran father. That guided me. Let Avram believe me now. Let Mon Trésor live.

The hallelujahs kept coming until the very end, the last note, that high F-sharp, and I was still there—we were still there—my prayer, the dawn, and I, in complete harmony for eight full beats.

"Avram, Avram," I said again, praying that I'd get it right this time.

"*Hineni.*" His voice quavered.

"Know that I speak the truth," I said, as gently and confidently as I could. "Know that you must renounce your vow. Know that you must never harm your son."

When I dared to look at him, Avram was staring up at me.

Please, please see me as your angel!

Then he looked down at his knife, still in his hand. He fell to his knees. He raised the knife.

No! I waited for the blue flash that meant Serakh had swooped down and saved Avram from himself. Distraught, I closed my eyes, praying she'd be in time.

In the seconds that followed, all I heard was a man weeping. When I looked down again, Avram had arched his back and was looking past the trees into the sky. His knife was on the ground, the long leather straps of his *tefillin* dangling from his upraised right hand.

"I renounce my vow," he cried. "My son will live to see his sons and his sons' sons. Let it be so."

Inhale. Slow release. "Then let us say amen."

"Amen."

Another amen echoed from the fir tree.

Avram curled in on himself and wept.

So did I.

CHAPTER FORTY-FIVE

GRANDPA'S ROOM FELT WARM and stuffy at 4:07. I was back in a flash, hours before dawn in my Berkeley world.

We sat on the floor, and as my body stopped aching, I tried to ease the anxiety plaguing my mind. "Will Mon Trésor be safe?" I whispered.

"I have no doubt," Serakh said.

"This potion can turn on you," I said, pointing to the paisley blotter Serakh had taken out of her pouch and put in my lap. There was still one dose left. "You can have flashbacks. Avram might get sick again—sick in his mind—next week or next year. Someone has to watch over him."

"I will do what I can. You cannot be his angel forever. This intertwining is over. You have done what you were meant to do."

"But I'll never know what happens. You can't leave me hanging." I took off my chiffon scarf. "So now I am supposed to be back on my own little spot on the *olam*, and we'll never see each other again?"

"Perhaps there will be another intertwining, as I have had with your grandmother Miriam. If it is the will of The One." Serakh cupped my chin in her hand, the gold flecks in her eyes bright, searching. "Until then be your own angel, my dear friend. And let us say…"

"Amen." Suddenly exhausted to the point of numbness, I turned away from the flash and let her go.

THE HOUSE WAS STILL quiet when I slipped downstairs in my bathrobe with Dagmar's things bundled under my arm. No Dagmar. I shrouded the last dose in toilet paper and flushed it away to a burial at sea. I collapsed under the covers. My arms and legs felt encased in cement and my body filled with lead. How many times had I traveled to Paris and flashed back again to Berkeley? How many days had I lived through twice? My eyelids closed. Darkness. A shallow breath.

"OW! SHIT!"

I jerked my eyes open. Full sunlight. Dagmar was balancing on my desk, her Morticia outfit snagged on the window latch.

"Hopey-Dope, you're just in time to free me from my bondage."

Struggling into wakefulness, I unhooked the material for her.

"I've gotta catch some sleep," she said, taking off her army boots. She was in a great mood. "Wake me in a couple hours."

As I sat back in bed, Dagmar waved two pieces of paper at me. "I was with Jerry and Marsha last night, and they are like Mr. and Mrs. FSM. I mean you'd think they'd been married by Mario Savio himself. They want us to call all the members of the Academic Senate today before their big confab at Wheeler. Here's the script. And here's my list. Twenty-five names was the least amount, so I took that. So, I mean, if they don't get called, it's no big deal. I'll see how I feel in a couple hours. There's, like, a thousand names."

"B-but you puh-romised them." I felt a bubble of anger rise in my throat about the LSD in our bedroom. And about all those promises my sister never kept.

"Everyone was taking a list, so I couldn't say no. But I can't call from home. This is a *shivah* house, and we're in mourning for Grandpa. We shouldn't be working and worrying about the mundane issues of the day."

The thought of Dagmar following etiquette—Jewish or otherwise—forced a smile on my face.

"Good going, Hope Springs Eternal. A smile in the midst of all this sorrow and strife."

"C-call m-me M-Miriam or Hope or M-Miriam Hope. N-no m-m-more silly n-names." My stomach knotted. I rubbed my bandage. *Do it. Do it now before you chicken out.* "And and a-nother thuh-ing."

"I am all ears, Miss Miriam Hope Friis."

"I b-buried your El-El SD buh-lotter."

One thousand one, one thousand two. Her eyes widened. "You did what?"

I took a breath and barreled on. "You puh-romised n-no d-d-doses in this room. You l-l-lied to me. It's ruh-otten r-r-rye. So let it r-rot in the guh-round, Duh-agmar. Don't l-let it ruh-ot your buh-rain!"

She paced the room in her Morticia getup like a demon professor on steroids. "I don't believe this. How did you find my stash? You went through my stuff without asking me! I take care of you, and I make phone calls for you, and I take you places, and I make one, teeny tiny mistake, and you have the gall—the gall!—to tell me how to live my life. Plus you have no idea how hard it was to get that blotter. Some Merry Prankster has up and gone, with the best LSD in the Bay Area, and you take the last of his doses and bury them. Bury them! I was going to sell them to pay back the dreidel money. Who do you think you are?"

"I...I..."

"And that was amazing stuff. Not like the crap they put in the licorice you stupidly ate. You would have had a great time at the Halloween party if you'd stuck with the dose I gave you in the blue cheese dip."

What?! "You...you..."

Dagmar glared at me. "Yes, Miss Friis. I slipped you one of my precious tabs when we first got to the party. Remember the crackers and blue cheese? You would have had a fit if I told you then, and I didn't want to spoil your good karma. Somebody had to loosen you up."

She'd given me a dose like it was nothing. To loosen me up?

I clenched my jaw. Hard. Pain streaked up the right side of my face. I sat there frozen.

"And this is how you repay me? You always keep your mouth shut, but now I see you're as judgmental as Josh. Well, I've had it with you. You march right upstairs to Grandpa's room and stay there. I'm not going to share my bedroom with my bratty kid sister for one more minute."

My pulse throbbed. I flew out of bed and grabbed one of Dagmar's army boots.

"Go on. Throw it!" She stood there, her hands on her hips. "I dare you."

I squeezed my hand around the leather and strode into the laundry room. I threw that damn boot into a laundry basket, strode back, and threw her other boot in the basket. Then I threw in assorted crap from the foot of her bed and headed upstairs.

Dagmar caught up with me in the kitchen, just as Josh came in the back door. He frowned at the overstuffed laundry basket.

"D-Dagmar's m-moving to Guh-randpa's room," I told him, trying to put words to the jumble of emotions raging through me.

"That is totally unfair," Dagmar shouted.

"Shut up, Dagmar," Josh said. "Let her explain."

"You always take her side," Dagmar whined.

They were at it again. Their problem, not mine. I dumped Dagmar's junk on Grandpa's rug and filled the laundry basket with the first load of things I wanted—the porcelain saucer Grandpa used for his coins, his afghan, the picture of Grandma on his dresser, Grandma's suffrage sash and Vote For Justice card, his bag of *tefillin*.

I marched back into the kitchen. They were still at it.

"J-Josh," I said, poking his side with the laundry basket to get his attention. "Puh-lease t-take Guh-randpa's jade puh-lant d-downstairs to m-my desk."

His eyes narrowed. "Hope, do Mom and Dad know about this?"

And then it hit me. They didn't know about Dagmar dosing me with LSD at the party. Otherwise, I would have heard about it. They would have had a fit.

I looked at Dagmar and arched my eyebrows. "No, thuh-ey d-don't," I said. "D-do they, D-Dagmar?"

She looked ready to kill me, but I wasn't going to change my mind. My workshop was downstairs. I'd have a bathroom to myself. Why move?

"No," she said.

We glared at each other. Even Josh had the good sense to keep his trap shut. Six beats of silence. Then Dagmar said, "Help her with the friggin' plant, Josh." She collected a shawl and her boots from Grandpa's old room and stormed out the front door.

I arranged Grandpa's things on my bed temporarily and stuffed more of Dagmar's crap into the laundry basket. I told Josh exactly where to put the jade plant and gave him the basket to take upstairs.

"You should ask Mom and Dad about this. They expected that you'd take Grandpa's room."

"D-Dagmar and I have an a-agreement." An arrangement anyway—for now. It seemed fair.

"Okay, but I'm just saying, you really should talk to them when they come back from their walk." He made a point of looking at my flannel pajamas. "You know it's nearly noon. You should get dressed."

Same old Josh. After he left, I stripped Dagmar's bed and rolled the linens into a bundle. The papers she'd showed me were lying on the floor. Clipped to the list of names was a mimeographed sheet with what she was supposed to say. The names and campus phone numbers started with Prof. Katzenbach in the math department and ended with Prof. Liles in economics. No names starting with M, which I was guaranteed to stumble over.

I shook my head and wiped my mouth with the back of my hand. Totally crazy. Too risky. I didn't even call to renew my own library books. And what difference did twenty-five phone calls make compared with the thousand or so faculty members.

Still…

I headed for the shower. As the steam built up in the bathroom, I focused on the towel rack and pulled off my bandages.

CHAPTER FORTY-SIX

I PATTED MY FACE DRY, wrapped my hair in a towel, and got dressed. Nothing fancy, nothing shlumpy. Black slacks; pale-pink and white, striped oxford shirt; black knee socks; and penny loafers.

By then the bathroom mirror had cleared. I took a good look. I sucked in my breath. Horrible.

Tiny stitch marks looped around from the back of my ear and spread down across my cheek to about three inches above my chin. In two places the raw, shiny skin puckered, as if tiny worms lived underneath. Ooze seeped out from the ragged strip along the top of my jaw.

I opened my mouth wider and watched my new skin ripple. For some strange reason, I thought of that snake in Celeste's bedroom. I was more than scarred. I was molting.

I bit my lip and stared at my molting self. Then I dumped clips and rollers in the bathroom sink, combed a part down the middle of my head, and strand-by-strand, put in the rollers. Whatever I was molting into, it might as well have decent-looking hair.

I stuffed cotton gauze around my right ear and consigned my head to the dryer hood. Then I decided that granddaughters in mourning could still tweeze their eyebrows and apply two coats of clear polish to their fingernails.

Josh shot me an approving look when I came upstairs. "Nice do," he said, which is a high compliment coming from my brother. I twirled my blonde curls, and his mouth dropped open. "That's some gouging you've got there. I can't believe you did that to yourself. You'll be scarred for life."

I put my hands on my hips and faced him. "So?"

He shrugged. "So, hey, I'm sorry. Does it still hurt?"

"N-not m-much."

He waved a banana in my direction. "Well, that's good. It'll be okay, kiddo. You take care of yourself and don't let Dagmar boss you around. You want half a banana?"

I shook my head and felt my hair caress my right cheek for the first time since Halloween. "I-I'm going to B-Barston's."

Who knew? My mouth seemed to be ahead of my brain, but at that moment it felt like the right thing to do. Dagmar wasn't going to make her twenty-five calls, so I might as well. I still had the five dollars I'd found in her clothes, plus a couple dollars more. Twenty-five calls at ten cents a call. I had plenty of cash.

Afraid that I might lose my nerve if I took the time for breakfast, I left a note for my parents and strode out the door. The sky looked glorious. Miracles do happen, I reminded myself. I had just finished a fantastical journey across the *olam*. I had a wondrous prayer shawl passed from generation to generation to me—Miriam Hope Friis, the granddaughter of Miriam Josefsohn Jacobowitz, wearer of the shawl embroidered by Miriam, the daughter of Rashi. A shawl that urged its owner to pursue justice.

Why not pursue justice like Mario? They said he stuttered like me except when he was giving a speech. I'd heard that for myself. Reciting my script would be like a public speech with no one watching. If I could pretend to be an angel, surely I could pretend I was speaking to the multitudes.

There were three pay phones at Barston's, and I didn't feel bad about monopolizing one for a good cause. No one else was using them.

The woman at the cash register gave me a sympathetic look and half a roll of dimes. I smiled. I was polite. I hardly garbled a word.

I reread the mimeographed message, and I thought of Gabriel. Maybe he was saying the same words to another set of faculty members at this very moment. Maybe he even wrote the message. It sounded like his style.

"Hello, Prof. _____. I am sorry to disturb you, but I feel compelled to urge you to vote on behalf of free speech at the Academic Senate this afternoon. Some students have been irresponsible, I admit that, but there's a principle involved here. A university should foster the free exchange of ideas for everyone in the campus community. It's a question of academic integrity and fairness. Berkeley has an opportunity to be the model for our broader American society, and to protect the First Amendment freedoms endowed to it by the Constitution. [Answer any questions politely] Thank you for your time."

Inhale. Slow release. I picked up the receiver, put a dime in the slot, and made my first call.

A baritone voice answered. "Professor Katzenbach, here."

"Huh-h-h-hello?"

"Yes, what can I do for you?"

My tongue glued itself to the back of my top teeth.

"If this is about your grade, you will have to review that with me in person during office hours."

I swallowed hard. "I ...um... I am s-s-sorry to duh-sturb y-you, b-but..."

My jaw locked in place.

"Please get to the point. I have a lot of work to do today."

I put the receiver back in its cradle.

Crap!

I retreated to the ladies' room and studied the pattern on the tile floor. No Serakh. No magical revelations. Then I got up the courage to look at my molting face in the mirror.

If you think I had glorious insights, you'd be wrong. Whoever I was turning into seemed to have a stubborn streak. Or maybe, I didn't care as much anymore. Or maybe I was ashamed at nearly killing myself because of my damn stutter. Or maybe I understood something new about taking risks. Or maybe I remembered what Gabriel said—that people could describe us but we shouldn't let them define us.

One foot in front of the other, I headed back to the phones. No way could I call Professor Katzenbach again. I hoped he was going to vote for free speech anyway.

I inserted another dime and dialed the next number on the list.

"Edith Keyser. May I help you?"

"Um...yes. It's ...ah ... about f-f-free speech on c-c-campus," I managed. "Pul-ease v-v-vote for our civil ruh-ights."

"Did you mean at the faculty meeting this afternoon?"

"Yes," I said, wishing nods, shrugs, and headshakes could work over the telephone.

"Are you one of my graduate students?"

"N-n-no, puh-ro-f-fessor. I'm a p-person." How stupid is that?

Two beats of silence. "Well, I wasn't planning to go, but since you made the effort to call, young lady, I will make the effort to attend. And I will vote for something in line with the FSM position. I agree with you, person to person."

"Thuh-ank you." And I hung up, my heart beating triple-time. Thank you. Thank you. Thank you.

I GOT THROUGH THE next six calls with my usual stuttering and blubbering. I changed the script, and said what I had to, the way that sounded best for me. Two professors didn't answer their phones, which I let ring for the full ten times, so I didn't feel like I was chickening out. I celebrated finishing the first dozen phone calls on the list with a hot fudge sundae, which tastes especially delicious in place of breakfast. Then I got back to work.

I had just checked off Professor Landau—number nineteen—when over my shoulder I heard Mr. Zegarelli clear his throat and ask, "What do you have to say for yourself, Miss Friis?"

CHAPTER FORTY-SEVEN

I STEPPED BACK FROM THE telephone and put the dime in my pocket. How long had Mr. Zegarelli been standing here? What was he doing at Barston's instead of school? I touched the soft new skin by my ear and turned toward him.

He shifted his gaze away from my face. For some crazy reason, instead of feeling ashamed at my scarring, I felt more solid, more me, as if I'd nailed the opening lines of a Bach cantata. *Here's when and where my new me begins.*

Mr. Zegarelli lifted the script from my fingers and read it aloud.

I folded my arms across my chest and waited.

He pursed his lips and flexed his nostrils, taking a commanding breath. "Miss Friis, it seems that your unfortunate accident on Halloween and the recent loss of your grandfather have clouded your judgment. Miss Nash has been kind enough to hand in your permission slip and trip deposit."

"I am r-ready to s-s-sing again, sir," I said.

"Yes, I agree. You are quite a talented young woman. I suppose you didn't realize that I buy coffee at Barston's after third period. Perhaps you forgot my admonishment that any student who becomes involved in the unrest on campus will be ineligible to represent Berkeley High School at the music festival. What do you have to say about that?"

Good question. The competition meant everything to me. If I didn't need money for the trip I wouldn't have gone to Sproul Plaza. I wouldn't have occupied Sproul Hall. I wouldn't have gone to the Greek Theatre. I wouldn't have understood.

Inhale. Slow release. "I-I am c-carrying out m-my r-respon-sibilities as a cit-izen. There is un-ruh-est on c-campus be-be-cause the ad-ad-m-m-ministration d-denies b-basic r-r-rights t-to the stu-dents. I am s-s-simply ruh-minding the f-faculty of that."

He practically snorted. "Miss Friis, I cannot tolerate this at-titude. Think about what you are saying."

I gazed at a crack in the floor and smiled. I thought that *what* I said came out pretty well. *How* I said it? Well, a stutter's a stutter—part of the package called Miriam Hope Friis. Not my favorite part, but still...

"I have, sir," I said. "I d-definitely have."

Mr. Zegarelli shook his head and let out a long and dramatic sigh. He refused to give the script back, since, as he put it, he had heard me paraphrase it several times before interrupting me, and it was evidence of my violation of the principal's order.

"I shall expect you in the principal's office tomorrow after school. I am very disappointed in you, Miss Friis. You might have quite a promising vocal career ahead of you if you'd learn responsibility."

"Yes, sir," I said, without a hint of sarcasm.

"Good day to you."

I nodded. He nodded. He left with the script but not the list. By this time I didn't need the script anyway. I fished out another dime. Of the last six calls, three professors didn't answer, one hung up on me, one engaged me in a long conversation about the Marxist imperative, and one complimented me on my clear soprano voice and asked me if I ever considered majoring in music.

TRUE TO MY NOTE on the refrigerator, I was home by early after-noon. Mom was in the kitchen, stirring a cup of tea and looking lost. I wanted to give her a bubble bath, sing her a lullaby, and send her back to bed.

"I'll share an apricot Danish with you," she said. "Mrs. Nash is bringing something from Andronico's for dinner. I couldn't manage without her." Mom lifted the hair away from the scarred side of my face. I winced at her quick intake of breath. But then she said, "Oh, sweetie, you gave me such a scare. And it's healing nicely. No flashbacks?"

"No," I lied. I didn't have the heart to tell her about Mr. Zipper Mouth or the monster screwdriver just then. She'd already given me permission to go to the music festival—not that I had much of a chance of going now.

Mom ran her fingers over the oak grain of our table. "I saw the handkerchief in the casket. That was your idea, I bet. Did you iron it for Grandpa?"

"Y-yes." Three gray hairs had snuck in among the black ones on the left side of Mom's French twist. "I'll take c-care of his juh-ade plant."

I got us another box of tissues.

A moment later, Mom said, "Gabriel called while you were out. I invited him to have dinner with us before we sit *shivah*. He'll come around five. The Academic Senate is meeting this afternoon, and he's busy with something to do with that."

Ah, sweet Gabriel. I practically waltzed over to the tray of pastries.

"He's a kind, sensible young man, don't you think? He'll be such a stabilizing influence for Dagmar. She's finally found someone we like."

What could I say? Deflated, I stood there in mid-stride and bit my lip.

Mom's expectations for Gabriel nagged at me through the rest of the afternoon, but Gabriel turned up in a mood to celebrate. "They're still deliberating," he told me as soon as I ushered him into the living room. "But an inside source says that most of the faculty will vote in our favor. Mario thinks we've won."

"That's f-fabulous!" I gave him a congratulatory hug and wondered when to tell him about my mother's plans for him and Dagmar.

"Hey, no bandages. Let me look at you." He put his hand under my chin and brushed my hair away from the ugly side of my face. I closed my eyes and wished I could close my ears, too.

"Hang on, Mime Girl," he whispered, his Mr. Zipper Mouth lips enticingly close to my ear. "You're going to be fine."

"I s-saw the script you m-made for the phone calls. And-And I even m-made some m-myself."

His eyes widened. "You're pulling my leg."

"No. R-really. From D-Dagmar's list."

Gabriel laughed. "I didn't think your sister would make those calls. Where is she?"

I shrugged. With Mom on Dagmar's side, did I really stand a chance?

Josh walked in from the den, hand extended. "Gabe my man, good to see you again."

Gabriel shook Josh's hand and thumped him on the shoulder. I had a momentary image of two male chimps.

"Hey, Hope, your music teacher called while you were downstairs."

Crap!

"He said he won't be talking to the principal. Did you rack up too many absences?"

"M-maybe." At least Mr. Zegarelli had the decency to save me from that bit of humiliation. No way was I going to tell Josh what happened at Barston's.

"Anyway, he said something about extra help for the music festival. You should take him up on that. You were pretty shaky with the Hanukkah blessings."

I creased my forehead and stared at Josh. He must have garbled the message.

"Hey, don't look at me. Ask him. He said something about cooling down and thinking about his Italian grandfather, and then he blathered about the Constitution. The guy sounded more like an American history professor than a music teacher." Josh shook his head. "Glad I never took his class."

"Me neither," Gabriel said. "Hope, is everything okay?"

"Y-yes," I managed, as it all started to sink in. "Definitely."

Josh raised his finger in the air. "One more thing. There's some strange girl waiting in Grandpa's old room for you. She says she's a friend of yours, but I doubt it. She looks like a nun."

CHAPTER FORTY-EIGHT

SERAKH. WHO ELSE COULD it be? I raced down the hall and then stopped. I remembered when I first heard her speaking to Grandpa. She was persuading him to give me my grandmother's prayer shawl. Now, in the worst way, I wanted her to meet Gabriel. It didn't make sense. It was a silly risk to take.

Still…

Gabriel was disappearing into the kitchen when I grabbed his hand. "Th-this is g-going to be a b-b-it odd, okay? I'll expuh-lain l-later." I snatched a half-sour pickle from the deli meat platter, stuck it on a paper plate, and told Gabriel to take it with us.

Serakh was standing next to a pile of Dagmar's junk. She had robed herself in black, from headscarf to sandals. I wrapped my arms around her and inhaled the goat smell clinging to her body. Before she could ask, I said, "It's fine. He doesn't know about Paris, but he's…um…a good friend. Gabriel Altman."

Gabriel nodded politely. Hanging out with Dagmar, he'd probably seen a lot of weird outfits. "Gabriel, this is Serakh. She's a…well, she's a friend of the family. It's complicated."

Serakh spread her arms out. "As you see, I have dressed in darkness as is your custom for mourning. Now that the intertwining is over, I give you my deep condolences on the release of your grandfather's soul from his earthly body. That is the first reason I have come. There are three."

"I'm so glad you're here," I told her. "I missed you already." I showed Serakh the pickle. "Have you ever had a sour cucumber? Try it. It's brined in vinegar and I don't know what else."

After the initial puckered surprise, she was delighted.

Gabriel bit his lip. Then he said, "Hope, I don't mean to sound rude, but what happened to your stutter?"

I grinned at him. "Sad to say this is only a temporary fix while Serakh is here. It has something to do with magical communication. I'll get back to my regular stuttering me as soon as she's gone."

Gabriel cocked his head. "I'm completely lost."

A case of the nervous giggles threatened to erupt. I cleared my throat and reminded myself that Serakh had come at a solemn time to pay her respects.

"The room has changed since Ephraim lived here," she said, wiping pickle-juice–covered hands on her robe.

"It's my sister's now. She hadn't organized the piles yet. We decided this morning, after... um...after my return." I heard the church bells again in my head, announcing matin services in Paris. Dawn. Avram.

My stomach lurched. "What happened to Mon Trésor?" I searched Serakh's face for an answer. "Avram didn't...I mean..."

She kissed my forehead the way she did when we first met.

"All is well," she said, and suddenly I had to sit in Grandpa's chair and take a deep breath. Too many ups and downs jumbled together in too short a time. Gabriel touched my shoulder.

"I'm fine now," I said, although he didn't look convinced. "Serakh, tell me the two other reasons you're here."

She reached into the pouch hanging from her belt and handed me the dreidels I had given to Dolcette and Avram. "The second reason is that I must return these to you. They are objects of the future and do not belong in that spot on the *olam*."

"Oh, of course. That makes sense, I guess. Do you want my William the Conqueror coin back?"

She shook her head. "The coin is acceptable to leave with you. It is a relic from the past, and you may do with it as you will."

Gabriel's eyebrows danced in surprise. "You've got a Saxon coin? It must be worth a fortune."

"It's only a replica," I lied, knowing I'd tell him the truth one day, now that he and I were...or were we?

"Serakh, I have a favor to ask, if you don't mind. I'd like to know what happens at the Northwest Choral Music Festival in Portland on January twenty-eighth, just a few weeks from now. And, um, Gabriel, when does the Board of Regents meet?" I didn't have the nerve to ask about the future of Gabriel and me.

"December seventeenth and eighteenth in LA."

"Right. Can we find out if the Regents support the free speech resolution? Gabriel can stay here. Please, Serakh, you know it won't take any time at all."

She shook her head. "This is not to be. You and I can travel only into the past, and even then at great risk. You must wait here and now for the future to become the present."

Gabriel coughed, his face a study in confusion.

"Serakh has a sort of loose relationship with time," I told him. "My dad the physics professor would get it."

"Well, I clearly don't."

Serakh grinned at him. "This does not matter. I trust that you are content to stay in the present with…what do you call her? Hope? She is a special person."

"Very special." Gabriel's voice was low and gentle, and round and deep.

For a moment I forgot Serakh was with us. I put my hand on Gabriel's soft woolen sweater. "What about Dagmar?"

"I've already told her she's just a friend. Your sister sees that as a challenge."

"My mother has the wrong idea about you and Dagmar, too. It's not going to be easy."

He caressed the top of my head. "It's going to be worth it."

Serakh cleared her throat. "Here is my third reason. This token you may also keep as proof that you were Avram's angel."

She gave me another coin, more refined than the silver one. It had Roman numerals on it and Hebrew letters, and the profile of a woman's face and upper body. The woman's dress had a high collar and she wore what looked like a ring of pearls covering a headscarf that draped across her shoulders.

"Gracia Benveniste. She is not much older than you," Serakh said. "They call her La Chica. She is partly of the line of Avram and Dolcette. No harm ever comes to their Isaac. He marries well. La Chica is born into his family generations later. Here is your proof."

La Chica was more than proof. I knew she would always remind me of my time in Paris with that beautiful baby, and his desperate mother, and his anguished father. Mon Trésor. My treasure. My eyes filled with tears. I brought the coin to my lips.

"What have you done with the rest of the potion?"

"I destroyed it, Serakh."

She smiled. "A wise choice."

One beat of silence.

My shoulders slumped. "You're leaving now."

She studied my face. "I see you are already healing. Perhaps I will meet you again with this man as I met your grandmother Miriam and her beloved Ephraim of blessed memory."

My face flushed. "Serakh, really?"

The gold flecks in her eyes sparkled with humor. "And perhaps not. It is time."

"Good-bye," I whispered.

"Nice to have met you," Gabriel told Serakh, as if this were a normal conversation. Poor guy. We'd have a lot to talk about.

I put the coin in my pocket and told him to turn away. I told Gabriel—my Gabriel—to shut his eyes, and keep them shut, until I said it was safe to open them. Then I took a breath and kissed him. The scar from his cleft palate repair pressed with an oddly satisfying firmness against my lips. I enveloped him in my arms and waited for the flash.

AUTHOR'S NOTE

"COMPLICATED"—THE WORD HOPE AND her physicist father use to describe their worlds—comes from a Latin word meaning "to fold together" or "to intertwine." Intertwining is one of my favorite words. Serakh intertwines people and events over the centuries—Hope and Avram, Paris and Berkeley, LSD and ergotism. That's what this book is all about.

I would like to elaborate on everything that's true in *The Ninth Day* and everything that's not, but that would take at least another fifty pages. Historical fiction is tricky that way—and fun. Gabriel's mnemonic "sober people don't find good in killing" is true. The lion-cruet menorah sits by my writer's desk. Yes, there was a Hanukkah celebration at Sproul Hall during the occupation and a pogrom in Bialystock (now in Poland), in 1906. Caffé Med is real. Tidbits on Telegraph is not. Neither is Barston's. I made up LSD-laced licorice and the choral music festival (although both could have existed).

Here's the big picture:

PEOPLE

THE BIBLE SAYS LITTLE about Serakh. It merely lists her (in Genesis 46:17 and Numbers 26:46) at events said to have taken place about four hundred years apart. People have spun tales about her for centuries. In *The Ninth Day* and its companion novel, *Blue Thread*, I take a turn. My Serakh flashes through the *olam*, which is my intertwining of space and time inspired by the ancient Hebrew word that can mean both "universe" and "forever."

Miriam Hope Friis and her family and friends are fictional. Hope is the granddaughter of Ephraim and Miriam, fictional characters last seen in 1912 in *Blue Thread*.

Stuttering is a part of Hope's life and the lives of an estimated three million Americans. It's a speech disorder with a physiological basis and can worsen through embarrassment, frustration, and fear. About one in twenty children aged two to five stutter. Some of these children continue to stutter as adults. I was one of them, although I rarely stutter now.

Gabriel's cleft palate is a relatively common birth defect involving fetal development of the roof of the mouth, and it can be repaired at a young age. Children born with a cleft palate or cleft lip (a similar defect) were once thought to be evil or cursed by a witch, or to possess supernatural powers.

While Hope's grandmother is fictional, Dolcette's mother, also named Miriam, is not. She's the middle daughter of the French rabbi Shlomo ben Yitzchak (or Solomon ben Isaac), known as Rashi (1040–1105). Miriam had a son, Yom Tov, and other children, including one named in a family tree as Dolce (my Dolcette). She might have worn a prayer shawl, although an embroidered one is my idea. The other Paris people are pure fiction.

TIMES AND PLACES

SINCE THE STORY TRACKS the Jewish holiday of Hanukkah, I used the Hebrew calendar as a starting point. Hanukkah begins on the twenty-fifth of *Kislev* (according to I Maccabees 4:59), and lasts from sunset to sunset for eight days. I used equivalent days in the Gregorian calendar for Berkeley and the Julian calendar for Paris. I added saints days for Paris 1099, as a more common way for most people to mark time then.

A Jewish community lived on Île de la Cité in 1099, near Saint-Étienne cathedral then, and the current site of Notre Dame cathedral (built 1163 to 1345). I made up the Paris events, including Avram's behavior, but the events in Mainz in 1096 are true. Pope Urban II proclaimed a "holy war" in 1095, to take back Jerusalem from Muslim rulers. An estimated 100,000 people, from noble knights to peasants, took up arms. One group of crusaders traveled toward Jerusalem through France and Germany. The ferocity of their attack on the Jews of Mainz, and several other cities along the Rhine River, gave rise among some Jews there to martyr themselves as an act of faith. In general, however, relations between Christians and Jews in France and Germany were generally civil during the early Middle Ages, prior to the twelve hundreds.

Although the Berkeley High School scenes are fictional, I stuck pretty close to the facts about the Free Speech Movement during those nine days on the Berkeley campus of the University of California. I wrote part of *The Ninth Day* there, at the university's Free Speech Movement Café. For the most part, events describing the actions of Mario Savio (1942–1996), as well as the Sproul Hall occupation, Greek Theatre assembly, student strike, and faculty vote, really happened.

In the early 1960s, student organizations used a twenty-six by forty foot area at the Bancroft-Telegraph entrance to campus to raise money and recruit members for various causes, including civil rights demonstrations. On September 14, 1964, the Dean of Students issued a statement that the area was officially part of university facilities. The statement noted that, "University facilities may not…be used to support or advocate off-campus political or social action."

Students from all parts of the political spectrum objected. The occupation of Sproul Hall marked the first major protest movement on an American campus and remains one of the most significant in our nation's history. The Free Speech Movement lasted many months—I've provided only a tiny slice of what happened. *The Ninth Day* ends just as the Academic Senate is meeting on December 8, 1964. Yes, the, faculty did support the students in an 824-to-115 vote.

CHEMISTRY

THE TRUE PARTS OF this story include *Claviceps purpurea*, a fungus known as ergot. In medieval times, nearly a third of harvested grain, particularly rye, might really have been hardened bits of the ergot fungus. Ergotism (the disease resulting from eating this fungus) is what caused Saint Anthony's fire and hallucinations similar to those experienced after taking LSD. Swiss chemist Albert Hofmann first synthesized LSD in 1938 as part of his research for the pharmaceutical firm Sandoz. He wasn't looking for a mind-altering drug, but he found one.

When I started *The Ninth Day*, I had no idea that LSD was connected to convulsive ergotism or Saint Anthony's fire. Whether it's about history or chemistry, research is full of surprises. Add imagination to that, and an astonishing world unfolds, as intertwined as the *olam*.

THE NINTH DAY PLAYLIST

Halleluyah (Psalm 150)
COMPOSED BY LOUIS LEWANDOWSKI

Under the Boardwalk
THE DRIFTERS

My Boy Lollipop
MILLIE SMALL

Now Is the Month of Maying
VIENNA VOCAL CONSORT

I Saw Her Standing There
THE BEATLES

You Don't Own Me
LESLEY GORE

Bachianas Brasileiras No. 5
JOAN BAEZ

We Shall Overcome
JOAN BAEZ

The Times They Are a-Changin'
BOB DYLAN

Artsa Alinu
RUTH RUBIN

Blowin' in the Wind
PETER, PAUL, AND MARY

Mr. Lonely
BOBBY VINTON

I Want to Hold Your Hand
THE BEATLES

Discussion Questions for The Ninth Day

How does the death of Ephraim Jacobowitz influence the lives and perspectives of Hope and her family?

If you could change one aspect of Hope's personality, what would it be? How would that have changed the outcome?

How do Henry Friis's religion (Lutheran) and his passion (physics) influence the story?

How might the story have changed if Dolcette's mother, Miriam, had made it to Paris?

Mario Savio had spent the summer of 1964 helping to secure voting rights for African Americans in Mississippi. How do you think that might have influenced his actions in the Free Speech Movement?

Based on what is revealed in the story, what are the chances that Hope and Gabriel might develop as strong and loving a relationship as Avram and Dolcette, or Rachel and Henry Friis, have?

What are the similarities and differences between the occupation of Sproul Hall in 1964 and the Occupy movement that began in 2011?

Why do you think that Hope and Leona are best friends?

If you were a student at Berkeley in 1964, would you have supported the Free Speech Movement even when the students went on strike and disrupted classes? Why? Why not?

Ergotism has played a role in several historical events, including, according to experts, the witch trials in Salem, Massachusetts. How much of individual and societal behavior comes down to chemistry?

How might the relationship between Dagmar and Hope been different if Hope didn't stutter?

How much history should an author put in historical fiction? What are the pitfalls for writers—and readers—of this genre?

What do you think would have happened if Hope had failed to persuade Avram that she was an angel?

Fantasy deals with what we welcome as "real" based on the internal rules of the story and external reality. What are some of the rules in Serakh's fantastical travel through the olam?

Suppose that Hanukkah did not happen to occur during the height of the FSM protests in 1964. What impact would that have on the narrative?

Acknowledgements

Many people went into the telling of this story, and I owe each of them my thanks. The Berkeley half of the T9D team includes Margot Adler, Bettina Aptheker, and Michael Lerner, all of whom were part of the Free Speech Movement in Berkeley and occupied Sproul Hall in 1964. The Hanukkah celebration at Sproul in T9D is based on one Michael Lerner (now a rabbi and the editor of *Tikkun Magazine*) organized back then. Several librarians and archivists at Bancroft Library opened their FSM files to me. I had the pleasure of touring the Berkeley campus several times with Keith P. Feldman, an assistant professor in the university's Department of Ethnic Studies—and my son.

Professors Natan Meir of Portland State University and Robert Chazan of New York University were particularly helpful in guiding me through the Paris half of the story and giving me a wider background in Rhineland Jewry during the First Crusade. A forthright friend broadened my understanding of LSD trips and flashbacks.

Yes, it's the truth. This book would never have happened without my writer's critique group, Viva Scriva: Addie Boswell, Melissa Dalton, Amber Keyser, Sabina Rascol, Mary Rehmann, Elizabeth Rusch, and Nicole Schreiber. My husband Michael Feldman also offered very real advice about my imaginary friends.

Michelle McCann and dozens of people at Ooligan Press polished T9D along the way. Thank you, thank you, and thank you.

OOLIGAN PRESS

OOLIGAN PRESS TAKES ITS name from a Native American word for the common smelt or candlefish. Ooligan is a general trade press rooted in the rich literary life of Portland and the Department of English at Portland State University. Ooligan is staffed by students pursuing master's degrees in an apprenticeship program under the guidance of a core faculty of publishing professionals.

ACQUISITIONS
Drew Lazzara
McKenzie Workman

PROJECT MANAGERS
Kate Marshall
Annie Whitcomb
McKenzie Workman
Kelsey Yocum

EDITORIAL
Gino Cerruti
Sarah Currin
Lacey Friedly
Emily Gravlin
Rebekah Hunt
Drew Lazzara
Tara Lehmann
Kathryn Osterndorff
Courtney Pondelick
Jonathan Stark
Whitney Smyth

DESIGN
Riley Kennysmith
Poppy Milliken
Lorna Nakell
Paige O'Rourke
Krys Roth
Adam Salazar

DIGITAL CONTENT
Kai Belladone
Camille Watts

MARKETING
Keely Burkey
Lauren Hudgins
Adam Salazar
Brian Tibbetts

Colophon

The Ninth Day is set in Adobe Caslon Pro and Essays1743.